If you have been waiting for Scott Kikkawa's latest book, you're not alone. I have been too! If you're not familiar yet with his gripping plots and searing characters, it's time to get to know them. I highly recommend Kikkawa's fantastic work.

—Pamela Rotner Sakamoto
author of *Midnight in Broad Daylight*

A gifted new voice in crime fiction, Scott Kikkawa delivers 1950s noir from a never-seen-before perspective with lead characters whose sparkling chemistry illuminates every page. Japanese American detective Frankie "Sheik" Yoshikawa and dazzling young reporter Ellen Park are a fantastic duo—sexy, funny, and engaging. Rich in culture and showcasing a neglected history with sensitivity and nuance, this is a series for our times.

—Ausma Zehanat Khan
author of the Khattak/Getty crime series

Scott Kikkawa's *Red Dirt* hits pay dirt with the second installment of his original yet classic detective series. Set in pre-statehood Hawai'i, Detective "Sheik" Yoshikawa is the kind of rough-edged, soft-hearted maverick fans of hard-boiled noir will love.

—Tori Eldridge
author of *The Ninja Betrayed* (Lily Wong #3)

Excellent! Scott Kikkawa manages to balance all the pieces here—a compelling mystery in an overlooked historical setting with characters worthy of discovery. Insightful and real, Kikkawa writes like an insider who knows how it feels to be an outsider, too.

—Frank Zafiro
author of the River City series

In the great tradition of hard-boiled detective fiction, Scott Kikkawa casts shadows on a sunny place.

—Steph Cha
author of *Your House Will Pay*

Step aside Raymond Chandler, Scott Kikkawa has arrived to put a new, fresh, and more delicious spin on the noir genre.

—Naomi Hirahara
author of the Edgar Award-winning Mas Arai mystery series

Detective Francis Yoshikawa is an original—handsome, street smart, literate, a veteran of the famed 442nd, and immersed in the multiracial mélange of the Islands.

—David Mura
author of *Turning Japanese: Memoirs of a Sansei*

Red Dirt

ISBN 978-1-943756-06-3

This is issue #120 of *Bamboo Ridge, Journal of Hawai'i Literature and Arts* (ISSN # 0733-0308).

Published by Bamboo Ridge Press
Printed in the United States of America

Bamboo Ridge Press is a member of the Community of Literary Magazines and Presses (CLMP).

Typesetting and design: Jui-Lien Sanderson
Cover art: *Yoshikawa Pays Beverly Machida a Visit* by Tommy Hite, 2021; oil on wood, 19" × 24"

Bamboo Ridge Press is a nonprofit, tax-exempt corporation formed in 1978 to foster the appreciation, understanding, and creation of literary, visual, and performing arts by, for, or about Hawai'i's people. This project was supported in part by funding from the National Endowment for the Arts. Additional support for Bamboo Ridge Press activities is provided by the Hawai'i State Foundation on Culture and the Arts (through appropriations from the Legislature of the State of Hawai'i and grants from the National Endowment for the Arts) and the Hawai'i Council for the Humanities.

Bamboo Ridge is published twice a year. For orders, subscription information, and back issues, contact:

Bamboo Ridge Press
P.O. Box 61781
Honolulu, Hawai'i 96839-1781

808.626.1481
read@bambooridge.org
www.bambooridge.org

5 4 3 2 1   21 22 23 24 25

Red Dirt

Scott Kikkawa

BAMBOO RIDGE PRESS

For Caroline and Cole, whose world is free of the witch hunts of the past, but not its injustices. Stay vigilant.

Prologue

Spies. Enemy aliens. *Traitors.* This is what they called us to our faces. The nicer ones whispered it behind our backs. In the days after Pearl Harbor, we all did what we could to make ourselves as invisible as possible. A lot of things went straight into the trash: the Hinamatsuri dolls, the calligraphy and brush paintings, the silk kimono. To-san even buried the swords in the back of the house under the ti leaves. Everybody stopped speaking in the mother tongue; even the old timers forced themselves to use English, and where they couldn't, they shut the hell up. We were all trying to prove we were Americans.

Dumping our sentimental ties to the old country wasn't proof enough. A lot of us stepped up and gave the ultimate proof: blood. We endured the taunts and racial slurs at Camp Shelby; then we shipped off to endure the artillery and bayonets of the Wehrmacht. I gave my blood. Wally Yoshida gave his leg. A lot of others gave their lives. We gave everything so that everyone would leave us the hell alone. We came home to some fanfare: fat carnation lei, a parade or two, luaus, and speeches.

Then came the new names.

Stalinist stooges. Communists. *Traitors.* Blood wasn't enough to appease the Gods of Sugar and Shipping. They didn't want sacrifice. They wanted docility. There were too damn many of us, and we were too close for comfort. We asked for fair wages. They painted us red.

I came back from the war and went to college in New York City on Uncle Sam's dime. There, I threw myself into *Le Morte D'Arthur* and learned a painful lesson about betrayal: it isn't a rejection, it's a choice. Like Lancelot choosing Guinevere over Arthur, I chose my country over my friends.

Traitor.

In atonement, or perhaps in denial, I took up sword and shield and swore an oath to defend. A .38 caliber sword and a shield that fit in my pocket.

Not for the first time, I rode out to seek the Holy Grail under the banner of a country that called me *traitor*.

I haven't found it yet.

Editors' note: In the story that follows, Hawaiian place names, street names, and the names of royalty do not include diacritical marks and appear as they would have been printed in English language newspapers in the 1950s.

PART I

Excalibur
Waialua

1

It stuck out of the ground like it was meant to be grasped by the lucky guy who found it. *WHOSO PULLETH OUT THIS SWORD OF THIS STONE AND ANVIL, IS RIGHTWISE KING BORN OF ALL ENGLAND.* I half expected it to bear that inscription in gold. It almost looked regal jutting out of the red dirt of Kunia in the middle of a burned-out cane field. It wasn't Excalibur's hilt, though, and I'd bet my entire pension that Sir Thomas Malory didn't have this particular object in mind when he described the sword in the stone. I was looking at a bone. A human bone. A big one. A femur, probably. And it was charred black.

All over the island, there were men at work. Haole executives sitting behind desks the size of mausoleums in their ballroom-like offices on Bishop Street, looking at papers that would double the size of their bank accounts. Pake shopkeepers on Kekaulike Street in their stores crammed with junk, looking with suspicion at loiterers, hands wrapped around baseball bats under the counters. Japanese and Portuguese and kanaka stevedores sweating on the docks, looking at the mooring lines and uttering silent prayers, hoping they wouldn't snap. Filipino laborers in the very field I was standing in, looking at the red dirt and picking up the burned stalks of cane and throwing them into the bed of a slow-moving truck. None of them had to see what I was looking at. None of their jobs required it. Mine did, for I'm a homicide detective—a hot, tired homicide detective whose wingtips would have to go into the trash after being assaulted by the red dirt. Shit. I should've worn an older pair.

It's 1953. The Year of the Snake to us Orientals. Maybe even the year of the same snake Sir Percivale saw battling a lion on his quest for the Holy Grail, the serpent a harbinger in Percivale's dream. Things to come. I wished I could see the future while I stood in the middle of that sun-blasted field in Kunia, choking on the red dirt swirling in the air and sweating like a man awaiting the gallows. I couldn't. There were no visions that day of maidens on snakes and lions heralding the future. There was just a burned bone sticking up out of the torrid soil.

Heavy, shuffling steps kicking up miniature orange-brown cyclones in the dirt came up from behind me then stopped on my right side.

"Dismembered and burned. Somebody took their time doing it," said the voice belonging to the steps.

"Yeah," I said. "It was done somewhere else, then the remains were brought here and buried, but not deep enough. The big harvester unearthed the femur, though at first glance it just looks like another burnt thing among the burnt cane stalks and leaves." I looked up to my right. Detective Lieutenant Gideon Hanohano of the Honolulu Police Department looked back at me with bags under his eyes. He always looked tired, but he always looked cool, too. Six-foot-two and three hundred pounds, the former lineman never broke a sweat. Not even in the furnace of Kunia. The cane fields of West Oahu thrived in this heat, the land situated on the leeward side of the island too far away from the Koolau Mountains to get the passing showers when the trade winds pushed the clouds over their peaks. All the water for the crops came diverted from the windward side or from reservoirs that seemed impossibly far away. The field we stood in was nasty hot and dusty after the stalks had had their leaves burned off prior to harvesting.

Gid Hanohano's big meaty fist came up out of his coat pocket filled with a couple of torpedo-shaped cigars. "Have one, Sheik," he offered. I took one of the cigars and rolled it between my thumb and middle finger.

"Thanks, Gid," I said. I looked at the brown and white band near the pointed head of the cigar. "Hey, Montecristo, from Havana. You've got great taste, Lieutenant."

"A page from your playbook. I can't go back to those smelly dime sticks since you introduced me to the Cubans. They're a pretty penny, though."

"You only live once."

"Like that poor soul." He looked down at the blackened bone. We bit the end caps off the Havana torpedoes and spit them into the dirt. Gid told me that he had talked to the luna about getting a couple of the boys to help us with shovels. While we waited for them, we puffed away and stared at the morbid bone in the hot earth. Some patrol guys in their olive drab uniforms came trampling through the blackened leaves and dust, dragging their shoes and raising a sinister cloud of the iron-oxide-rich dirt. They strode across the burned-out field erect and proud, like knights coming to tournament at Camelot. Shields, pinned to their chests, flashed defiantly in the angry Hawaiian sun. Only the banners and horses were missing. Trailing behind like squires, lab guys in their white coats, which wouldn't be white for very long, carried their implements of battle: satchels of chemicals, boar's bristle brushes, cameras and flashbulbs. Lots of flashbulbs, as if necessary on a near cloudless day in Kunia at high noon.

"Cocoa," I said to Gid, "and cinnamon and leather on the palate. Montecristo is pretty damn good."

Gid laughed a dry, wheezing near-silent laugh. The only way you could tell he was laughing was by the way his massive shoulders quaked. Even his smile looked more like a grimace of pain.

"Cocoa and leather," he said. "You crack me up, Sheik. It tastes like a cigar to me, but a good one." Gid always had a way of taking something I just said and making it simpler and more efficient. Like a Zen monk. Or like a kindergarten teacher. It made me feel foolishly baroque, but it made me smile too, for a lot of what came out of the mouth of Gideon Hanohano was so much like the solitary note from the keyboard of Count Basie over the blare of his orchestra. Simple. Definitive. Absolutely on the mark.

I loosened my tie and adjusted the porkpie hat on my head, pulling the snapped-down brim in the front a fraction of an inch lower over my bloodshot eyes, as if it would somehow increase the amount of shade it made over my face. When not drawing on the cigar, I could taste the rust red soil on the back of my tongue. Breathing the stuff in, we probably shaved off a few hours from our short, miserable lives every time we inhaled. It was times like that that made me wish, just a little, that I had listened to Ka-san and gone to law school like Wally Yoshida. But only just a little.

FRANCIS HIDEYUKI YOSHIKAWA
DETECTIVE SERGEANT
HOMICIDE DETAIL
HONOLULU POLICE DEPARTMENT

That's what my calling card said. This batch of them from the printer even had my name spelled correctly. Most people who knew me well called me Frankie. My Japanese parents who named me couldn't even pronounce that name so they called me Hide-kun. My fellow dicks in Homicide called me The Sheik. By any name I was tired. Hot and dirty. Call me what you wanted that morning, just not *cheerful*.

The mob in olive drab, along with their attendant brains in lab coats, arrived at our position. Superfluous flashes went off in the white noonday heat, capturing the black bone in its charred splendor from several different angles. Two young Filipino laborers in wide-brimmed straw hats and thick-soled boots caked with red dirt came scurrying up with large spades resting on their shoulders like rifles affixed with wide, flat bayonets. I almost thought they were going to salute us when they came to an orderly halt at my side.

"Thanks for coming out, gentlemen," I said to them. I took another draw off the Montecristo as they eagerly awaited direction. "Just do as that man says," I told them, inclining my head toward a squat figure in a lab coat and eyeglasses with lenses as thick as the Sunday *Star-Bulletin*.

"Thank you, Sheik," said the M.E. "This way, guys," he told the laborers, and directed them to the mound where the bone was sticking up. The M.E. was having the two diggers carefully make a trench in a three-foot radius around the protruding bone. More red dirt billowed up into the hot air and into my lungs. I took a handkerchief out of my breast pocket and covered my nose and mouth, momentarily letting my cigar hang from between the fingers of my free hand. Gid let out a deep cough and covered his mouth, too.

After a few minutes of trenching, the M.E. had the laborers stop and called in the lab guys with their brushes. Two technicians squatted and brushed around more black pieces of what was once a human being. Like archaeologists, they stopped every now and then to photograph the grisly shallow excavation. The sun was at its zenith and beat down angrily on insignificants like us, stupid enough to expose ourselves to its wrath. The only dead bodies polite enough to turn up in air-conditioned venues were tourists in their Waikiki Hotel rooms smothered in their sleep by their drunk, resentful spouses. Or those who died alone or by their own hand. Most others were found in places like this that were miserable to wear a suit. Sugarcane fields were a favorite place for making and disposing of corpses; when the fields were burned to get rid of the leaves and concentrate the sugar in the stalks prior to harvesting, almost anything in the middle of the conflagration got consumed and destroyed,

including evidence. This poor soul was brought in burnt pieces and buried
in a shallow grave; ironically, it was the burn and harvest that normally
consumed all traces of a corpse that exposed this one.

As the rust red-orange cloud around us settled to ankle height,
I removed my handkerchief from over my mouth and wiped my face
with it. My sweat was stained the same dark orange hue as the field. I
started puffing again on the cigar. I looked over at Gid, who had begun
to do the same. He stood, watching the technicians unearth black bone
after black bone between photographs, serene and uncannily dry in
the shade of his brown fedora. Beyond Gid, I could see Pearl Harbor
and the gray vessels crowding its piers, and beyond the harbor, the vast
azure expanse of the Pacific. The irony that I was standing in a dirty
field burning up in my suit within sight of the deep blue ocean was not
lost on me. When we were huddled together in a canvas tent in the
freezing rain of Northern Italy with the boom of artillery all around
us, Wally Yoshida, my high school teammate and foxhole neighbor,
had often remarked to me that he missed the "warmth" of home. Too
often I had stood in the "warmth" of home since and found myself
missing the chilly mornings of Belvedere, Italy or Bruyères, France
or the silent white snow in Central Park that I had trudged through
while at Columbia on the G.I. Bill. I thought of how that snow had
sparkled in the moonlight with the Upper East Side skyline behind
it and how breathtaking the sight of it all was from a horse-drawn
carriage while wearing a tweed overcoat and wool scarf, with Rachel
Levinsky bundled up next to me. It seemed ridiculously far away from
the red dirt of Kunia. A world and a lifetime away.

The brushing stopped and the flashes went off again. One of the
technicians reached carefully into the shallow pit and pulled something
out of it. He straightened up and walked a few steps over to the M.E.,
who looked at the item, took it from the technician, and walked over to
me and Gid.

"Sheik, Gid," he said. "The victim was dismembered postmortem, including decapitation. No sign of the skull, though. This was found around the cervical vertebrae."

"English," I said. The M.E. reveled in his bombastic speech. I knew what he meant. I just liked knocking him down a couple of pegs for the hell of it.

"I'm sorry, Sheik. Neck bones," he said, smirking. "Have a look." He placed the item in my outstretched hand; it was a pair of blackened dog tags on a blackened ball chain. I had seen enough of them to know the shape and size. I took out my handkerchief and rubbed one of the metal tags vigorously while Gid and the M.E. looked on. The soot came off the raised letters with some effort. Sweat was pouring down my face when I could finally read the glinting metal characters.

"Holy shit. Jiro Machida."

2

Jiro Machida. Sugar worker organizer and part-time reporter for the *Honolulu Record*. Activist and labor advocate. Military Intelligence Service veteran. Intellectual. Communist.

Honolulu was still in the grips of the Red Scare, the verdict in the Smith Act trial of the so-called Hawaii Seven close to being reached. The HUAC, the House Un-American Activities Committee, had convened hearings in Honolulu a couple of years before in the wake of the crippling longshoremen's strike of 1949, stirring up the paranoia of the local haole establishment. Communists were everywhere in the islands, the HUAC concluded. The Communists came in all stripes from outside the country club gates: haole agitators from San Francisco, labor union leaders, UH professors and their wives, even a couple of Negro transplants from big cities. But most were Japanese. We were clandestine agents of the Kempeitai during the war, who became Stalinist stooges after it, to hear it told by the landowning elite from their cool Manoa lanais, sitting on their rockers and sipping iced tea.

It didn't matter that scads of us were shipped off to Europe as Uncle Sam's expendables against Hitler. I got a Purple Heart for taking a bullet to the shoulder while rescuing a bunch of Texas haoles in the Vosges woods. Wally Yoshida, my best friend from McKinley High, lost a leg in Italy. Yet, we were still considered *Red* to the haole sugar-and-shipping overlords. Probably because we Japs were spawning at an uncontrollable rate, busting the confines of our sweltering pens in

Kakaako, Sheridan Tract, and Moiliili. Territorial elections were around the corner and the haole oligarchs were circling their wagons. The Red Scare was their latest volley.

Jiro Machida was Public Enemy Number Eight, Nine, or Ten after the Hawaii Seven, depending on which *Honolulu Star-Bulletin* or *Honolulu Advertiser* editorial you read. He was as colorful a character as one could be for a Japanese guy while most of us were as colorful as day-old rice. Jiro Machida was outspoken, eloquent, and smiled a lot. Unlike local men, he dressed with care and was someone Kakaako matrons considered "very handsome." Jiro Machida, according to station bulletins, had been missing for almost a month.

"Well, looks like we've done another job for Missing Persons," said Gid, as if reading my mind.

"Yeah," I said. "Maybe we should get two paychecks." A soundless laugh shook Gid's body. He dropped his spent Montecristo stub onto the red dirt and killed the ember under his mammoth cap-toed Oxford.

"Well, I got two meetings to get to—one at the station and another at the Prosecutor's. Follow up on this, okay?" he said.

"Okay, Gid. See you." Gid lumbered over to the waiting stake truck, his ride back to his car, its bed laden with burned sugarcane stalks. He hauled his mass up into the passenger seat and the truck pulled away, leaving a huge rusty cloud in its wake. Gid walked with a permanent limp, courtesy of an opium addict in Chinatown who stabbed him in the thigh with an ice pick, narrowly missing his femoral artery. It happened long ago when he was a uniformed beat man trying to break up a riot in a gambling den. It was, sometimes, painful to watch him move.

I watched the cane truck bear him back to his car at the plantation office about a mile down a rough dirt road. I had parked along the highway. After thanking the M.E. and his crew, I began the arduous trudge back through the burned-out field. My shirt stuck to my back and chest under my coat. I could imagine the pink-orange hue my soaked white collar had picked up after nearly three hours out in that cane field. Ka-san had a method for getting the red dirt out of white clothes, something she had perfected after years of living on the Waipahu plantation To-san worked at before he moved us all out to Kakaako. It involved immediate soaking in a bucket overnight, then a series of soaks in clean water before washing the garment in the usual way. I couldn't be bothered. I'd probably end up throwing away the shirt along with the shoes. Ka-san would click her tongue and shake her head if she knew. "Mottainai!" she'd say.

I reached my car after what seemed the same eternity it took Percivale to find the Holy Grail. I dusted myself off as best I could before I got into my new Cadillac Eldorado. It was red with a black leather interior, and I had put the top up and closed the windows as a precaution. While my foresight kept the upholstery clean, it had also turned the interior into an oven. I took the top down and scorched my palms and ass on the leather seats. The shiny new car's down payment represented all that was left of my G.I. Bill money after getting a degree from Columbia University in Medieval and Renaissance Literature. Both the degree and the car were flashy and impressive and something no one in Hawaii had—paid for with my blood. The difference was that the car actually got me from place to place, and the degree for all intents and purposes was as useful as an inflamed appendix. Gid disagreed. He told me if I had the capacity to analyze stuff written by folks who were dead for hundreds of years, then I'd have no problem figuring out folks who'd been dead for a lot less time. He called me a thinking man and said the Department could use a few more like me.

I hoped he was right. Most days it didn't feel that way. I chased my tail the same as every other dick in the Detail, maybe with a little more poetry, but definitely a lot more angst. It was nice, though, to have a man as smart and respected as Gideon Hanohano have such confidence in me; he was both friend and mentor. His endorsement

of my ways saved my job and pension after I had drawn the ire of a
particularly important haole just a month earlier while investigating
the death of a young Japanese woman who turned out to be his
daughter's lover. And my high school sweetheart. The occupational
hazards of being a homicide dick were, despite the occasional scrape
with suspects, mostly emotional. The fallout from the Miyasaki case
nearly ended my career, but Gid shielded me with a reputation, a
reputation as big as his body, absorbing the shit from the brass, who
were really dumping on me the shit they got from the territorial
governor and the haole elite. No doubt Harcourt Billings, Sr. pushed
as hard as his cufflinked wrists could to strip me of my pension. It
was Gid's quiet logic that persuaded the brass to keep me on the
Department payroll. He even got me a commendation, though it was
hushed and without any press fanfare.

  In fact, on the day I received the commendation from the Chief
in his office, I thought he was calling me in to personally sack me. There
was bile in the back of my throat and my palms were still wet with
apprehension when the Chief stood up from behind his huge koa desk
and extended his hand.

  "Congratulations, Detective," was all he said as he shook my
hand. Then he handed me a certificate and a medal in a black jewelry
case and sat back down. He lowered his eyes back to the paperwork
on his blotter, clearly signifying the end of our three-second meeting.
When I walked out of the huge double doors, Gid was waiting for me in
the hallway with his hat in his hands.

  "Everything okay?" he asked, with just the faintest trace of a
smile.

  "Swell," I said. "What did you tell them?"

  "Not much. I said they had a choice of pissing off either one rich,
powerful haole or almost half the island. I said it was up to them, but I'd
think about next year's elections."

I said, "Oh," then smiled. It probably didn't take Gid any longer
to tell that to the brass than it did me. It was that single *splank* of a note
from Count Basie's piano. Gid didn't take many shots, but all the ones
he took hit home.

As I thought about the day that Gid saved my job, I pulled a
Lucky Strike from out of the battered pack in my sweat-soaked coat
and stuck it in my face. I flipped the chrome lid of the Zippo Gid had
given me for Christmas and lit it up. The smoke disintegrated into the
withering heat of the Kunia air, and I started the Caddy, threw it into
gear, and headed down the long asphalt road makai toward the highway
and town. The drive back took me along the edge of Pearl Harbor
on Kamehameha Highway. The cane fields of the Ewa Plain loomed
green and quiet in the midday heat in the distance to the left like the
rolling sea, making me feel small and mean and petty as an insect.
After a few minutes the green had begun to erode in Aiea, giving way
to patches of white houses and bald tracts of red dirt being leveled for
more houses. The sugarcane was slowly disappearing, being replaced by
a crop of humans. Most of that crop bore a striking resemblance to me.
Change hung in the balmy air all about Hawaii like betrayal waiting to
happen in *Le Morte D'Arthur*, Mordred waiting in the wings, hot to take
Arthur's crown. That's probably how the haoles saw it. The Camelot of
the Navigators' Club and Punahou School and Manoa were about to be
overrun by the yellow horde. To them, the Red Scare was not so much
about wholesale slander as it was about survival. Their Camelot was
about to slip into the cesspool of memory, forever irretrievable.

Soon I was past the sun-blasted kiawe scrub of Red Hill and the
bleak utilitarian edifices of Fort Shafter and in the hot, crowded sprawl
of Kalihi, meandering my way from Kamehameha Highway onto King
Street. Laundry lines of Hell's Half Acre—replete with house dresses,
brassieres, and pillowcases, hanging like tournament banners from the
pages of Malory—adorned each side of King Street. Hoodlums and

drunks loitered on the sidewalks with cigarettes hanging out of their bronzed faces, waiting for something interesting to happen but not holding their collective breath. I drove steadily through the colorful bustle of Chinatown, then entered the brownstone-and-Spanish art deco business district that in a few blocks dissolved into the civic center of the courts and Iolani Palace.

A few more blocks on King, and I hung a right turn makai on Sheridan Street and pulled up in front of the humble building that housed the *Honolulu Record*, a small newspaper with a circulation of a little better than five thousand. It survived on its scant subscriptions and newsstand intake, donations, ad revenue from Japanese-owned businesses in Honolulu and Hilo, and generous contributions from the longshoremen's union. The paper was printed on an old hand-cranked press right in the middle of the office. Koji Ariyoshi, one of the Honolulu Seven, was the *Record*'s founding father. He had been an Army Intelligence language specialist during the war, plucked from internment to serve in Indochina translating intercepted Japanese messages and then eventually in China, where he met and befriended Mao Tse-tung himself. He got to compare firsthand the treatment of peasants under the British colonial system, the Kuo-min Tang, and Mao's communists. After returning from the war and raising consciousness about the plight of Hawaii's labor class, Ariyoshi started up the *Record* in 1948 as its Editor-in-Chief with financial help from the union.

Koji Ariyoshi was on trial for Smith Act violations along with six others; the *Record* faithfully covered the trial's progress with a healthy dose of accompanying editorial. The HUAC had already pronounced the *Record* a Communist Party front, though the Committee could do virtually nothing to halt its operations. Despite its small circulation, the *Record*'s influence was far-reaching, serving as a political counterbalance to the haole-run *Advertiser* and *Star-Bulletin*. The *Record* attracted

a few bright minds to grace its pages with their insight. In addition
to Ariyoshi himself, there was the Negro poet and journalist Frank
Marshall Davis, who came to Hawaii from Chicago and penned a
column called "Frank-ly Speaking," which was as muscular and bracing
as his poetry. One of the stanzas from one of his many poems about
Chicago: *Between the covers of books lie the bones of yesterdays/ Today is a
new dollar/ And/ My city is money mad.* Bold stuff that told it like it was.
"Frank-ly Speaking" was an entertaining and thought-provoking read,
where Davis would often rant eloquently about subjects as diverse as
racism, labor, sports, jazz, and vitamins.

I didn't drive straight to the *Record* to talk to Ariyoshi or Davis.
I was interested in a couple of the paper's other bright minds. One of
them was Jiro Machida, who obviously wouldn't be there because his
bones were on their way from Kunia. To the M.E.'s office. The other
came out of the building onto Sheridan Street as soon as my less-than-
inconspicuous red Eldorado pulled up to the curb fronting the *Record*'s
offices. In her gloved hands, she held a small purse and straw hat. She
wore a smart black dress covered in red polka dots and shiny black
pumps on her delicate little feet. Her black hair was up in a serious,
business-like bun and adorned with a red bow. A pair of glasses with
wide frames perched on her little nose, magnifying the dark, pretty eyes
behind them, her fresh lipstick accentuating the pout she gave me as she
closed the front door to her office.

She was one of the brightest minds I had ever met, and that
included the Rhodes Scholars who regularly put me to sleep with
lectures on Middle English and Abelard and Heloise at Columbia. Also,
the most beautiful of the lot by far. She was some lucky guy's girl. For a
change, I happened to be that lucky guy.

3

"You're late," she said. I got out of the car and walked around to the passenger door, holding it open for her.

"I'm sorry, darling. I got held up at a scene over in Kunia. I need to talk to you about it." Her expression softened and she stood on the tips of her black pumps, giving me a kiss. I could taste her lipstick, sweet and waxy. She sat down in the passenger seat and tucked her polka dotted hem in so I could close the door.

"I never could stay mad at you," she said. She cast her eyes coyly to the side and batted her lashes once behind her enormous lenses.

"Well, that's a relief." I got back behind the wheel and pulled away from the curb.

Like Jiro Machida had once been, Ellen Park was a part-time reporter at the *Record*. Most of the staff had been part-timers, as the paper could not afford to have many full-time reporters on its modest payroll. When not at the *Record*, Ellen worked in her parents' Korean grocery on the Kapalama Canal in Kalihi. While at the University of Hawaii, she was the Editor-in-Chief of *Ka Leo*, the school's paper. She read a lot of my case reports for fun, correcting the grammar with a perpetually sharpened pencil. She always kept one in her purse for the purpose of proofreading the work of mere mortals. Nitpicking was her hobby.

I met Ellen when she was covering the Miyasaki case for the *Record*. She tagged along and wrote a small series on the Japanese girl found chained to an anchor in Honolulu Harbor and the gallant Nisei detective assigned to the case, chronicling his dogged pursuit of the killer. He had the same name as me, but the man Ellen wrote about was something out of *Le Morte D'Arthur*, a Kakaako Sir Galahad. The readers of the *Record* would have been mortified to learn that his Kaimuki apartment was strewn with dirty socks and empty whiskey bottles. During that week in hell amid three gruesome murders—including one of my partner and friend, two suicides by self-inflicted gunshots to the head right in front of me and Gid being sent to the hospital with lead in his shoulder—I somehow fell hard for Miss Ellen Park. I was damned lucky she stuck around despite seeing the socks and bottles.

Ellen's sigh brought me back out of my reverie just after we had made the turn onto King Street. She was looking at me again with her gaze of appraisal, and I could already tell I wasn't earning any high marks from the judge.

"You're filthy," Ellen said. She ran her white-gloved finger along my grubby collar and made a face at the red-brown stain. "What were you doing this morning, gardening?"

"More like landscaping. I told you I was out in Kunia and I needed to talk to you about what we found out there."

"So, talk then." Ellen's interest was piqued. She always liked hearing about my cases and offering her investigative opinion. Her instincts had helped me on several occasions, but this case was a little too close to home to be a detached diversion for her.

"Later," I told her. "I'll tell you all about it once we've had our lunch."

"That's not fair. You can't just tell me you have something to talk to me about then not talk to me about it. You have to tell me *now*." Ellen hated surprises and she hated suspense. Much of her existence was spent eliminating the possibility of either in her life; it was that instinct to never to be caught off guard that made her such a great reporter. That same instinct also sucked a little of the mystery out of our romance, but Ellen more than made up for it in many other ways that made my pulse race and my breath heavy. I'd trade a little mystery for a truckload of thrill any day of the week.

"I'm not purposely trying to build up any excitement here," I told her. "The news isn't good, and I think I shouldn't rush it."

"Bad news? Then you really have to tell me about it right away!"

"Let's get our food first."

"You mean you want me to wait until we've waited for our seats at the Kress counter before you'll tell me anything?"

"I had something else in mind. Something faster and a lot nicer than the Kress." I stopped at a small okazuya on King Street for some assorted Japanese delicatessen fare and headed makai toward Kewalo Basin. All the while, Ellen bugged me about the bad news I was supposed to break to her. She stopped asking momentarily when I pulled into the dock area of the basin.

"Are we eating here by the water?"

"That was the idea. This is a special place for me. My dad used to bring me here when I was a kid." I parked next to the water where some fishing sampans were tied up and grabbed my raincoat from the trunk. I led Ellen by the hand to the shade of a large tamarind tree and spread my raincoat out on the grass. Ellen removed her gloves and folded them neatly before tucking them away in her purse. We sat down and I opened the paper sack from the okazuya and pulled out a couple of light green glass bottles of Coke. I pried the caps off with the can opener of my Swiss Army knife and handed one to Ellen.

"Have you ever brought a girl here before?"

"No. I always come by myself. It's my favorite place to think, after the furo at my mother's house." Ellen took a sip of cola and smiled triumphantly. She pulled a cone sushi out of the bag, holding it by the square of wax paper it was wrapped in. She took a bite, then held it in front of my mouth for me to do so.

"I must be pretty special to you, Frankie Yoshikawa."

"Of course."

"Good," she said sweetly, then instantly turned her face and tone back to business. The way she was able to do that, so suddenly, disconcerted me. "Now tell me about your morning in Kunia." I was beginning to learn that non sequitur was part of her nature and was probably a by-product of being such a fast thinker. Still, it was a little disturbing when in the throes of passion, she'd stop mid-kiss to wonder if she had locked the door at her parents' shop or proofread one of her articles. Her mind could be several places at once; I was a one-track thinker.

"Gid and I took a ride out there after some luna at the sugar company called dispatch early this morning. One of the laborers in the field grabbed what he thought was a burnt stalk of sugarcane and let go quickly when it didn't feel right. It turned out to be a human bone—one of many that were hacked up and burned."

"That seems fairly routine," she said. "I don't mean to sound cavalier about it, but you've found other victims that way, haven't you? Didn't you tell me that it was one of the more popular places to dispose of a body—putting it in in the middle of a cane field?"

"Yes," I said. I continued to eat, but I suppose it was too much to expect her to do the same. She folded her arms and gave me an interrogation stare.

"Then what makes this one special, as far as I'm concerned?" she asked. I laid my cone sushi back down on the wax paper square on my raincoat. No way to break it gently.

"There were Army dog tags around the neck," I said. "They were Jiro Machida's." Ellen was silent for a few heartbeats. She stared at me through her big lenses and blinked once or twice.

"Oh, my God," she mouthed soundlessly, then threw her arms around me and buried her face in my shoulder. Ellen had tremendous respect for Jiro Machida and always admired his work as a reporter. She along with others on the *Record* staff had expressed a great deal of concern over his disappearance. I lifted her chin and removed her glasses. I took a clean handkerchief out of my pocket and wiped her eyes. I relished any excuse to get her glasses off. I kissed her gently on the forehead and placed the handkerchief in her delicate little hand. She composed herself in a matter of seconds.

"I knew something like this would happen," she said, frowning.

"What do you mean by that?"

"Jiro and that thing he had with Harry Kurita. It was way beyond rivalry. I think they really *hated* each other. They had shouting matches in public. Jiro punched Harry in the face when Harry came by a few weeks ago to the *Record* to call him out. He bloodied Harry's nose pretty badly before Koji and Frank pulled him off." Ellen used a pair of hashi to fish out a bright yellow piece of shrimp tempura and held it up for me to bite, left hand cupped under it to catch any crumbs. I took a bite and then she did. Her legs were folded to her side in alluring feminine fashion, calves peeking out from under her polka-dotted skirt which was spread out over my raincoat and the grass next to it. I admired the contour of her hips beneath the flowing skirt and watched her sip from her Coke bottle while I pondered what she just said.

Like Jiro Machida and others at the *Record*, Harry Kurita was also under investigation by the HUAC. He was a doctoral candidate at UH and lectured there in English Literature. I had met Harry a while back in passing: he was a serious character with horn-rimmed glasses. He smoked a briar pipe and his mother probably ironed his clothes. He kept a stylish apartment in a brand-new building on Kapiolani Boulevard near University Avenue that was probably crammed with leather-bound editions of Dickens and Byron and Keats. He probably

seduced young Oriental coeds in that library-like parlor of his. Harry
Kurita and Jiro Machida were remarkably similar for a couple of guys
who hated each other's guts. They were even the same size. Maybe
that's why they hated each other's guts. Both were a couple of brilliant
intellectuals who aspired to change the world and made sure the world
knew and admired them for it. Harry was a rising Communist Party star
just like Jiro. Harry had also been missing for a month.

Ellen put her small, elegant hand in mine as we watched the
sampans cast off in search of ahi and aku and mahimahi. I lit a Lucky
Strike and we shared it between sips of Coke. We rubbed each other's
knuckles gently with our thumbs like children, feeding the pigeons
tempura crumbs and sushi rice. Time always passed so quickly with
Ellen. We idled in the shade of the tamarind tree for almost a half hour
with my head in her lap while she absently ran her fingers through my
tangled and heat-dampened hair before I broached the subject of Jiro
Machida again.

"Tell me more about Jiro," I said. I looked up at the seductive
curve of her bosom under her polka-dotted dress and her dark eyes
above it. She leaned down and gave me a quick soft kiss on the forehead.

"Jiro only stopped by the *Record* to drop off his articles. He didn't
keep a desk there—he told me he preferred to type on his lanai at home
in Waialua. He said it was quiet there and he put up screens to keep the
mosquitos out. Besides, there wasn't any room at the *Record* for a desk
for him or any of the part-time reporters for that matter. I sit at a small
typewriter table next to Ida's desk. Ida Furuta, the press's secretary, is
probably at the office for more of the day than anyone, including Koji
Ariyoshi. If anyone deserves a desk there, it's Ida."

"Why so much bad blood between Jiro and Harry Kurita? You'd
think they'd be natural allies against the modest world."

Ellen slapped my cheek playfully. "You're terrible, Frankie
Yoshikawa. Jiro and Harry were rivals for control of the Palolo Group."

"The *what?*"

"The Palolo Group of the Hawaii Communist Party."

This was news to me. Palolo Valley had its own cell? Literally, my backyard. I lived in a small, cramped cinderblock apartment near the corner of 10th Avenue and Waialae on the mauka side in a building owned by the miserly Old Chang, proprietor of Chang's Liquor and Sundries at the mouth of Palolo Valley. Of course, Hawaii CP cells were a fairly harmless and buffoonish lot of intellectual hotheads and labor leaders talking strategy for wringing more money out of their membership—money that would be used to print leaflets and send local CP leaders to San Francisco to attend "classes" on Marxism and the fine art of "organizing." When not talking about money, they were talking about increasing membership so they'd have more people to hit up for more money, like a sewing circle or stamp collectors' club. Nobody was planning the next great overthrow. The HUAC took such gatherings very seriously, though, and judiciously inflated the "threat" posed by these cells.

"I can't believe they'd come to blows over who gets to bang the gavel at those silly little meetings of theirs," I said.

"It isn't silly, Frankie Yoshikawa. Not to them." Whenever Ellen addressed me by my first and last name, she was trying to make a point. After proofreading, point-making proved to be her favorite pastime. Counterpoint-making was a close runner-up.

"Okay, darling. It's not silly." I rolled my eyes and got another playful slap on the cheek. "But why the viciousness over something like control over their little club? I thought communists were supposed to be deferential by definition. Let's all get along and share with one another and all that."

"In those circles, competition *can* be vicious. It can mean who gets a paid position within the CP and who has to do it just for the love of it. With Jiro and Harry, it was personal. There was a rumor that

Harry was seeing Jiro's wife. Harry and Jiro are about the same age, in their early forties. Beverly Machida is in her mid-twenties. I met her at a *Record* party at Lau Yee Chai. I guess she's what men would consider attractive." Ellen made a sour face she thought I didn't see.

"Harry and Jiro's wife? That might do it." I stayed there for a moment with my head in her lap, watching the sampans cast off, obscured by the brilliant reflection of the afternoon sun on the water. I thought about To-san and regretted that he would never meet and get to know Ellen. "Tell me about their fight at the *Record*," I said, after watching the fan-like sails of one of the vessels slip into the channel.

"It happened on the last day I saw Jiro. He came in to drop off an article he finished and stayed around to talk to Koji and Frank Davis. Harry pulled up in front of the office and came in and started yelling at Ida, demanding to know if Jiro was in. Jiro came out from Koji's office and asked him what all the noise was about. Harry told Jiro he knew what it was about. Jiro told Harry to go home. Harry said not until he got the answer he came to get from him or something like that. Then Jiro punched Harry in the face and Harry fell backwards. Jiro kept hitting him until Koji and Frank came out and pulled him off. Harry's face was a bloody mess. He got up and told Jiro, 'I'm going to kill you.' Then he left."

"What? Are you sure Harry said *that*?"

"I'm positive. Ida and Koji and Frank heard it, too." I sat up and shook my head. It was still full of Ellen's lingering perfume and the warmth of her lap. Her last statement jarred me out of that wonderful place in a Sinatra tune where nobody existed except me and her.

"I've got to go," I said and stood up.

"Remember to come over for dinner tonight. My mother is making something special just for you." Ellen took my hand and I gently helped her to her feet. I picked up my raincoat and shook the grass and sticky tamarind pods from it.

"I haven't forgotten. Your mom's bi bim bap or a cold baloney sandwich? It's one of the easier choices in life."

"She's bringing the stone bowls out for you."

"That's nice of her."

"It's nice of *me*. Who do you think is going to wash them after you eat?"

We got into the Cadillac and I drove Ellen back to the *Record*, where she was going to finish her article before being picked up by one of her older brothers and taken home to help her mother prepare dinner. As I held the passenger door open for her and helped her out she asked, "Where are you hurrying off to now?"

"I'm going to Harry Kurita's little love den. From what you told me, he's probably our front runner for suspects. He's been missing for as long as Jiro has been. Maybe I'll get an idea as to where he might have gone. Maybe not. It's been a while. Then I'll head out to Waialua and call on the Widow Machida." I put my arms around Ellen's waist and drew her in and kissed her. Her body seemed stiff and wooden and her lips were hesitant.

"What's the matter, darling?"

"Frankie Yoshikawa. If you so much as smile at her, we're through." She tapped the tip of my nose lightly with her index finger, grinned an icy grin and walked for the office door. "See you tonight," she said without turning around.

4

Harry Kurita's apartment on Kapiolani Boulevard wasn't a
very large place. New, it had the smell of fresh paint and wall-to-wall
carpeting. The new apartment smell carried a faint overlay of black
cavendish, Harry's pipe tobacco of choice. Sophisticated. Worldly. Just
like the tomes on his shelves with raised leather on the spines and gold
leaf lettering, the tiny parlor crammed with them. But furniture did
not crowd the room; there wasn't enough space. An off-white loveseat,
a walnut lectern with a large volume of Keats pretentiously opened
to "Ode on a Grecian Urn," a small coffee table piled with more old
books, and a decanter of scotch were the only things in the cramped
room, apart from the shelves stuffed to the gills with Romantic English
Literature or criticisms on it.

There was no radio. I met Harry Kurita in passing at a cocktail
party hosted a year before by my sister Iris, a high school geometry
teacher and advocate for political change. Harry was spouting some
diatribe about the evils of professional sports. He stood in the middle of
my sister's parlor with a martini in his hand ranting about professional
sports being a bourgeois tool used to control the masses, or some
such shit. He made this speech of his while I was trying to listen to
a previous day's ball game on my sister's radio. I asked him to hold it
down, please—Mantle at bat in the bottom of the ninth. Harry called
me a "case in point" and shook his head with exaggerated sadness. Iris
kicked me out of her house and wouldn't talk to me for a couple of

weeks. It was nice to see that the exalted Harry Kurita practiced what he preached. Or maybe he just couldn't afford a good radio like me and a lot of other people on a government salary.

Besides, Harry didn't need a radio to seduce the UH coeds he brought back for "study sessions." All he needed was his magnetic personality along with the loveseat and the books and the scotch. He didn't need competition from Frank Sinatra.

Harry's tiny apartment was on the ground floor of a new three-story apartment building. Its exterior done up in brown moss rock faced the boulevard, the building was dubbed "Kapiolani Suites" in modern white script on the rock wall. Ferns and ti leaves flanked the wall with a handful of black gas tiki torches skewed at stylish angles. All the new buildings were either "suites" or "arms" or "gardens" or "manors." I guess everyone wanted to feel like their new address was swankier than their last, even though it was just as hot and miserable as the old place and a hell of a lot smaller. Only the new paint and carpet made it nicer. The new place certainly wasn't more exclusive than the old place, either. In fact, it was probably much less so. Flashing my badge and a suggestion to the manager that he get an after-lunch drink with the dollar I slipped him got me access to Harry Kurita's little love nest. Try that with any daikon-cutting housewife in Kakaako and you're likely to end up posting bail for a trespassing charge.

The parlor didn't yield any interesting or relevant information. It was so sparse except for the books that there wasn't much of anything to look at. I moved to the bedroom. It's where Harry probably spent most of his time there, anyway. Even—and especially—during his "study sessions." The bedroom was stuffy and tiny, smaller than the parlor. The twin-sized bed in the middle of the room dominated the small space. There was a small nightstand and lamp and a maroon alarm clock with brass bells perched on it. A dresser stood against the wall at the foot of the bed, and next to it, stood a closet door. I started my methodical search with the nightstand. It had an open space under a single drawer where Harry kept more old books. The books were all poetry collections—Keats, Shelley, Oscar Wilde, and W. B. Yeats—all stuff set aside for post-roll-in-the-hay recitations in the nude no doubt. The books had nothing in them except poems. I opened the nightstand drawer. Condoms. No big surprise there. Loose change. The poor girls needed bus fare home after the "study session" was over. Aspirin. Actual conversation with tittering coeds was probably less than fascinating for a big brain like Harry. And panties. Lacy, silky panties in assorted colors. Trophies. They were typical of someone with Harry Kurita's ego. He probably watched those girls in his lectures the way Uther Pendragon watched Igraine when he was a guest at Cornwall and probably plotted to bed them in pretty much the same fashion: in the guise of something he wasn't—a trusted academic who was solely interested in the intellectual "development" of young, impressionable women. Judging from the number of panties in his nightstand drawer his appetite was large. Half a pack of Choward's Violet mints to sweeten the breath rounded out all that was in the nightstand. All were indicators of nothing I didn't already suspect.

The bed itself was neatly made. Harry seemed like the kind of intense and obsessive individual who did this every morning. There was nothing under the bed or under the mattress. I moved to the foot of the bed and opened the closet door. Empty. Nothing in there except for a winter coat twenty years out of style for the occasional mainland trip and a whole lot of wire and wooden hangers with nothing on them. The top shelf of the closet, which was usually the place for a suitcase, was also empty. No shoes on the closet floor. No neckties or belts on the hooks inside the door.

I shut the closet door and looked at the dresser that had nothing on it but a fine film of dust. I opened all of the drawers. Empty, every single one.

There were only two more rooms to look at in the tiny apartment. The bathroom's soap tray still held a slightly used bar of soap and half a bottle of shampoo. The medicine cabinet was full of talcum powder and green and brown glass bottles of little pills from a University area pharmacy: sleeping pills, pills for back pain, vitamins, but nothing critical or life-or-death necessary. There was no toothbrush, cologne, razor, or shaving brush—stuff the well-groomed man on the lam couldn't do without. The basin and the tub were dry and looked like they had been for quite some time. The manager had told me that he hadn't seen Harry Kurita for a month and that the rent would soon be due. He had reported Harry's absence to Missing Persons a couple of weeks earlier and complained about the lack of progress. The Missing Persons guys hadn't asked to see the apartment. Not yet.

I went back out to the parlor and sat down on the loveseat. It looked fairly obvious that Harry Kurita had blown town. The Missing Persons guys would have checked the airlines and the passenger ships; I'd remember to ask about it later, when I got back to the station. I started to perspire more profusely and the urge for a cigarette became overwhelming. I got up off the loveseat and walked to the opposite side the parlor to open the window. It took me all of three steps to get there. When I put my hands on the frame, I looked down at the sill and saw splinters. I squatted to eye level with the sill and looked more closely. The catch was bent slightly and scraped underneath. I stood again and opened the window and examined the underside of the frame. Someone had taken a sharp-edged object and undone the catch.

I pondered this while I lit up a Lucky Strike by the opened window. I took my hat off and let the slight breeze play through my limp, sweat-soaked hair while I smoked. If Harry Kurita killed Jiro Machida then fled the island, he took his time. The body was dismembered and burned and the charred remains were buried in a shallow grave in the middle of a Kunia cane field. He came back to

his apartment and packed a suitcase with all of his clothes and some
necessary toiletries then he disappeared. Why not? Who knows when
anyone would have discovered Jiro's remains? Leaving the dog tags
was sloppy, but he may not have known about them. Evidence showed
clothing incinerated to hell with the flesh, and they had probably
hidden Jiro's dog tags. Only the bones remained, if you could call the
brittle, barely solid state as "remaining." And the dog tags. The tags were
probably the only metal Jiro wore on his person. The skull was missing,
probably to prevent dental identification. It was the work of a man who
knew how to use his brain. Harry Kurita was such a man who knew how
to use his brain and he probably used it more discriminately than he
used other parts of his body.

I discarded my cigarette butt by flinging it into the mulch under
the ti leaves and ferns outside the parlor window. Then, just for the hell
of it, I turned to the kitchen and walked off the shag carpet onto the
linoleum.

They invented the term kitchenette for the little space I stood
in. To call it a kitchen would be stroking its ego. There was a porcelain-
coated iron basin under a tiny window hung with rough cotton curtains,
no doubt sewn by Harry's doting mother. Fronting the basin, the icebox
and the range were both within arm's reach in opposite directions. I
pulled the chrome handle on the icebox door and peeked inside. The
sour smell of old milk hit me in the face, and so did other food items
in varying stages of decay. The freezer was fuzzy with accumulated ice.
Somewhere in there, a chicken and a box of peas, and one of those
stick-in-the-oven dinners in compartmentalized foil trays: a bachelor's
teishoku.

I shut the icebox door and jiggled the chrome handle to make
sure it was sealed. I then saw it—a small wastebasket next to the stove. It
occurred to me that nobody had emptied the thing since Harry went on
the lam, so now here sat a veritable time capsule of the day he skipped

out. I opened a small drawer next to the range, pulled out a pair of tongs, and went fishing.

There was old tin foil with a crust of what was once brown gravy from the top of a frozen dinner. Under that, papers: mailers for some correspondence course on how to "increase your stamina" with some Charles Atlas look-alike in leopard briefs and oiled biceps, an old baking soda box, a paper bag from a liquor store, and a newspaper.

I pulled the newspaper out with the tongs and set it on the counter next to the range. It was a *Honolulu Advertiser* dated exactly one month before—probably a couple of days before both Jiro Machida and Harry Kurita were reported missing. I flipped through the pages, looking at every article and advertisement. I thought about Gid Hanohano and his habit of reading the newspaper every day cover to cover, missing no detail. Gid told me that it's something every good investigator should do. I tried to follow his example, taking in every column inch. The headline on the peace talks at Panmunjom and the weather report with its promise of miserable humidity brought back memories of the week I spent in hell working on the Miyasaki case. The paper was from that week. I thought of the heat and the kona winds. I thought of the friend I had to put down, the friend I almost lost, and the friend I did lose. I thought of meeting and falling for Ellen. I thought of what started it all, the poor girl we fished out of the harbor.

The harbor.

There it was, staring me in the face. Page three. Someone had circled the name of a ship under the vessel departures portion of the shipping announcements. The *Iwakuni Maru*, a Japanese-flagged fishing boat, had been scheduled to depart from Pier 32 at 11:00 a.m. on that date. I tore page three out of the paper and folded it and stuck it in my coat pocket. I threw the tongs back in the little drawer and I put my porkpie hat back on my head, snapping the brim down in front. Once outside, I tapped out another Lucky Strike from the pack and lit it. I stood in the cool green shade of the torch ginger leaves fronting Harry Kurita's apartment, enjoying the cigarette. Missing Persons would have talked to the airlines and to the big passenger ship lines that went regularly between Honolulu and the mainland or the Orient. They probably would not have talked to anyone manning the tramp steamers and they definitely would not have talked to the crew of a Japanese fishing boat. If Harry Kurita hopped aboard a Japanese fishing boat, he might have gone far, far away indeed.

5

Waialua. A long drive. Hot. Red dirt. Biting insects.

Waialua was a little plantation town on the North Shore blasted
by the sun and full of the sickly sweet smell of cane being processed at its
mill, a place on the edge of nowhere—if Oahu was nowhere. I couldn't
believe I was headed out to the cane fields again that day, and this time,
to fields even farther than Kunia. To Jiro Machida's house, one of a row
of rickety structures all covered with the same dark green paint meant to
hide the red dirt but not doing a very good job of it. I had gone through
three Lucky Strikes on the drive out from town. I lit up one more as I
pulled up the driveway of white sand and crushed coral dumped and
spread out over red dirt where the small lawn ended, where a vehicle was
parked on the lawn, a nondescript gray-brown Ford about ten years old. I
parked next to the Ford on the sand driveway and cut the engine.

The lanai was hemmed in by metal screen, rusted by the salt air
of the nearby beach and sporting its own screen door at the top of the
three rotten-looking plank stairs leading up to it. Inside the screens, I
could make out a small whitewashed table and an old office chair. On
the table a black typewriter. I crossed the little lawn and put a foot on
the first plank stair just as the front door slammed and light, rapid steps
thumped up to the lanai screen door. Suddenly, the door flew open,
narrowly missing the brim of my hat. I came face-to-face with a bald
head with dark, round sunglasses and long black goatee. The sunglasses
were so dark and large they looked like two gaping black holes in his

face. The rest of him was a spry, compact body wrapped up in the robes of a Buddhist monk. He smelled of Bay Rum aftershave.

"So sorry. Excuse, please," he said, blading his right hand vertically and holding it in front of his face in reverent greeting, bowing deeply.

"It's okay. Daijobu," I replied, bowing reflexively. The monk smiled at me with a mouthful of yellowed but sturdy-looking teeth, bowed again while passing me, and got into the Ford. He hit the starter, nodded goodbye, and then reversed off the lawn onto the road back toward the sugar mill and town. I shook my head. A homicide dick encounters all kinds of characters in the line of duty, but that monk was definitely one of the stranger looking birds I had seen in broad daylight. I climbed the steps to the lanai. Off to the right side of the door was a getabako full of ritzy high heels. I knocked on the frame of the front door.

"Did you forget something, Basho?" a high, slightly nasal voice called from the gloom of the interior of the little house. The voice had the sound of unintentional allure, of a trap set unwittingly by a child. It was the sound of a sleeping cobra, if a sleeping cobra made a sound.

"I sure did. I forgot to come at a better time. But I'm not Basho. Basho just made a beeline back toward town, like I should have. It's too hot to be in Waialua today."

"Some of us don't have a choice," said the voice, getting closer. Small steps padded toward the door until I could smell the warm spice of her body. A silhouette emerged from the darkness, graceful and curvy.

"Can I help you?" she asked through the screen. I could see black hair piled high and red lips through the screen and, I thought, the flutter of eyelashes downcast demurely.

"Mrs. Beverly Machida?" I asked. I pulled my badge from my pocket and showed it to her through the screen. "I'm Detective Sergeant Yoshikawa of the Honolulu Police Department. Could I trouble you for a word, Mrs. Machida?"

"You *could*," said the sleeping cobra, languidly with subtle heat. A small hand undid the iron hook that held the screen door closed. "Won't you come in, Detective?"

She was about five-foot-six if you didn't count the hair piled on her head. With the hair, she was almost as tall as I was and most unusually tall for a Japanese girl. She was built like a Radio City Music Hall Rockette with skin bronzed by the sun, though not in the way Ka-san's was from years of hard labor in the cane fields; hers was the bronze of health and vanity, the tint of swimming and tennis. She had exceptionally large eyes and full, wet lips that glistened in the faint light of the sun through the lanai screens. She wore a simple white dress with the palest gold floral brocade that purposely drew attention to the dark, sensuous luster of her skin. She looked at me from under hooded lids, lazily and dreamily, as if she were looking through me at a pastoral Van Gogh full of gold and blue, something infinitely more interesting than my face.

"Thank you," I said. I removed my red dirt-dusted wingtips and followed her into the warm little parlor, shutting the screen door behind me. The room had a homey, rustic, island feel to it, furnished with a koa-framed sofa and koa-framed seats. The cushions were upholstered in white shantung silk and the coffee table held a large koa bowl filled with colored glass globe floats from Japanese fishnets. Across the sofa and the coffee table against the far wall, there was a credenza and, on the credenza, a white porcelain vase full of freshly cut torch ginger, bird-of-paradise, and lobster-claw heliconia. The opposite of Harry Kurita's cramped little seduction library, this place revealed a woman predator.

"Won't you have a seat, Detective?"

"Thank you."

I sat down in one of the koa armchairs with my hat in my hands and my hands on my lap. Beverly Machida's manicured fingers pushed an ashtray on the coffee table toward me. I pulled my pack of Lucky

Strikes out of my pocket and offered her one. She pulled one of the cigarettes out of the pack in a sensual, slow manner. I held the Zippo out for her and she grasped my hand while she lit up. Her hand was soft and warm and felt like something only felt in a bedroom. She let her fingers slide slowly off my hand when she was lit up and tossed her head back lazily while she slowly blew white smoke toward the ceiling. I lit up my own cigarette and stuck the Zippo back in my pocket. She regarded me from under dark, thick lashes.

"What brings you out to Waialua on this hot day, Detective?"

"News," I said. "Bad news."

"Jiro?"

I nodded. I was staring at the glass globes in the bowl on the table. I brought my eyes up to meet hers and found she was looking at nothing, staring right through me as if I weren't there at all. She suddenly had the dead, dull eyes of a reptile on a wet leaf with no spark of thought behind them. Or maybe her eyes were always like that and I failed to notice them when I first looked at her; there was a lot more about Beverly Machida to notice at first glance. I braced myself for the wail and the convulsions. They didn't come. Instead, she stood up calmly and walked over to the credenza. She bent down and opened a pair of doors and produced a tray with a crystal decanter full of scotch and a couple of tumblers. She padded back to the coffee table in small, mincing steps like a kimonoed geisha and set the tray down next to the koa bowl full of glass globes and removed the diamond-like stopper from the decanter. She looked up at me with a wide smile.

"Drink?"

"Why not?"

Her graceful hands lifted the heavy decanter with improbable ease and poured the dark amber liquid generously into the cut crystal tumblers. It was the most dumbfounding thing I had ever seen. In my short time in Homicide, I had broken the horrible news to newly made widows a number of times. I had witnessed the loud, terrible wail from the Portuguese matron who clenched her flour-covered fists and beat them on her huge apron. I had witnessed the silent, intense stare of the Japanese housewife with watery eyes who was broken into a thousand pieces under the quiet façade of dignity. And everything else I had seen was something between the two: the young kanaka newlywed who repeated "Oh my God" over and over again, the old Filipina plantation matriarch who crossed herself and bawled into her brown hands, the haole socialite who dug her fingernails into your forearm and asked, "Are you sure? There must be some mistake . . . ."

Beverly Machida was something I had never seen before.

She coolly handed me the tumbler and stood close enough to my chair so I could feel her heat, watching me take my first sip of scotch. Her right hand rested on the dramatic curve of her hip and she reached out with her left hand to fix the lapel of my coat, all the while humming a Cole Porter tune with lascivious huskiness just under her breath. I stiffened unnaturally when her hand touched my clothing and my blood ran cold. This was the strangest manifestation of shock I had ever seen.

She sat back down and took up the other tumbler, draining half of it in a single pull. She set it back down on the tray, looked up at me, and smiled some more. I thought I smiled back but I didn't really. I flinched. It only felt like I smiled.

"We found remains in a cane field in Kunia," I said, just to fill the air with something other than my discomfort.

"I already knew he was gone," she said, almost dreamily, still smiling and still looking right at me but not really *at* me, like she was looking at a spot in the air where my head was.

"How?"

"I felt it. And Bashō told me so."

"The monk in the Ford?"

"Yes. He's my spiritual counselor."

"How did *he* know?"

"He said it was the way of things. That Jiro yearned to be one with the fabric of eternity, to add his own light to the lights of those who had already achieved that oneness. Basho said he was there in the tapestry of lights, shining more brightly than ever, even more so than he did here with us."

"He said *that*? Just now, before he left?" I took another sip of my scotch. It burned on the way down.

"Yes," she said, almost giggling.

"Lucky guess."

"In our lives, there is no guessing, Detective. There is only clarity in varying degrees."

"Sure."

I was beginning to feel like a drunken peasant watching a medieval passion play, admiring the pretty colors and the pretty noises paid for by his hard-earned coin but completely missing the point. Beverly Machida sat there staring in my direction with a vacant smile on her tanned face. She raised her tumbler to her lips and drained the rest of her drink. I did the same.

"Another drink, Detective?"

"By all means."

She poured another drink for both of us, just as stiff as the last. I watched her raise her tumbler to her lips with both hands and nearly empty it. I didn't touch mine. I looked at her trying to determine if her queer behavior was some off-the-deep-end reaction to the news that her husband was dead.

"I'm a Homicide Detective, Mrs. Machida," I said, trying to elicit a more normal reaction from the strange young widow.

"Beverly."

"Pardon me?"

"Call me Beverly. Mrs. Machida is my mother-in-law."

"I'm a Homicide Detective . . . Beverly."

"It sounds like an interesting job." She continued to smile and poured herself another drink. At this, I lost it.

"*Interesting job*? I'm not trying to small talk you into a *date*, Beverly. I'm trying to tell you your husband was the victim of foul play. Murder. Murder most foul. Someone hacked his body to bits and burned it and dumped it in a cane field. Does that mean *anything* to you?"

She set her tumbler down on the coffee table and her smile became a spoonful sweeter. "It doesn't matter how he got there, Detective," she said, now looking just a little medicated as well as inscrutable. "He's one with all existence, the way he always wanted to be."

"Stop. No more mystic proclamations or introspective talk of the fabric of existence or any other assorted Buddhist mumbo-jumbo. I'm trying to tell you that someone killed Jiro Machida and cut him up and incinerated his pieces then buried them in the middle of a Kunia cane field. Jiro Machida. Your husband. Would you do me a big favor and play along just a little bit? If you don't want to cry, you can sit there and look astonished. Or angry. Or even catatonic. But not serene. I might get hysterical if you give me more *serene*."

"You're tense," she said, smiling like a jade carving. "Would you like a massage?" I shot up out of the koa chair and nearly sent my tumbler of scotch hurtling to the floor.

"I need to use your bathroom," I said.

"It's in the back, behind the kitchen." Beverly Machida continued to sit and smile and drink like we were at some hotel lounge trying to put up the show of getting to know each other before angling for a kiss goodnight. It was more than I could wrap my brain around. Her strange behavior actually made my head hurt. I made my way through the cozy little parlor into a clean plantation kitchen with new Formica on the counters and new linoleum on the floors. The bathroom was a little annex attached to the rear of the main house, like it was in most plantation houses of the era in which it was built. I exited the back of the kitchen through a windowed door and descended two steps to reach the bath annex. A whitewashed board with hinges and a handle served as the door. I pulled it open and yanked a chain dangling in front of my face to rouse the naked light bulb.

The floor of the bath annex was a bare poured concrete slab which replaced the original pine boards. There was a drain in the middle of the floor, a deep wooden furo, and a commode and basin on a wall opposite the furo. Mounted on the wall above the basin was a medicine cabinet with a mirror door. I walked over to the basin and twisted the "C" knob for cold tap water. I splashed my face with it and looked in the mirror at a haggard, irritated face. It was the face I imagined on Arthur after he had been betrayed by Lancelot and Guinevere, lined by grief and haunted by his burden of rule. At the moment, though, my grief and burden were being caused by my inability to read a strange young widow's bizarre reaction to her husband's murder. It made for a dramatic picture all the same.

I dried my face and hands off on a fluffy white towel on a hook on the wall then opened the medicine cabinet. It was full of man's stuff: shaving brush, razor, aftershave lotion—Bay Rum. Basho's scent. Was the strange little "spiritual advisor" spending the night? Neither of them was even supposed to know Jiro was dead until I told her that afternoon. Then again, if what Ellen said about Beverly and Harry Kurita was true, Beverly wouldn't have much of a problem carrying on with the monk right under Jiro's self-righteous nose. All of the girly stuff was probably in the bedroom on some dressing table, and there probably was a dressing table in the bedroom. Mrs. Machida was pretty continental for a girl who lived in a Waialua plantation village house. There were aspirins, too. Lots of them. The way she sucked the scotch up, she probably needed them.

I looked down. The floor was wet near the furo. Someone just had a bath. Either Beverly took one just before coming to the door or Basho did before getting in his jaunty Ford and high-tailing it out of Waialua. The whole place still had the smell of soap and a little Bay Rum. Basho. It didn't surprise me at all. Beverly may have offered *me* a bath if she thought it would make me less "tense." Maybe I was overreacting. Maybe she was just really eccentric and this was her way of dealing with terrible news. Maybe I should just get the hell out of Waialua and pick up some flowers to take to Ellen's and just forget about the whole damn thing. What the hell. I tried. Sometimes breaking the bad news to a new widow wasn't all the drama it was supposed to be. With Beverly Machida it wasn't even close. I had spent enough time on the fringes of the island up to my knees in red dirt and misery. Time to call it a day and clock out.

I got my head together and exited the bath annex. The sun was now dipping toward Kauai and shining directly in my eyes. I took a quick look at the little yard and garden in the back, fenced in by a makeshift barrier of bamboo stakes and chicken wire, no doubt meant to keep the chickens at the Filipino's house next door from wandering into Beverly's little cucumber patch and pecking away at the long green fruit near the ground. I climbed the two steps to the kitchen door and went back into the house.

I crossed through the kitchen and my socked feet nearly tripped on something on the parlor floor. It was a white dress with gold brocade flowers. I looked up and saw Beverly Machida sprawled on the sofa with her hair down and her eyes closed and the same empty smile gracing her dark face. She was wearing nothing but her brassiere and a slip, both starkly white against her tan skin. She held her tumbler of scotch high on her bare midriff just below the breathtaking swell of her lace-sheathed bosom.

"I'm sorry," she said vacantly but with a seductive undertone. "It's hot."

"Just like I said."

I was already headed toward the door. This bizarre display was too much. Eccentric or not, no grieving widow ever shed her clothes for me as a reaction to the terrible news I gave her.

"Would you like to join me?" she asked, eyes still closed.

"Thanks, but I've got to run."

I took a calling card out of my coat pocket and dropped it on the coffee table next to the scotch decanter. "Sorry about your husband. Call if you have any questions." I put my hat back on my head, snapped the brim down in front, and opened the screen door. As I got back into my wingtips, a husky giggle came from the sofa.

"Don't go," she said. She hadn't budged.

"I have to."

"Please stay and lie down with me, Harry."

Harry? Maybe it was the shock. More likely it was the scotch. I tied my shoes quickly and started for the lanai screen door. For no reason at all, I looked at Jiro's typewriter and walked over to it. It was clean and well maintained and there was an old towel draped over the back of the chair, probably used to cover up the typewriter when not in use to protect it from dust and the salt air of the North Shore. I opened the top, yanked the ribbon spool out and stuck it in my pocket. I listened to the sound of nothing floating through the screen door one last time. I got off the lanai and into my car and drove as fast as I could out of Waialua.

6

Park's Grocery, a two-story wooden structure painted light blue, was just across the street from the Kapalama Canal. I pulled up across the street from the little store on the canal side at just about six o'clock. I had stopped by a King Street florist on my way back into town from Waialua and my strange visit with Beverly Machida. I had a bouquet of bright yellow chrysanthemums for Ellen's mother and a dozen white roses for Ellen. Gid told me about the florist. He happened to know where all of the florists were in town; it was the kind of knowledge he acquired from reading the newspaper cover to cover every day. The big sage wasn't just my advisor on things police and investigative; he also took it upon himself to guide me through my life, and especially, my love life since Ellen.

Gid could see my falling for Ellen before I did. The week I was immersed in solving the Miyasaki case, I literally fell for her, or, I should say, *because* of her, I fell right out the second-floor window next to my desk down onto the sidewalk on Merchant Street. I was trying to get away from a prying little girl reporter who had the brains to single me out as the dick assigned to the case when the rest of the press was content to get the lowdown from the brass's official release. Ellen cornered me outside the Homicide Division office and insisted on covering the case for the *Record* as "my story." I stalled her and jumped out the window. In the end, though, I was lucky she was so persistent. We both got our exclusives: Ellen got her story and I got Ellen. Gid saw it coming. He told me where I could get long-stemmed roses on sale. "Flowers, Frankie," he told me. "It's the best way to show a wahine you really care about her."

"How's that?"

"You wouldn't buy flowers for *yourself*, would you? Women like that—it shows you're willing to do something *just for her*. In the end, it's what they all want. Someone who will do things *just for her*."

"Right," I said. "Just for her." And he was right. Gid was always right. He was right about his feeling that something was going to go south when we drove up to Sam Makuakane's house in Papakolea, where we found Sam, an old friend of mine from high school, who turned out to be the man who unwittingly drowned Millie Miyasaki. He shot Gid in the shoulder and I shot him before he confessed and died. Having Gid around was better than having Sir Percivale's visions of serpents and lions and maidens foretelling the future. He never talked in riddles. He attributed most of his "correct guesses," as he called them, to something called his na'au, or gut, an inner feeling from the digestive tract rather than from the brain or heart. He taught me how to use mine, and I'm still not sure if I'm grateful. Using your na'au properly can be a curse as well as a blessing. Just ask Gid. This is why he rarely smiled.

I got out of my car and carried my two bouquets across the street. I was greeted with a punch in the face by the scents of kimchee, garlic, and fish. Since I started dating Ellen, the smells had become less overwhelming and more welcoming. They started to be the smells of home, whether they were at the Park's or from my own icebox from food Ellen brought over for me.

Ellen's mother sat behind the counter, half hidden by the cash register. Young looking for her age, she wore glasses with rhinestone-studded frames and had jet-black hair. She looked up from the counter and smiled widely at me.

"Konbanwa!" she shouted in flawless Japanese. Her voice was soft and gentle as a fire truck siren, and Ellen had inherited her mother's volume.

"Hello," I told her, returning her smile. "It's nice to see you again. Thank you for inviting me to dinner. These are for you." I held the chrysanthemums out for her to take. She accepted them with a bow.

"Totemo kirei! Domo arigato gozaimasu!" she boomed. Ellen's mother had gotten into the habit of addressing me in Japanese. She and her husband, Ellen's stepfather, both spoke it perfectly having lived through the Japanese occupation of Korea when young. I think her speaking to me in Japanese was her way of making me feel welcome, though I never spoke it back to her out of embarrassment. My feeling was that she could not have been very thrilled at the fact that her only daughter had chosen a Japanese boyfriend. Ellen's father was much more aloof with me, but then again he was with everyone. He ran roulette and craps games in the back storeroom of the shop and his game patrons referred to him as "Pohaku" Park. Pohaku was Hawaiian for "stone," and it was a reference to his expression as well as his demeanor. Ellen went out of her way to assure me that both her parents were actually quite fond of me, and if they resented me for being Japanese, they hid it well.

This was much more than I could say for my own mother. Though Ka-san actually liked Ellen very much, she often made crass comments on Sundays when I brought Ellen over for dinner in Kakaako. Things like, "Sorry, there's no garlic in here," when passing her the bowl of namasu or "Not karai enough, yeah?" whenever Ellen took a bite of something. I cringed whenever those comments came out and reprimanded my mother. The reprimands slid off her back unnoticed. Ka-san actually thought she was being nice to Ellen by being concerned about her "taste." My mother didn't get the memo that had proclaimed the Japanese to be the most polite and tactful of all peoples. She even told Ellen once that she was a "nice" Korean girl, in a tone

that suggested that "nice" Korean girls were in short supply. No doubt
Ka-san believed this to be a compliment of the highest order. She was
soundly scolded after a while by not just me but by all four of my older
sisters whenever those comments came out. Still, Ellen bore it like a
trouper, smiling indulgently and thanking Ka-san for her concern. Ellen
got a lot of support from my sister Pansy's husband Eldred Wong, who
was Chinese, and from my sister Iris, who had been friends with Ellen
from before we met as they both attended the same Democratic Party
fundraisers and events.

Ellen's mother was bustling about, chopping the bottom inches
off the chrysanthemum stems and arranging the flowers in a green
ceramic vase when Ellen appeared on the store floor, looking fresh and
pretty in a simple tropical floral print dress with her hair down.

"For you," I said. I extended the bouquet of white roses.

She took them, smiled into the flowers, and took a good, long
sniff. "Thank you," she said. "Are these an apology?"

"An apology for what?"

"For seeing that . . . *woman*." She said the word begrudgingly.

"Come on, darling. You know it's a part of my job. She's Jiro's, uh,
widow, after all. If it's any consolation, I found her to be quite strange
and disturbing. And I didn't so much as smile at her."

"Then apology accepted, Frankie Yoshikawa." She smiled
angelically and tiptoed to give me a kiss. I took it for what it was worth
and didn't belabor the point. Flowers. The best way to show a wahine
you really care. Thanks a lot, Lieutenant.

Dinner was every bit as good as it was billed. The bi bim bap
was a kaleidoscope of colors—red, green, yellow, orange, brown, and
white—and flavors—sweet, salty, spicy, and savory. It was all made nice
and crispy by the hot stone bowls it was served in and there was plenty
of beer and Korean floral tea to wash it all down. Ellen's brothers had
all moved out years ago when they married and acquired homes of their

own, so on that particular night it was just me, Ellen, and her parents. Her stepfather excused himself early to set up his games for the evening. After dinner, Ellen left me at the dining table with a beer to enjoy while she cleaned up with her mother. When they were done, she returned with a plate of sliced fruit for dessert and suggested we take it out to the canal across the street to enjoy.

We sat in my Cadillac with the top down and admired the moonlight on the sluggish waters of the Kapalama Canal while we enjoyed slices of the sweet, water-filled pears the Parks brought in from Korea. We kissed for a little when we thought nobody was looking. Then Ellen did it again: she wanted to talk business just when I thought I could lose myself in her embrace and forget about everything that had happened that day.

"What happened out at Jiro's?" she asked, pulling her mouth away from mine. Non sequitur. Annoyingly, I was getting used to it.

"What happened? Nothing, strangely enough. I broke the news to Beverly Machida and she acted like it wasn't news. She said she already knew he was dead. She *felt* it. She offered me a drink and gave me some Buddhist philosophy. Some monk was over at their house— he was leaving as I arrived. Mrs. Machida called him her 'spiritual counselor' or something like that. She called him Basho and said he was the one who told her Jiro had gone to the great Nirvana cement mixer. I told her he was murdered. She didn't cry, didn't scream, didn't babble like an idiot. Nothing. So, nothing happened. It was perturbing." Of course, I did not relate the fact that Beverly Machida had gotten undressed and invited me to join her on the sofa. I knew Ellen. No good could have come of that. I did tell her one last thing, though: "She begged me to stay as I was walking off the lanai. She called me Harry."

"Harry? Why?"

"I don't know. She was nice and drunk by then, I guess."

"Then I suppose it was true—about her and Harry."

"I don't know. Maybe. I took a look at Harry Kurita's apartment just before I drove out to Waialua. I couldn't find anything tying him to Beverly *or* Jiro. It looks like he's skipped town." Ellen thought about this. She had that frown on her face she got when her thinking cap was on. So much for more kisses.

"It's funny what you said about the monk," she said at last. "Beverly didn't strike me as particularly religious or philosophical. In fact, I kind of thought she was quite the opposite—shallow, vacant, self-absorbed. Jiro, on the other hand . . . Jiro had lately taken to discussing Buddhism with Koji and Frank, which was kind of weird."

"Weird? Why? I thought he was a deep, intellectual thinker."

"He was, but not in a religious way. Jiro was a communist to the core, and we all had quite a time trying not to talk about it with HUAC investigators. He went to school in Russia, you know, when he was younger. I think it was called Sun Yat Sen University, in Moscow. It's not there anymore. He met an old Japanese communist there named Sen Katayama and learned how to speak Russian. In fact, he was recruited to the MIS because he was able to communicate with Russian intelligence units in Japanese-occupied Korea. He even spoke a little Korean, and pretty well." I thought Ellen averted her eyes and blushed a little in the moonlight. It irritated me that Jiro may have flirted with her in Korean, though it probably happened long before I met her. She must have read my mind and said, "Are you pouting, Frankie Yoshikawa? Are you jealous?" She laughed like little pieces of silver falling. I turned away and didn't answer. I was probably scowling, which only amused her more.

"I must be pretty special to you, Frankie Yoshikawa." She was still flush with laughter but her eyes were serious.

"What do you think?" I pulled her to me and we blissfully lost ourselves in each other for a precious twenty minutes. It was as if we both quaffed the same potion that set Sir Tristram and La Beale Isoud upon one another on the boat from Ireland to Cornwall. In this case the potion was a couple of beers and some little porcelain cups of Korean tea. We set our lips and tongues and hands loose with reckless abandon.

It all came to an end with Ellen's mother bellowing for her. It was something in Korean. Ellen bellowed back, also in Korean, from the passenger seat of the Eldorado across the street. The two of them had what sounded like a heated argument from several yards apart. They probably woke all the fish in the Kapalama Canal. It wasn't an argument at all. According to Ellen it was a simple exchange about hanging laundry in the back of the store the next day because it didn't look like it was going to rain.

"Still," she said in breathless fashion, though I couldn't tell if the breathlessness was my doing or all that shouting she did at her mother, "I think I'd better get back inside. Dad's night customers will be starting their games soon."

"Okay, darling. Could I trouble you for something before I leave?"

"For you, anything."

"How about a large envelope and a couple of postage stamps?"

"Huh?"

I pulled out the ribbon spool I yanked out of Jiro Machida's lanai typewriter. I said, "It's Jiro's. While his liquored widow was babbling away on the sofa, I put this in my pocket."

"Is it evidence?" Ellen asked.

"No. It's a *clue*, possibly. If it were *evidence*, I probably should have acquired it properly. I'm going to mail it to myself at the Station."

"A matter of semantics to suit your purpose, I suppose. Why mail it to yourself?"

"Call it a feeling. I don't want it on me tonight." Naʻau. That's the feeling I had. Gid Hanohano's guts-before-brains philosophy. It always served him well and it served me well, too. A little too well. Gid taught me how to trust it and I've cursed him for it ever since. Sometimes it was better to live in the dark.

Ellen nodded and shouted for her mother with instructions in Korean. Her mother came out smiling, holding a large manila envelope and about five postage stamps.

"Hai, dozo," she said in Japanese, presenting me the items with both hands and bowing her head.

"Thank you," I told her in English, and returned her bow with a nod and a smile. I appreciated her efforts, but somehow could never speak back in Japanese knowing what she must have gone through growing up in Japanese-occupied Korea, despite the fact that she understood and spoke Japanese better than she did English. I thanked her again for dinner as well, and she invited me to come any time, again in Japanese.

Then she said in English, "No more baloney." She smiled a great, big smile.

"No more baloney," I replied. Ellen had told her about the dinners I usually ate when not being fed by Ka-san or restaurants. It was nice to be wanted somewhere. Ellen walked me out to the front of the store and gave me a long goodnight kiss. She warned me to be careful and told me to call her in the morning. I told her I would be careful and I would call her in the morning. Then, I crossed the street and got into my car and drove away.

I stopped at the downtown post office and stuck the typewriter ribbon into the envelope Ellen's mother had given me. Not knowing the correct amount of postage, I stuck all the stamps on it, addressed it to myself at the station, and dropped it in a bronze mail slot.

The night air was warm and a slight breeze moved the fronds of the coconut palms along King Street as I drove back to my little apartment in Kaimuki. The palm leaves moved and shined metallically in the moonlight like black Christmas tree tinsel buffeted by a ceiling fan. Occasional neon signs flickered in the windows of Japanese bars and tinny kayokyoku music spilled out of the doors when red-lipped bar girls pushed them open to get some air. The rest of Moiliili and Kaimuki were a lot less lively, though. Behind the bars on the main drags were deep bedroom communities where decent folks lived and slept. They'd had their chazuke and their evening bath and had put out the lights for the night. Only grubby homicide dicks with one more cigarette to smoke and one more shot of whiskey to drink were still out driving around. And I was about to put an end to that nonsense.

I pulled the Eldorado into its usual space on the side of Old Chang's storefront and put the top and windows up in case it rained. Then I dragged my soiled wingtips up the concrete stairs, scraping the soles as I went. The occasional hum of a motor on Waialae Avenue was the only other sound.

I got to my apartment door and opened it. I kicked something on the way in. It was the wastebasket. It wasn't propped up in the kitchen the way it was when I left it. It was lying on the floor in the foyer. I could feel the kochoojang paste from the bi bim bap come up to burn the back of my throat. Na'au. Something stunk and not just the trash on the floor. I pulled my .38 out of my shoulder holster. I turned on the lights and looked around the apartment.

I said: "Shit."

7

Ransacked. A hurricane had torn through my apartment. The wastebasket overturned in the foyer, all of the trash strewn about the linoleum, every kitchen drawer and cabinet door flung open. Some of the contents were on the floor, some haphazardly placed on the stovetop or counter, others just thrown and resting wherever they fell, with the parlor and the bedroom and the tiny bathroom in pretty much the same state. Before Ellen had blown into my life, I may not have noticed. Lately, she was in the habit of tidying up for me and the mess was a stark contrast to the order she brought to the place. The thought made me smile sourly.

I made a quick survey of the damage and took inventory of my meager worldly possessions. The place looked like shit but nothing was missing. To-san's gold pocket watch and the two hundred bucks I kept stashed in the nightstand drawer were scattered on the rug next to my bed when the drawer was pulled out and dumped. Whoever broke in appeared uninterested in my valuables. Whoever it was upended the mattress and threw it up against the wall. Dumped even the ashtray on the rug, though I couldn't imagine what anybody could have possibly thought I might've hidden *there*. This mess—out of sheer malice!

I stepped over the trash, wooden spoons, and broken dishes on the kitchen floor and found my bottle of Haig & Haig Pinch mercifully untouched. I uncorked it and poured a stiff drink into an unbroken glass. I took the glass out of the apartment and down the stairs with me to the

Eldorado. I opened the driver's door, slid behind the wheel, and used the radio on the dashboard to notify police dispatch that I had been the victim of a Breaking & Entering job. A B&E. *Me.* I had to smirk at the irony. Then I got out of the car, closed it up, lit a cigarette, and waited on the steps. I was angry, red dirt-stained, and tired. Mostly, tired. I was probably more peeved about the fact that my sleep would be delayed than the fact that someone had broken into my apartment and made a mess of it. The street light from Waialae Avenue came slanting through the cracks between the buildings on 10th Avenue, throwing warped blue shadows on the asphalt in front of Old Chang's store. I felt as immaterial and drawn out as those shadows and puffed my Lucky Strike sullenly.

By the time the prowler finally appeared, the scotch was gone and so were two cigarettes. I caught the glint of the badges of the two patrolmen through the windshield before they got out of the car and walked up to the steps. They were both young, sturdy kanaka boys fresh out of recruit school by the look of the sharply creased, brand new olive drab uniforms. Both wore their hats with the shiny visors pulled low over their eyes, big six-foot-tall specimens who could have been twins. I put my empty glass down on the step I was using for a stool and pulled my badge out. It gleamed dully in the muted street light. Number One extended his hand in greeting while Number Two pulled a pad out of his breast pocket.

"Sergeant Yoshikawa?" said Number One.

"That's what they call me in some circles." I shook his hand. He had a nice, firm grip like a boa constrictor.

"I'm Kealoha and this is Kapuniai." He inclined his head toward Number Two.

"Good evening to you both, gentlemen. It's nice of you to come on such short notice." I lifted myself off the concrete step with monumental effort. I picked up my empty glass and led the way back up to my apartment. The two big patrolmen looked absolutely gigantic in the tiny foyer. I tiptoed through the mess on the kitchen floor off to the side and refilled my glass with scotch.

"Can I offer you guys a drink? I think there might be two more unbroken glasses up here somewhere."

"No thanks, Sarge. We're on duty." Lately, the Chief had made a concerted push to get cops to stop taking swigs on the job. Like the two in my apartment—these younger, newer guys, clean-cut and earnest, took not drinking on the job very seriously—unlike the older ones who got caught and were written up. Many of them were losers who had already pissed their pensions away on bad investments or marriages that they busted up with their Hotel Street hooker habits or Chinatown gambling addictions or both, their paychecks and liquor all they had in the world. I straddled the line between the two groups, with an unsteady foot in each world. For the most part, I kept my own on-duty drinking discreet. It helped that I no longer wore a uniform regularly.

"Okay, Kealoha," I said. I raised my glass in salute toward the serious young patrolman. "Suit yourself."

"I'm Kapuniai."

"Right." I drained my glass in one long pull and poured again. Kapuniai smiled patiently at me and started asking the questions with his stubby pencil and dog-eared notepad recording my answers while Kealoha took a thorough look around the place.

"What time did you get in, Sarge?"

"About 9:30."

"And you found the place like this?"

"I didn't leave it this way." I told Patrolman Kapuniai that the last time I was in the apartment was about seven in the morning and that nothing appeared to be missing. He asked a bunch of other questions, questions I had heard before, but from my own mouth to other people.

Regular people. People who had their homes and lives broken into. Now I was one of them. He nodded solemnly with every response and licked the tip of his pencil each time before writing anything down.

"That habit can kill you, Kapuniai."

"What habit is that, Sarge?"

"Licking your pencil. You can get lead poisoning."

"Nah. It should be okay. These days there's almost no lead in these things. It's basically just graphite, Sarge." He smiled good-naturedly and licked the tip of his pencil once again. I shook my head and smiled along with him. Graphite. At least the rookies were getting smarter. Kealoha emerged from my bedroom and ducked into the bathroom.

I thought about calling Gid at home, but quickly pushed the thought out of my mind. It was just a B&E. Nothing had been hurt except my self-respect, and lately there wasn't a huge premium on that. Gid would be sore that I didn't call him, but I didn't think it was worth waking him up and his whole army of a family just to tell him some stellar citizen had entered my humble abode and threw all my dirty and clean laundry on the floor.

I put on some coffee. Kealoha and Kapuniai finished up their routine and sat down at the dining table with me. They took some coffee like the clean-cut troopers they were and talked amiably and aimlessly for a little bit about some of the brass and which ones were smart and which ones were not so smart and had a good laugh over some of the instructors at recruit school who were still around saying the same old things. The talk eventually came back to the matter at hand and just who the hell I thought had done this.

"Sorry for asking, Sarge, but do you think it might be somebody who's still sore about your last case?" Kealoha broached the subject like he was peeling a bandage off of day-old wound. And he was. That these two young patrolmen knew about that case shouldn't surprise me; the whole damn department knew.

Harcourt Billings, Sr. The thought made me shudder involuntarily. The Miyasaki matter was only one month or so in the books, and Billings was still smarting from the hurt I put on him for pressuring his daughter's poor secretary into taking a few lives, including her own. The heartless scum was footing the hospital bill for Ruth Makuakane Prentiss's mother and had been asking her for favors— favors which facilitated the movement of black-market rice while prolonging the longshoremen's strike of '49. Billings reaped a huge profit while letting Ruth do all the dirty work as a go-between with the secret scabs who moved the rice by night and prolonged the strike by day. Ruth killed Millie Miyasaki, then her own boyfriend, a union organizer, when she found they had concocted a botched blackmail scheme targeting Billings' daughter, Peg, who they thought was responsible for the black-market rice scheme. Ruth, Peg's secretary, was secretly in love with Peg, and to further complicate matters, she was also Sam Makuakane's kid sister, and Sam took the fall for dumping Millie in the harbor to protect Ruth.

Harcourt Billings, Sr. ended a bunch of lives with his greed. He had a paid lapdog in our own division who killed my partner Jack Morris when Jack got too close. I brought an end to his stooge when I found out, right before his stooge could put an end to me. Billings wrecked another life, too, if you counted Peg. I couldn't legally pin those deaths on him, so I hurt him the only way I could. Ruth gave me evidence of Billings' engineering of the black-market rice scheme in her moment of reckoning before putting her gun in her mouth and pulling the trigger. I used that evidence to make Billings' life hell on earth when I turned it over to Ellen, who did a sweeping exposé of the scheme in the *Record*. Shortly thereafter, Old Harcourt was dragged before a Federal Grand Jury and raked over the coals. In the end, his money and his lawyers would likely prevail. Ruth and her boyfriend, union organizer Danny Boy Cadiz, would receive the brunt of the blame for the scam.

Both were six feet under the loamy earth of Nuuanu and in no position to speak on their own behalves. The brass gave Billings' flunky, Clancy "Luau" Lewis, a hero's burial, the same as they gave to Jack Morris, all to cover up the black-market scandal. Anyone who read about it in the papers would never have made the connection. But Billings got a taste of what it was like to be treated like a common criminal and it must've scared the shit out of him. His hair went from steely gunmetal gray to snow white.

He probably held a grudge. He did everything he could to end my career with HPD, and Harcourt Billings' everything was a lot. Still, tossing my humble abode didn't make any sense or seem like his style.

"No," I told Kealoha after a while. "I think Billings would've just bought the damn building from Old Chang and evicted me. He could've. I don't think I had anything he wanted anyway. He knows he'll be cleared of the rice scam by a grand jury. Somebody was definitely looking for something here. I don't think it was anyone connected to my old case." Old case. Like it was years in the past instead of days. "It was probably from something a lot more recent."

"What's that, Sarge?"

"I took a drive out to Waialua this afternoon," I said. Then I told the two young flatfoots a little bit about the charred bones in the cane field and how the dog tags led me to the strange widow. "Mrs. Machida is more likely to have come in here and tossed my apartment than anybody connected to my other case."

"Why do you think this lady would be snooping around your place?" asked Kapuniai.

"A typewriter ribbon, probably."

"I'm sorry?" I explained that I had taken the ribbon spool out of Jiro's old typewriter and that she may have discovered I did so after I left, and that I had taken precautions to put in a mail drop addressed to myself at the station.

"You think this Beverly Machida did this?" Kapuniai licked his pencil again. I winced as he did it. I think he got a kick out of watching me cringe.

"The typewriter ribbon is the only thing I can think of that anyone may want from me."

"What about that Buddhist monk, Sarge? Maybe she thinks he took it."

"I don't know. Maybe there's a Hongwanji somewhere that looks like this shit, too."

Kealoha started busying himself checking out the door frame and lock for about the third time. My head was pounding like the surf at Makapuu and my mouth was dry and filmy.

"I'll go down and get the dusting kit from the prowler, Sarge," he called from the foyer.

"I wouldn't bother," I told him. The thought of staying vertical for another hour was enough to make my cranium pop. "She . . . or whoever probably didn't leave any prints. Entry wasn't forced. Old Chang's cheap piece-of-shit lock was picked, and probably not even with locksmith tools. A bobby pin or toothpick would do it. I know. I've done it before when I couldn't find my keys. And I wasn't even sober."

"You think this Beverly Machida drove all the way out here from Waialua and did this?" Kapuniai ventured.

"She or somebody who wants whatever Jiro Machida was working on."

"And what is that?"

"I don't know yet. I didn't look at the ribbon. I won't know for a couple of days when it arrives at the station in the mail."

"You think it might've been whoever clipped this Jiro?"

Harry Kurita? It might make sense. Ellen did say he came to the *Record* for an answer or something. But I didn't think it was Harry. I thought about a two-bit seducer of coeds who preened and pontificated and pissed his little existence away until he was forced to give it all up. His passions were his undoing. Now he could never come back to his Kapiolani Boulevard *salon*. No more Keats recited in that pompous drone. No more scotch on the little loveseat.

"I don't think so. He's gone," I said.

"Where, Sarge?" Kapuniai licked the tip of his pencil but didn't write anything.

"Out to sea."

8

"Why didn't you call me?"

He said it without looking at me. Gideon Hanohano wasn't
happy. He never really looked happy even when he was, but I could
tell he was really annoyed. I sat in his office nursing a paper cup of
cold, lousy coffee and listened to the ticks of my wristwatch, loud as
consistent claps of thunder in the stale air.

"It was late."

"It was *important*." Gid took up his morning paper and turned
a page. He donned his ridiculous little spectacles. They looked like a
spindly gold insect on his massive head. Gid always did this when he
was upset. He'd play like he was ignoring the offending party, never
making eye contact but talking out of the side of his mouth as if
passing on some secret information. That he was pissed off was secret
information only to those who didn't know him well. I had gotten the
treatment from him a handful of times and I knew the score. It wasn't
fun, but it wasn't dangerous, either. The time to start worrying was
when Gid looked you in the eye and raised his voice. The last guy to get
looked in the eye by Gid while he was upset ended up in the Emergency
Hospital. I was there with him when the bouncer of some Hotel Street
jazz club told us it was "No Cop Night" when we were trying to get in
to interview a girl singer who was a key witness to a stabbing in the alley
next to the club. The bouncer looked Gid in the eye and spit on his shoe.
Gid hit him in the nose with one of his stone fists and laid him out. He

told me it was faster than getting a warrant, but I knew he was really pissed off.

"I'm sorry, Gid," I told him. My words bounced off the dark granite wall of his downturned face. "I thought it could wait. I didn't want to wake Emma or the kids."

"She's used to the telephone ringing in the middle of the night. They all are." The silence returned as he scanned the page he was looking at. After a while, he incongruously announced, "Two Army guys from Schofield are on the undercard at the Civic tonight. Welterweights. I've seen one of them fight before, this Kid Collins. He's pretty good. And this place on Piikoi Street is giving free eye exams on Tuesdays." He was determined to torture me. I couldn't take it anymore.

"Come on, Gid. I said I was sorry. It won't happen again. I'll call next time. I promise." Gid flipped another page then he took off his little wire spectacles and tossed them onto the open paper. He rubbed his eyes with his right thumb and forefinger and looked up at me and smirked with the left corner of his mouth, letting out a hippopotamus-sized sigh. It was really a smile, though. I could tell because his eyes softened up.

"Ah, it's okay," he said. "Emma snores so loud I probably wouldn't have heard the telephone anyway. But call next time and remember that the bell would never wake her."

"Okay," I said. I smiled and relaxed a fraction. I was relieved that the silent treatment wasn't going to last all day. Gid was always concerned about all of us under his wing. He also hated missing out on anything having to do with a case. My little apartment being turned upside down was one of those things he needed to know about. Gid Hanohano was a cop twenty-four hours a day. Most dicks were barely a cop for two hours; their badges only came out when it was time to shake down a Chinatown gambling den for a kickback or to impress the pretty haole heiresses at the bar at the Royal Hawaiian. They were otherwise

in search of a free lunch and a nice shady tree to nap under while they
waited for the next watch party where they could booze it up and grab
the dispatch girls' asses. Not Gid. The Great Hanohano didn't have time
for any of that shit.

We lit up cigarettes and I told him what happened since we
parted ways in Kunia the day before. As always, while I gave him
my narrative, Gid nodded thoughtfully and stared right through his
venetian blinds and the Yokohama Specie Bank Building across the
street clear up to Mount Kaala and Alaska beyond it. Every now and
then he'd lift an eyebrow or shrug his gigantic shoulders. Half of Gid's
vocabulary was gestures and he was still more eloquent than most
professors I knew. When I was finished, he pushed his chair back from
his desk on its squeaky wheels and killed what was left of his cigarette
in a rough clay ashtray fashioned by one of his eight kids. I stood up and
squashed the butt of my smoke, too.

He said, "Let's go see Pinky."

Wilton "Pinky" Davis was the Honolulu Harbormaster. He was
greedy, lazy, and lecherous and his ethics would have made him right
at home in Al Capone's Chicago. In other words, he was a typical civil
servant in the Territory of Hawaii. Pinky was one of a growing breed of
island-born haoles whose mouth was missed at birth when the stork was
passing out the silver spoons; his father was a crewman on a commercial
vessel. Pinky had a complex from growing up haole and poor and he
spent his entire life sucking up to the Punahou set to get ahead. His
bootlicking won him the Harbormaster's post after years of being a port
pilot. He was also married to Gid's cousin. That made him Gid's relative,
which put him in the same company as about half of the island.

Gid and I took the tiled stairs down from the Homicide Detail
offices to the main floor where the receiving desk was located. The
hapless desk sergeant was trying to deal with the surge of wretched
humanity waiting to be booked. The hookers and winos all had faces

like broken clocks, breathing in the stale air while they waited their turn under the slow-moving ceiling fans and growing a minute older for every second that ticked away into oblivion. They were the corpses twisting in the wind in rusted suits of armor, failed grail-quest knights whose lifetime pursuit of a prize ended in abject failure at the bottom of a pile of used condoms, dirty hypodermic needles, and empty gin bottles. Failure had a smell—cheap perfume, rotgut booze, and piss-soaked rags—all mixed with the clammy sweat of fear and desperation. The receiving desk was ripe with it.

Gid and I slipped past the stew of misery and down more tiled stairs in the Spanish style art deco foyer to Bethel Street. Beyond the giant doors of the foyer everything was different. Outside the station, the world was awash with glorious Hawaii sunlight and the sky was tinted postcard blue. Pretty office girls in their jewel-hued finery giggled demurely behind white gloves at the corner of Bethel and Merchant. Mynah birds sang clearly over the dirge of traffic. It was a beautiful morning. I had had a half hour nap on my sofa amid the wreckage of my apartment after the rookies cleared out, and I killed the rest of the Haig & Haig. More pretty girls crossed Merchant, basking in the sun while it hit their silky raven tresses. It was a beautiful morning and I felt like a turd on a birthday cake.

We walked a couple of blocks makai down Bethel toward the harbor. Our destination, Aloha Tower, loomed over us with its flags flying in the wind like birds circling the crown's patina. As soon as we crossed Route 92, the smell of the harbor hit us, marine and industrial. When we reached the tower entrance, the same OUT OF ORDER sign that must've graced the elevator doors since before the attack on Pearl Harbor greeted us. Gid gritted his teeth and steeled himself for the task of hoofing it up the stairs to the top office. As usual, he dove into the task of dragging himself up, keeping a steady pace, aware that he was setting an example for me. Gid was always setting an example.

When we reached the top floor, we took some time to catch our breath before opening the door with the pebbled glass window stenciled with HARBORMASTER in gold leaf. It was the fruit of Pinky's years of ass-kissing to sit behind those gold letters. Behind the door, a pretty young kanaka secretary in a yellow dress looked up from her typing. She recognized us from our last visit. She may have smiled but her eyes grew wide with something between worry and panic.

"Mr. Davis," she shouted over her shoulder. "You have visitors. I'm going on my break." The girl grabbed her purse and blew by us in a yellow blur, practically throwing herself down the stairs. She didn't want to hang around for our interview. She remembered the last one.

"*Break?* Who said you could take a . . ." Pinky had emerged from his office to berate the poor girl and froze when he saw me and Gid. "Aww, shit."

"Hello, Pinky," said Gid. Pinky started backing slowly into his office, arms raised defensively in front of his near-fuchsia face. His complexion gave him his moniker.

"Goddamnit, Gid! The last time you boys were here it took Samantha and me two whole days to clean the place up. I just replaced all of the wrecked furniture. This shit's all brand new, so please . . . ." He cringed again.

"Relax, Pink. We just want to know about a Japanese fishing boat that called here about a month ago."

Pinky let out a roaring laugh that was cracked through with nervous relief. "Japanese? Shit, Gid, I can help you boys with that. Come on in and have some coffee." Pinky was happy as hell that information on a Japanese fishing vessel would not likely cause a stink of any kind with his keepers. Our last visit involved getting information on a Billings boat for the Miyasaki case and Gid had to be a little more persuasive. We walked into Pinky's inner sanctum, decorated with all kinds of maritime junk: a shiny brass bridge compass, colored glass

Japanese floats in nets, pilot's charts, giant conch shells, and framed photographs of Pinky and all kinds of *de rigueur* port celebrities from a Kewalo Basin ice house proprietor to a Pearl Harbor rear admiral. His view, though, was nothing short of spectacular. There were windows on three sides of his office which afforded him a panoramic view of Honolulu Harbor from Kewalo Basin and Waikiki behind it to the lush green Koolau Mountains behind the piers, and between them beyond Sand Island was the Pacific, sparkling like a giant sapphire with a billion facets.

We had a seat at a large koa conference table cluttered with charts full of reef notations and sounding depths, which were probably more for show than practical use. Gid and I were served coffee in paper cups by an obsequious Pinky, fawning and bowing like a houseboy. He hefted a large green ledger from the top of a low credenza next to a gleaming deep-sea diver's helmet. He balanced the big book on his enormous gut and brought it over to the conference table, where he let it drop with a dramatic slam. Pinky took a pair of bifocals out of his shirt pocket and opened the book.

"What was the boat called?"

"*Iwakuni Maru*. It called about a month ago," I told him. Pinky leafed through the pages then stopped and smiled with his yellow teeth.

"It's your lucky day. Or I should say tomorrow is. She's due back to lade supplies tomorrow, probably at about first light. The chandler requested the Pier 32 gates opened at five a.m. for his truck. The Japanese like to take care of their shit as early as they can. Hell, you know that, Sheik."

"Sure. That's why I always roll out of bed at noon when I have the choice."

Pinky laughed raucously. "You crack me up, Sheik. You want to hear something else that's funny? You know that colored writer at the *Record* who writes that funny column? Samantha asked me the other day if we were related because he's named Davis, too!" He laughed some more, holding his gut like it had just been hit. He carried on for a few seconds until he noticed Gid looking at him with a straight face, withering his joy. Pinky quieted down to a chuckle.

"*We're* related," said Gid, "and I'm not laughing about *that*."

Pinky stopped his chuckling immediately. We stood up, grabbed our hats off the table, and walked out the door.

9

Gid and I returned to the station after our little talk with Pinky Davis. The three-block walk from Aloha Tower woke me up a bit but did little for my flagging constitution. I needed a drink. But I didn't dare take the flask out in front of Gid while on duty. Gid was determined to enforce the Chief's no-juicing-on-duty mandate. "Looking sharp is half of being sharp," he told us as he read us the riot act. I asked him what the other half of being sharp was and he simply replied, "Coffee." I'd have to settle for a shot of that until I could get out from under his shadow.

The problem with coffee at that moment was that it was made by Delilah. Delilah Kamanu was the Homicide Division secretary, a curvy, honey-voiced part-time hula dancer who was talented in a great many things. She could take dictation more accurately than any stenographer, type faster than she could talk, and squeeze a steak dinner out of even the most miserly date. As a dancer she was spellbinding to watch and she was quite the songbird, too. What Delilah couldn't do was make coffee. But that never stopped her from trying.

Gid and I entered the Detail office to find Delilah sitting on the blotter of my desk in a tight yellow dress with red anthuriums printed all over it. Her bronze legs were crossed, red heels dangling over the linoleum. She was buffing her nails and stopped to jab the daruma doll under To-san's banker's lamp every so often, watching it spring back up indifferently. As soon as she saw me, she gasped.

"Sheik! You look like hell! Gid told me what happened last night." I shot Gid a frown and he shrugged.

"Thanks for the broadcast," I told him.

"Don't mention it."

Delilah came running up with a paper cup full of her steaming coffee. "Here, Sheik," she said. "You really need this."

"No, you don't," warned Gid.

"Shut up, Gid," she said. She forced the cup into my hands. I took a sip and my eyes watered.

"How is it?" Delilah asked.

"Like liquid turd," I gagged.

"I told you. You didn't need it," Gid repeated. He lit a cigarette and rocked slowly on his heels with his hand in his pocket.

"Actually, I did. I needed a reminder that I'm still alive. A shitty cup of coffee will make you appreciate the fact that you can still tell it's a shitty cup of coffee."

"That's what I love about The Sheik," said Gid. "Always the philosopher."

"I don't have to take this," said Delilah. She stomped out of the office like a petulant child. I took another sip and grimaced. Gid was still laughing his dry, wheezing laugh when the telephone on my desk rang. I picked up the receiver and cradled it in the crook of my neck while I pulled a Lucky Strike out of a pack in my desk drawer and lit it.

"Homicide, Yoshikawa."

"Detective?"

"Yes. Who is this?"

"Beverly."

"Well, hello, Mrs. Machida. What can I do for you?" At mention of the name, Gid stopped rocking back and forth and looked in my direction.

The high, slightly nasal voice drifted through the receiver with a distant, ethereal quality, like a mournful violin concerto floating over a sea of years from some sepia-toned memory, alien but at the same time intimate. It was the voice of Morgan Le Fay, full of dark enchantment and expectation. It said: "I need you."

"I beg your pardon?"

"I need you. Do you know Pearl City Tavern?"

"I know it. The Monkey Bar?"

"Yes. Eight o'clock." A click broke the spell and the line went dead. Once again, I was back in the yellow-gray world of Homicide Detail. The ceiling fans turned slowly and batted the cigarette smoke around in the hazy sunlight that spilled in through the blinds. Gid stared.

"Got yourself a date?" asked Gid.

"An appointment," I corrected.

"Need backup?"

"No. Thanks, though. I think she's going to tell me something and I think she'll only do so if I come by myself."

"Sounds like a date," said Gid.

"My date's for lunch." I thought about Ellen and what her probable reaction would be to this development. I saw a long afternoon. Ellen Park was sweet, ebullient, intelligent, and the most beautiful, desirable woman I had ever known. She was all I ever wanted. When it came to having to talk to other women, though, being with Ellen was like holding a lit firecracker in my hand. I never knew when it was going to go off. Inwardly, I groaned at the prospect of meeting Beverly Machida at night.

"You may be wise to have a little backup, though. Just in case," said Gid's back as he lumbered into his office.

"She's just a girl. What makes you think I need backup?"

Gid sat and his chair groaned. He put his little spectacles back on and looked up at me from over them. He said one word: "Naʻau."

Great. Gid had another one of his feelings that never turned out
to be wrong. He was always telling me to trust my own gut feeling on
case matters and I was far from perfect when it came to my *own* naʻau. I
always trusted Gid's, though.

"Okay, Lieutenant," I said, resigned. "But keep your distance. I
don't want her spooked into clamming up if she spots the cavalry."

"Don't worry. I'm discreet," he said. He was looking down at his
newspaper. "Like a mouse."

I rolled my eyes. A six-foot-two, three-hundred-pound mouse.
Discreet. A damn good thing the Monkey Bar was dark. Gid may
have been one of the best detectives anywhere, but what he wasn't, was
inconspicuous.

"I'll buy your steak tonight if you can blend in and disappear," I
told Gid. "This is a finesse interview."

"You won't even see me."

I shook my head in despair. I turned my attention to the daruma
on my blotter and gave him a poke. The blank eyes looked back at
me. Ka-san gave me the daruma when I finished recruit school. I was
supposed to draw one of the pupils in when I set a goal for myself and
the other one when I attained it. I poked it again and watched it bob on
my blotter.

I was supposed to pick up Ellen for lunch. She told me she would
have some information for me. Ellen. I thought about her loud voice
and her red lipstick and the way she bounced from place to place, full
of boundless energy. I thought about her shimmering hair and her eyes
in the moonlight and her question or answer for everything. I thought
about what life would be like without her; I didn't like it. So, I took out
my pen and drew a dark circle in the daruma's empty left eye. I thought
he winked at me when I was done.

PART II

Morgan Le Fay
Town

10

"Why didn't you call me?"

Not again. Not her, too. I went through it with Gid earlier. Now Ellen was bent out of shape, too, for not getting an annoying telephone call from me in the middle of the night. I had just gotten through telling her that my apartment was turned upside down. She was livid.

"I didn't want to wake you."

"You didn't want to wake me? I thought I meant something to you, Frankie Yoshikawa."

"You did—I mean you do. Of course, you do. Why else would I not want to wake you for something so trivial?"

"Trivial? Someone broke into your apartment and that's *trivial?*"

"Nothing was taken."

We sat in a booth next to a window at Kau Kau Korner. The place touted itself as "The Crossroads of the Pacific." I couldn't see the Pacific anywhere near it, unless you counted the stagnant Ala Wai Canal. It was more accurate to say it was the crossroads of Kapiolani and King Kalakaua, the busiest intersection outside of downtown Honolulu. We sat on the same side of the table and shared the chop steak—a "New Taste Thrill" according to the menu. The chop steak was really nothing more than tough little pieces of beef fried in a wok with celery, carrots, onions, and other stuff with Chinese oyster sauce. It wasn't bad, but only someone from Kansas might consider it a "New Taste Thrill" and only if they liked their beef on the chewy side. Ellen had an iced tea and I had black coffee. We shared all of our food when we ate out—Ellen hardly ate enough to justify getting herself a full order and I didn't need a full order. I hadn't played ball in the AJA league since I got into Homicide and the meager time I spent in the gym with the dumbbells wasn't enough to offset the huge amounts I used to put away as a first baseman at Columbia. I was becoming a sedentary creature and I didn't like the feeling. I thought about rookies like Kealoha and Kapuniai. I used to wonder how guys like that turned into the guys at the receiving desk until I saw signs of the alarming transition in myself. I was resolved to stave it off as long as I could, though I wasn't naïve enough to think sharing a chop steak with my girlfriend would do the trick all by itself.

It took me about fifteen minutes of apologizing and dessert to get Ellen to stop being upset about not being called the night before. As I did with Gid, I promised to inform her immediately on all things similar in the future, no matter what the hour.

"Things are different with us, Frankie Yoshikawa. They're different from what they were before. We belong to each other, so you need to start telling me about the things that affect you as soon as they happen. It's what people do when they care for each other."

"Okay, darling."

Ellen was often saying things like that. Things that made me want to roll my eyes and smile at the same time. Ellen was like that. To hear her tell it, she knew almost everything, and for those few things she didn't know she had a litany of educated guesses. It was exasperating and occasionally annoying, but it was also strangely arousing, and I was addicted to her presence. It was weirdly nice to have someone in my life that was always there to tell me what to do, beside my mother.

When she was finished with her apple pie, she leaned over toward the window and pulled a letter envelope out of her purse. She turned back and handed it to me with her dainty hands, like a Shinto priest making some kind of New Year's offering. I took the envelope from her.

"What's this?" I asked.

"It's a list of names. I found it in Jiro's things that Koji kept in his desk. He didn't turn these things over to the HUAC investigators. I need you to give it back to me after you've looked at one name in particular. If this list gets out, a lot of people could be in a lot of trouble, and that's not why I'm showing it to you. The name I want you to remember could help you figure out what happened to Jiro—and Harry."

I opened the envelope. I withdrew the single sheet of folded paper contained within it. As Ellen said, it was a typewritten list of names. Preceding each name was a "group" number—Group 1, Group 2, Group 3, and so on. Each "group" was followed by a different name and there were thirty "groups." The names were ethnically mixed, about half of them haole, nearly the other half Japanese with Hawaiian, Filipino, or other names thrown in here and there.

"Take a look at Group 12," said Ellen.

I looked at the name. Marlon Wilde. It was just a name to me, like all the others, and one I didn't recognize. I looked back up at Ellen. Her dark eyes were aglitter with excitement behind the giant lenses of her glasses. Her eyes were particularly beautiful when they were excited.

"Who is he?" I asked.

"Group 12 is otherwise known as the Palolo Group," Ellen said in a low whisper. "What you're holding is a list of the cell leaders."

The Hawaii Communist Party's leaders. I folded the list and stuck it into the envelope and handed it back to Ellen. I resisted the temptation to look at the other names and see if I recognized any of them. I didn't want to know. I didn't care. Smith Act stuff was out of the ballpark for a local homicide dick. Ironically, the work I did was a lot dirtier and more dangerous than the work the HUAC investigators did, though their stuff was always on the front page and my work made it there only if the victim was haole and rich. The exception to that, of course, was the Miyasaki case, which reflected a noticeable shift in the political climate.

Still, the whole nation was enamored with the red witch hunts taking place on the waterfronts of every U.S. port, and Hawaii's docks were no exception. And it wasn't just the piers that attracted the hunters: the cane fields and classrooms were under the microscope, too. *Big Jim McLain*, a Warner Brothers picture depicting the exploits of a HUAC Investigator in Hawaii, had opened the prior year in Honolulu at the Kuhio Theater in Waikiki, but it wasn't one of John Wayne's biggest box office hits. However, it was wildly popular here. Real life HUAC Investigators were actually the opposite of John Wayne. Most were pencil-necked haole former accountants from the mainland who had little or no success infiltrating local labor circles. They would have loved to get their clammy little hands on the list Ellen showed me.

I finished my cup of coffee and gratefully accepted a refill from the passing waitress. I was tired and sinking fast. I lit a cigarette and grabbed Ellen's gloved hand under the table and squeezed it affectionately. She had come through once again for me. Outside the window a parade of automobiles rolled by on King Kalakaua Avenue to and from Waikiki. They always reminded me of a school of reef fish.

"Can you tell me anything about Wilde?" I asked, knowing Ellen had probably dug into the matter as much as she could before passing it on to me.

"Not much," she replied, though I knew Ellen's "not much" was probably a complete dossier. "He's thirty-six years old, born in Milwaukee, Wisconsin, moved to San Francisco to take a job aboard a tramp steamer as a deckhand when he was sixteen. He did that for about a year then started to work on the docks. He was sharp enough to move up the ranks of the longshoremen's fledgling union as an organizer—he could read and was fairly articulate. When the union was looking to make inroads here with the stevedores and sugar workers, they sent Wilde as one of their advance party. When Kempa left the party to testify against the Hawaii Seven, he left a leadership vacuum in the

Palolo Group. Jiro and Harry's in-fighting for control of the cell led to the elevation of the neutral Marlon Wilde as a compromise choice."

Robert McBurney Kempa. The red turncoat whose testimony was instrumental in eventually bringing Smith Act charges against the Hawaii Seven: Jack Hall, John Reinecke, Koji Ariyoshi, Jack Kimoto, Jim Freeman, Charles Fujimoto and his wife, Eileen Fujimoto. Wilde's personal history was similar to Kempa's. He may have been a natural choice for a replacement all along, though Jiro and Harry's egos had fought it. Now they were both gone.

"I don't suppose you know where Wilde lives or works these days?" I asked in a tone that implied it was difficult information to come by. I knew Ellen wouldn't be able to resist responding to a challenge.

"He's only about two or so blocks into the valley from your apartment. He's renting a room in the back of a house near the corner of 10th Avenue and Kaau Street. As for work, he's a Territory employee. He's currently a groundskeeper at the Ala Wai Golf Course." Ellen took a sip of her iced tea with a sweet, self-satisfied expression. I smiled back at her.

"Your 'not much' was more than most dicks at the station uncover in an entire year. I'd better keep you close by, darling."

"Very close." She threw her arms around my neck and kissed me on the cheek. I asked for the check and paid it. I took a toothpick from the steel dispenser by the cash register to dislodge any remaining New Taste Thrill in my mouth and drove Ellen back to the *Record*. She told me that she would be busy that evening making kimchee with her mother. I told her that I would be busy, too, but that I would call her when I was finished with my business.

"Good," she said. "You're learning, Frankie Yoshikawa."

"I understand it's what people do when they care for each other."

11

The skinny Japanese boy with the crew cut was leaning against the clubhouse wall with a marijuana cigarette dangling from his mouth. He wore an argyle sweater vest with a white shirt under it and was suffering for his sartorial statement, sweating like a fugitive in a broom closet. He had just finished prying the cap off a bottle of cola, the one luxury of a caddy on his break at a municipal golf course. He looked like a punk who had found twenty bucks on the sidewalk and spent it all on the ridiculous clothes he was wearing.

I joined the kid in his meager patch of shade under the clubhouse awning. The sun had just begun its descent in the west, but not by much. The Ala Wai fairway was empty; all the doctors and dentists and insurance salesmen, who crammed their rounds in the morning when it was cooler, were long gone back into their air-conditioned offices. I took a cigarette out of a pack and lit up. He eyed me suspiciously as I undid the top button of my shirt and loosened my tie.

"Can I help you?" he asked, though in a way that wasn't at all helpful.

"I sure hope so."

"I'm off duty right now if you want a caddy. My break ends in fifteen minutes," he said, surly and suddenly no longer enjoying his cola.

"Do I look like I'm dressed for a tee time?"

"How the hell should I know?"

"You're the one wearing the Ben Hogan getup in eighty-three-degree weather."

"What the hell do you want?"

That did it. I wasn't taking any lip from a Kakaako punk, especially because I used to be one myself. I grabbed him by his collar and snarled, "You mean, 'What the hell do you want, *sir*?' You sure say 'hell' a lot for someone who lives on tips." The kid's eyes grew wide with fear.

"Okay, okay! I'm sorry! I'm sorry . . . *sir*. No need to get violent. It's been a long day."

I released my grip on his collar. "Yeah, for you and me both." I took a five-dollar bill out of my pocket and held it between my index and middle finger in front of his face. "As I was saying, I was hoping you could help me."

The kid rubbed his close-cropped head. He looked at the five longingly. "Sure, I can help you, sir." His manners had improved a hundred per cent.

"I'm looking for Marlon Wilde. He's a groundskeeper." The kid gave me a dubious look. He shifted his weight from one foot to the other. I put the five back in my pocket. "What's the matter, kid? Don't know him?"

He stared at my hand in my pocket, where the five had gone. "Are you a loan shark . . . sir? I don't want anyone to get hurt on account of my talking . . . ."

I pulled the badge out of pocket and showed it to him. His eyes got huge and he started wheezing. "I'm no loan shark," I said. "And nobody's going to get hurt. As long as they tell the truth."

"He gets off when my break ends. He comes out this way. That's his Buick out there, the dark green one. He usually goes straight to the car," he stammered. I could see the unspoken prayer he uttered behind his eyes that I wouldn't turn my professional attention somehow to him.

"Thanks, kid," I said. I stuck the five in the V-collar of his argyle sweater and yanked the reefer out of his gaping mouth. I threw it down and ground it up under my heel on the asphalt. "You shouldn't smoke that shit," I told him. "It kills brain cells and you'd better save the ones you have left."

"Yes, sir," he croaked, then ran off, and disappeared into the clubhouse without his cola.

I returned to the Eldorado and put on a pair of sunglasses and moved it under the shade of a banyan tree. Then I sat and waited. In less than ten minutes, a haole man in gray coveralls with grass stains on the knees strode out from behind the clubhouse toward the green Buick. He looked like he was between five-foot-six and five-foot-eight with sandy hair, prematurely aged skin from exposure to the Hawaiian sun, a stevedore's broad shoulders, and a large gut from too many brown bottles. He got into the Buick, started it up, and pulled out of the clubhouse parking lot onto Kapahulu Avenue. As soon as he was out in traffic and headed mauka on Kapahulu, I eased out and followed about three cars behind.

After proceeding for a handful of blocks on Kapahulu, the Buick hung an abrupt left turn onto Kaimuki Avenue. I stomped on the accelerator to keep up before the oncoming makai bound traffic on Kapahulu cut me off. I was still a comfortable three to four cars behind him when I saw him make a left turn into Kaimuki High School's driveway. I idled across the street and saw two men and two women get into Wilde's Buick. Too far away to see what the people looked like, I could only tell how many of them there were and their gender by their clothes: hats and suits on the men, light-colored skirts on the women.

The green Buick pulled out of the high school and back onto Kaimuki Avenue, heading toward Kapiolani Boulevard. I followed. It occurred to me that what I was witnessing was a Communist Party group or cell meeting; Kempa had testified that meetings were often conducted in moving vehicles with no written minutes taken. The Palolo Cell's pick-up location for meeting attendees used to be the Sears Roebuck parking lot on Beretania Street. The rendezvous location had apparently changed since Kempa ratted out the CP before the HUAC, but the *modus operandi* remained the same.

The Buick headed ewa on Kapiolani until it hit University Avenue and turned right, toward the UH campus. I thought about Harry Kurita and his den of iniquity which was just a block or so away. It dawned on me that Wilde's car was probably full of Harry and Jiro's associates, a veritable gold mine of information about the last days either man was seen.

The Buick then hung a hard and abrupt left turn onto Date Street, nearly being broadsided by the oncoming makai bound traffic on University. He had spotted me tailing him. I cursed the fact that I was in a fire engine red Cadillac Eldorado convertible—the quintessential automotive sore thumb. When I thought about it, I was surprised he hadn't seen the tail much earlier. Now I had nothing to do but to keep following and get him to pull over, having all those cell members to interview too big a prize to pass up. I made the turn onto Date in time to see him turn right on Hausten Street. At that point, I decided to gamble that the Cadillac was a faster machine than the Buick.

I continued on Date, headed ewa past Hausten, and turned right on Isenberg Street. Once on Isenberg, I floored it, flying by the east end zone of Honolulu Stadium, then fishtailing a right turn onto King Street. I hit the gas again going Diamond Head down King until I saw the nose of the Buick inching out from Hausten onto King. I came to a screeching stop right in front of it in the intersection and prayed that he'd stop, too, before he broadsided my pride and joy. He stopped. He tried reversing away, but ended up hopping the curb in his panic and bending his rear bumper on

a lamp post a few yards down Hausten. I blocked his front end
diagonally, pinning him between the Eldorado and the lamp post.

I got out of my car, mad as hell. I pulled my .38 from my shoulder
holster and my badge from my inside coat pocket and thrust it at his
windshield and bellowed: "POLICE! GET OUT OF THE CAR!
NOW!"

The driver's door opened slowly and Wilde's sandy head rose
slowly above it, along with his hands. As soon as he was clear of the
vehicle, he started protesting.

"Hey! What the hell is this?"

"SHUT UP! Get your hands on the hood and don't move!" Wilde
sullenly did as he was told. I walked up behind him and savagely kicked
his ankles apart. I frisked him and found a bone-handled switchblade
in the back pocket of his coveralls. I threw this into the bushes. When I
was convinced he didn't have anything else on him that could be used to
puncture me, I turned him around by the collar. All this time, the other
shadowy figures sat petrified in the Buick, not daring to move.

Marlon Wilde stared me down with an icy insolence born of years
of dockside bravado. His hazel eyes were full of defiance. He held his hands
aloft at shoulder level but bent slightly at the knees like a prizefighter.

"Are you crazy?" he demanded. "You almost got us all killed! We
weren't doing anything wrong!"

"Then why the hell did you run?"

"What was I supposed to do? Pull over so you could harass us
freely? We weren't doing anything!"

"You want to tell that story to the HUAC, Mr. Wilde? Do you
think *they'd* believe that you weren't doing anything?" At that, Wilde
looked as if someone had pulled a cork out of his ass and deflated him.
His big shoulders drooped.

"Okay. What do you want?" he asked in a resigned tone. He blew
a sigh and looked down at his boots.

"Answers, Mr. Wilde. From all of you." I peered into the car and looked at the man in the front seat. The brim of his hat was pulled low over his eyes and he sunk back into his coat, as if it were a fortress of some kind that made him invisible to me. "All of you—out of the car," I said. "Line up on the sidewalk. You can stand next to them, Mr. Wilde."

The man in the front seat got out first and walked over to the sidewalk to stand next to Wilde. He was an Oriental man with gold-rimmed glasses and gray hair at the temples in a smart gray flannel suit. Next the rear door on the driver's side opened and a stocky haole man in a brown suit and brown fedora got out. He was red in the face and sweating profusely. He was followed by an Oriental woman in a pink floral dress with a black pillbox hat and white gloves. She wobbled on her high heeled pumps unsteadily, looking nauseous from the wild ride in the Buick. The man in gray helped steady her as she stood next to him in the line on the sidewalk. They all stood there, dazed and unwilling to make eye contact with me. I didn't lay a hand on any of them, but I didn't have to; I knew that the blood ran cold through their veins. They were terrified. They had been stopped by a law enforcement officer while they were conducting a mobile Communist Party meeting at the height of the Red Scare. I looked at them, each face individually, one by one. I didn't recognize any of them.

Then the second woman got out of the back seat. I could see the top of her curly black head and a gloved hand grasping the top of the door frame to steady her as she pulled herself up. She was wearing a simple green dress and she looked up at me slowly, grinning sheepishly.

"Hello, Frankie."

I said: "Shit. Iris."

12

Iris Imada. My sister. Member of Hawaii Communist Party Group 12. I suppose I shouldn't have been surprised given her politics and tendency to talk people's ears off. What shocked me is that she would take the risk. She must have known the HUAC was arresting anyone who was stupid enough to get caught and anyone the stupid ones were ratting out. I felt unsteady, suddenly, and not just because I was exhausted. I really needed that drink.

"What's this about, Frankie?" my sister asked, clearly not as scared as her friends.

"That's my line."

"Are you working for the Feds now? Is *that* what this is?" The others cringed, including Wilde. Iris was still tough, though. She always was. And it still got on my nerves.

"Shut up, Iris. How the hell can you do this?"

"I'm not afraid to do what needs to be done."

"I don't care about *you*. How can you do this to Chester? And your kids? *What about Ka-san?*"

"Shut up, Frankie!" The others cringed again. Iris looked disdainfully at them. "Oh, don't worry. This cop is my baby brother."

"We'll talk about this later," I told her. "As for the rest of you, this doesn't let you off the hook. If my smart-assed sister continues to make me mad, you will all—and that includes you, Iris—you will all be turned over to the HUAC for their pleasure." I glared at Iris. She folded her skinny arms across her chest and glared back.

"You can't prove we were meeting, Frankie," said Iris in the mocking, self-righteous tone she used to use on me when we were kids.

"I don't care about your little red meeting-on-wheels. I don't give a rat's ass if you were planning the next glorious revolution. I need answers about Jiro Machida and Harry Kurita and if I don't get them then you can all explain to the HUAC that you were only taking an afternoon motor tour of Moiliili. And you know *they* don't need any proof to make your lives hell."

"What about Jiro and Harry?" asked Iris. She suddenly stopped being so smug and combative.

"Jiro's dead and Harry's gone." Five empty faces looked at me. It was the first time I had ever known my sister to be absolutely silent for more than two seconds. "My sister can tell you I'm a homicide detective. And I could not care less about your politics."

"Okay. We'll talk," said Wilde. The sun started to beat down on the six of us standing around under a lamp post on Hausten Street. There wasn't enough shade in the sickly looking lauhala tree overhanging the sidewalk to make more than two people comfortable. Down the block and across the street at The Willows, the syrupy music made by a trio of fat ladies in matching muumuus drifted over to our side of the street. Colorful stuff, it told of the little fish in the sea and flowers adrift on the surf and how a person would come back for someone or some such shit. It was the kind of thing that made me realize just how badly I needed a drink. Hawaiian music always made me reach for a glass. In a nice way.

"Not here," I said to Wilde. "Come on across the street. I'll buy you all a drink." I looked at Iris and narrowed my eyes. "Except you." She stuck her tongue out at me. I reached out and smacked her beauty parlor curls. Suddenly, I was in the third grade again. Wilde got back into the Buick and straightened it out so it was parallel to the curb. I parked behind him. The others waited on the sidewalk, then we all walked together across the street to The Willows. The girl in the little thatch-roofed stand that housed the cash register looked up at our approaching party while doing her nails. It was after the lunch rush and she was working her little emery board as if to stay awake, as well as to make her fingers look pretty. She laid down the board beside the register and put on her Welcome-to-The-Willows face.

"Late lunch, folks?" she almost giggled the words. It takes a certain kind of personality to meet and greet at The Willows and this girl had a bad case of it. "Are you all from the same office?" Small talk fell out of her cute little face like water through a sieve.

"*They* all work together," I said. I reached for a toothpick. "I'm just measuring compliance."

"Sounds complicated," said the girl, still bubbling over. She grabbed a stack of menus.

"It isn't," I said. I stuck the toothpick in my mouth and started chewing it. "Just drinks this afternoon. Thanks." She put the menus back down and led us to the verandah overlooking the koi pond. She seated us at a rattan table long enough for twice our number. Near the little waterfall, the plump trio sang. I could smell the pikake strands around their thick necks even from as far away as our table. I ordered a Four Roses with a cola chaser and Wilde had a beer. The rest of them declined to have anything and Iris had a cup of coffee, sulking. My first few swallows of bourbon made some of the pain of being awake and alive go away.

Introductions were made around the table. The gray-flannelled cadaver who sat up front with Wilde was Tetsuo Fujioka, an English professor at UH. He was Harry Kurita's mentor, though it was Harry who brought him into the CP and not the other way around. The short red-faced dripper in the brown suit was the unfortunately named Dick Wiener, a labor attorney from San Francisco. He pronounced his name "Wine-er," though I suspect his folks changed it from "Weener" to prevent him from growing up with a complex. Too late. He looked at the tablecloth and muttered to himself. The pink dress was Sally Leong, one of Fujioka's graduate assistants. She was a little too refined to be one of Harry's former conquests, so I suspected that she was Fujioka's mistress. She sat a little too close to the gray flannel jacket and made worried eyes at him. Then there was Iris. All in all, an impressive lot on paper but sorry to look at in person. It was like a collection of all the kids who got picked last when teams were chosen on the playground. Except for Wilde. If it weren't for his massive gut, he could probably swing the stick in the cleanup position.

"Jiro's dead?" Wilde asked. He finished his first beer and ordered another.

"Cut to pieces and burned. He was found in a cane field on the ewa side." I pulled my Zippo out and lit a cigarette, unintentionally punctuating the statement with a flame.

Wilde shook his head. "I never thought they'd take it this far. They hated each other—that was no secret. Kempa recommended at one point that one of them move to a different group, but neither would budge. Both of them were stubborn as hell. And the shit they had with each other escalated. But I never thought that he . . . that they . . . would end it like this."

"Escalated? How?"

"It started with Jiro making Harry look bad at meetings, always contradicting him, putting his suggestions down. Harry retaliated in kind. Then the shit with Beverly."

"Harry started seeing her?"

"Nobody knew for sure." This was Fujioka who spoke up. He was staring through his spectacles at the fire-hued koi moving in circles in the pond. "Jiro made accusations and Harry wouldn't deny them. He called the accusations weak and pathetic, just like Jiro."

"I think Harry enjoyed letting everyone think he was carrying on with Beverly," said Leong. She glared at Fujioka.

"Come on, Sally," Fujioka hissed softly. He never took his eyes off the koi. "I know you never really cared for Harry, but you need not assassinate his character so. It's unbecoming."

"How can you defend him, Tets? How can you defend him even now, after what he's done to Jiro?" Sally Leong's pink fingernails were clawing into the gray flannel on Fujioka's upper arm. Her face looked stretched out over her skull, like Saran Wrap on a cold chicken. Obviously, there was something else at play between the two academics, but something I wasn't interested enough to ask about.

"Harry didn't kill him," said Fujioka flatly. "He was a peace-loving soul."

Leong blew air out of her face and shook her head. "If you love him so much, why didn't you run off with him, Tets? The two of you could've read Keats to each other naked." Everyone else at the table shifted their weight uncomfortably in their seats.

Wiener turned beet red. "I'll have that drink now, if you don't mind, Detective," he said, wiping his forehead with a handkerchief.

"You and me both," I said. I signaled the waiter who took our orders and withdrew quietly back to the bar. I looked at Fujioka and Leong, who were still fuming from their exchange. "Now if you two erstwhile lovebirds are through debating the relative merits and demerits of your sordid little triangle's third leg, I'd like to get back to the trouble between him and Jiro Machida."

"Side," said Iris. I almost forgot she was there.

"What?"

"*Side*, Frankie. Triangles have *sides*, not *legs*." My sister the geometry teacher. She never missed an opportunity to correct me. I rolled my eyes and looked back at Wilde.

"Why all the hate?" I asked him. "Was it really all about who got to drive the rest of you around Moiliili while you talked about leaflets?"

"A couple of petty dictators, the two of them," said Wilde. "But it wasn't just about that. Or about Beverly." Wilde looked at his "comrades" one by one, searching their faces for the go-ahead before continuing. All returned his glance, nodding their tacit approval to disclose what he was about to disclose.

"We came into some money. Some old lady with a mansion on the slopes of Diamond Head at the far end of Waikiki dropped some cash on Group 12. She took a shine to your sister who called on her in one of her fundraising efforts. It turns out though she's old, haole, and rich; she was some reporter who covered the Bolsheviks in Russia starting from about two years before the revolution. She was kind of like a one-girl fan club for them. Beatrice Walker Crane. She was a freelance who sometimes did stuff for *The New York Times*. She liked Iris so much that she gave her two thousand dollars for the Group."

Two grand. Chump change to the likes of the local Rotary Club or Masonic Lodge but big money for a small neighborhood communist cell in Palolo Valley. Iris smiled smugly at Wilde's mention of her wheedling the money out of Old Lady Crane.

"Jiro and Harry came to blows over a lousy two grand that didn't even belong to them?" I asked.

"It wasn't the money necessarily, Detective," said the sweaty Wiener. He mopped his wide forehead with a linen napkin when he really needed a sponge for the job. "Jiro and Harry clashed over how the money should be used. Jiro wanted to set up a fund to support striking dock workers and Harry wanted to . . . well, Harry wanted to go to China."

"China?"

"Yes, China. Harry felt that the money should be used to send one of the Group to China to study Maoist doctrine. He felt that because Hawaii is largely Oriental that the working people may have more of an affinity to Chinese ideas than to Russian ones."

"But Jiro had studied in Russia and met Mao himself in China during the war," I said. "Wasn't he something of a first-hand expert on how Maoism compared to Bolshevism or Trotskyism?"

"That was Jiro's argument against sending someone, especially Harry. And that only made Harry more upset. Harry said Jiro's interpretation of what he saw in Russia and China couldn't be trusted because Jiro couldn't be trusted."

"We all thought both ideas had merit," said my sister. She sipped her coffee like she was the Duchess of Windsor. "We saw they would clearly never agree so we put the money aside while we figured out another neutral use for it."

"It sounds like just another one of their petty arguments," I said. I was working on my third bourbon. "What makes you think this was what broke the camel's back?"

"Because the money went missing around the same time they did," said Wilde. "The Group voted for me to hold it. My place was broken into. Someone turned it upside down. Nothing was taken but the money. I couldn't go to the police because ... well, you know why. We were set to question both Jiro and Harry at the next meeting but neither of them showed. We didn't see either of them again." When Wilde mentioned the break-in, I thought of my own apartment being ransacked.

I looked at all of them. They all affirmed Wilde's statement with mute, slight nods. Fujioka hung his head with shame for his protégé. I killed my bourbon and ordered one more. Two grand couldn't buy you a new house or even an old one on Oahu. But it could buy you a new life. It could get you to China and then some. For two thousand dollars, Harry Kurita could rut his way through Peking's prettiest Red Guards and set up shop with one in some mud plaster hut with a clay tile roof while she taught him to recite Keats in bed. In Mandarin. He could also buy himself a new name or even a new face. And a Japanese fishing boat might take him in the right direction.

I stood up after downing the last Four Roses, burning my throat. Group 12 of the Hawaii Communist Party stood with me. I dropped a ten-dollar bill on the table. The three fat ladies wailed "Kaimana Hila" at our backs as we walked back out to Hausten Street. The happy girl in the little shack put her emery board down long enough to ooze a "Mahalo" at us while I snatched another toothpick and a handful of after-dinner mints from her counter.

"Mahalo yourself," I told her. I grinned and she grinned back, then returned to the important business of her nails. I put the mints into my handkerchief and folded it up.

We parted at the curb across the street. Wilde and his little club got into his dented car. My sister got into mine.

"So long, comrades," I told them. "Thanks for the little talk. It was a gas. Power to the people." They stared sullenly back at me from under their eyelids, all of them looking about ten years older. It's what happens when you live for a cause. You'll never catch me doing it. I've got plenty of other things to make me old before my time.

13

Iris was as quiet as a mollusk during most of the drive to her Kapahulu home. So unlike her to shut up, it was creepy. I grew up in a house in Kakaako with four older sisters, each one of them thinking she was a mind reader. They all knew what drove the world to hear them tell it, but never agreed on anything for four women who knew everything. My sisters all had flowers' names—names my poor parents couldn't pronounce any better than mine: Violet, Daisy, Iris, Pansy. At McKinley High School, the boys referred to the pink house on Kawaiahao Street we grew up in as the "Yoshikawa Garden" owing to the four "flowers." I never understood their fascination with my sisters. To me they were just bossy toilet hogs in silly curls and clown makeup. Iris was the loudest and most pompous of them all. She had an opinion about everything and her favorite thing to do in the world was to make sure you knew it. Still, she, like the rest of them, managed to find an unwitting man to marry and ride like a carnival pony.

That man was Chester Imada, Certified Public Accountant and sashimi aficionado. He wasn't really passionate about his work, though he was one of the best when it came to finding loopholes in "The Code." His one true love after my sister was raw fish. He would steal down to the auction at Kewalo Basin early on Sunday mornings before dawn, before my sister made him put on his dark suit for church. I went with Chester once just to see what all the noise was about. Cold and wet, the place smelled like dead fish. Not my cup of tea. But Chester was in heaven, sampling little bits of ahi tail meat and going home with several bundles of pink paper-wrapped cuts of fish. He was even persnickety about the shoyu he used to dip his sashimi in—stuff from Japan that cost three to five times as much as the shoyu from the brewery in Kalihi. To me it was pretty much the same—dark, warm, salty. Chester swore he could tell the difference. Then again, he smoked the kind of dime cigars that my landlord Old Chang sold in his liquor and sundry place and wondered what I tasted in the Cubans I bought from the hat check girl at the Moana.

Chester wasn't home when I pulled up in front of my sister's white house on Mooheau Avenue. The house was quiet and the front lawn was littered with dead yellow leaves from the mango tree. My niece, Carrie, was sitting on the rattan chair on the lanai, reading *Little Women*. She looked up when I pulled the Cadillac into the driveway. She put the book down and came bounding down the concrete steps, pigtails flying. She was ten years old but looked more like eight.

"Hi, Uncle Frankie! What are you doing here?" She smiled a big smile showing me a mouthful of orthodontic metal.

"I had to arrest your mom," I told her. Carrie laughed like a baby seal, croaking in a high pitch. Iris shot me a blood-chilling look. She didn't find the remark nearly as funny as her daughter did. "I took the cuffs off her so she wouldn't be embarrassed walking into her house."

"What did she do?"

"She disturbed the peace. You know how your mom gets when she starts talking."

"I know how she gets." We both laughed. I got out of the car and gave my niece a hug. Iris sat still in the passenger seat, sulking like she missed out on the after-dinner mochi. I opened the door for her, then reached into my pocket and pulled out the handkerchief of the mints I pinched from The Willows. I gave them to my niece.

"Why don't you go in and split these with your little sister," I said to her. "I need to talk with your mom for a little bit. Okay?"

"Okay. Thanks for the candy, Uncle Frankie!" I gave Carrie a pat in the head and she ran up the stairs and blew through the screen door, shouting, "Patty! Patty! Candy!" I shoved my hands in my trouser pockets and looked at my sister, raising my eyebrows once. She got out of the car and stomped up the stairs to the rattan chair, sitting where her daughter had been. I followed her up and sat down next to her, picking up my niece's book and flipping through the pages rapidly just to give my hands something to do.

"So, talk," Iris said, staring straight ahead at the mango tree.

"Look, I'm not going to tell anybody about your little meeting today or your club membership. Quite frankly, I'm too damned embarrassed to do so."

"You mean you're too damned *scared* to do so."

"You're welcome. Anything for my grateful sister."

"Oh, Frankie. Get off your high horse. You just don't want the red taint on you."

"This isn't about *me*, Iris."

"You think you're doing me a favor? That's so patronizing. You sound just like the plantation lunas who gave To-san a nickel more on payday than the Filipinos got and told him it was because he was such a good worker."

"Will you shut up and listen for a second? The Feds are *arresting* people like you and your friends. Don't you read a newspaper every now and then? I don't care about a 'red taint.' I care about those two little girls in there. What do you think it's going to be like for them when their mom goes to jail? Maybe years from now they might be proud of your 'sacrifice,' but right now they'd be terrified. And they'll never forget *that*."

"Shut up, stupid."

"*You're* the stupid, *stoopid*."

"*You* are."

We glared at each other. Then we smiled. Then we laughed. It was just like when we were kids. No matter what we argued about, our disagreements degenerated into name calling of the most infantile nature. Stupid. It was the one thing both of us hated to be thought of as. I pulled a cigarette out and lit it and sat on the railing of the lanai with my back to the street. Iris shifted on the rattan seat and crossed her legs the other way and looked at me.

"When did you find out Jiro was dead?" she asked.

"Yesterday. In the morning. Dispatch got a call from a sugar company luna in Kunia. They found his burned bones in a shallow grave in the middle of a stripped field. I went out there with Gid."

Iris flinched at my description of Jiro's remains. She chewed her lower lip. I guess lip chewing is what people do if they don't smoke. "Did you tell Beverly?" she asked.

"Yeah, I went out to Waialua yesterday."

"How did she take it?"

"She didn't."

"She didn't believe you?"

"It wasn't denial. It was more like the news was about the same as finding out the score from yesterday's Yankees game. If you didn't follow baseball."

"Oh. Maybe it was the shock."

"I think *I* was more shocked than she was. She got Buddhist about it. Very Buddhist. More than the bonsan at Uncle Toshiro's funeral."

"Really? She didn't seem the type to me, but then again, she's a strange one . . . ." Iris chewed her lip some more then stopped abruptly and looked me in the eye. "Frankie? Don't you get mixed up with her, understand? She's trouble. You and Ellen are good for each other. Don't screw it up." There was something in my sister's voice that sounded like genuine concern. She wasn't just preaching like she usually did.

"I won't," I told her. I couldn't help smiling. My big sister was worried. About me. It would've been cute if she wasn't so serious about it, making that weird, ugly frown of hers. What Chester saw in her I would never figure out. I thought about the daruma with one of its eyes filled in. Ellen was my dream and my destiny. Whatever else I let fall by the wayside in my life, I wouldn't let that. I took another drag and blew smoke up at the lanai roof rafters at an old wasp's nest of dried mud. "Don't worry," I told her. "I like my women somewhat more predictable. And yeah, you're right—she does seem like trouble. Do *you* think she was carrying on with Harry?"

"I don't know for sure, but I'd put money on it."

"Why?"

"Because of the way she is. And the way Harry is. But I don't think it lasted too long. Neither of them could be in love with anyone but the person in the mirror."

"No kidding. I remember Harry from that cocktail party here last year you booted me out of. But Jiro sounds like he was head over heels with himself, too."

"Yeah, that's what they were like, the three of them. Jiro and Harry were always trying to outdo each other. They both made pitches at Mrs. Crane, and she was so impressed she eventually ended up giving me the two thousand dollars for the ... uh ... Group. I went to her house on Diamond Head and she had me sit down and have tea with her and all she could do was chatter about the two of them. She thought they were absolutely brilliant. She called them 'The Future.'"

"Wilde told me she coughed up two grand because of *you*."

"Aw, I just made the collection," she said, though the downplay was obviously for my benefit. I don't know why she bothered. All those years growing up she never bothered. Modesty suited Iris like stiletto heels on a gorilla.

"Tell me about the collection."

Iris recounted her visit to the house on the slopes of Diamond Head overlooking the azure sea. She spoke longingly of the garden out of Scheherazade's tales, the Moorish tile work fountain surrounded by an emerald lawn, and lush ferns and ti plants lining the edge of the space fronting the white stucco walls. I couldn't share her appreciation at the moment. My head hurt like hell. The bourbon from The Willows was beginning to wear off and I needed another slug to stave off the pain. I puffed away on my Lucky Strike while she blabbed on about the Ottoman ceramics and the rosewood furniture.

"Sounds like a nice place," I told her. "Like something out of *Little Orphan Annie*. What did the old lady say about your two windbags?" I rubbed my forehead with my thumb and forefinger. I needed another drink but wouldn't take one in front of my nieces. To them I was still Galahad, righteous and gallant. I was really more like the fallen Lancelot, trying vainly to hide the bad habits under a shining breastplate and a string of tournament victories. Every day the armor gleamed a little less. It was getting harder to stay in the saddle.

"Are you okay?"

"Yeah. Swell. What did she say?"

"She said that both of them came over often to talk to her about their plans for the Group. Not together, of course. She told me she was very impressed with them and then she gave me the cash. She said it was for their plans."

"Why didn't you just give each of them a thousand?"

"It was for The Group, Frankie. We decide everything together."

"Like good little comrades."

"Shut up."

I looked out over the mango trees across Mooheau Avenue to the crown of Diamond Head rising above them. On the other side of the crater was the Cranes' place with its Garden of Eden and its rosewood dining set. It was a short drive and I had a little time. Not much, but more than I was willing to spend sitting on the porch with my sister with my head coming apart at the temples. I gave Iris a weak grin and headed down the lanai steps.

"You going?"

"Yeah," I said over my shoulder. "Stay out of trouble. I mean it."

14

The flask was empty by the time I reached the other side of Diamond Head. My head hurt a little less and I could appreciate the white stucco starting to turn gold from being blasted by the slow sinking sun over the ocean. Mrs. Crane's place wasn't a house. It was a temple. It was a mosque. A place of worship for the lost souls who rode to tournament under Marx's banner but dragged a conscience weighted down with the backbreaking mass of old money. Done in Spanish mission style with a red tile roof, the house—terraced in layers with gardens on each level to match the downward slope of Diamond Head toward the sea—was big enough to be a small hospital. I imagined that all you could see was the blue Pacific from most of the windows in the house. Haoles and their millions. The conservative ones strived to be British with their country club whites and tea on the lanai. The leftists, on the other hand, thought they were French, embracing the ways of a darker, stranger people, so long as it wasn't the dark, strange people they happened to live with; they loved to import touches from exotic places they had lived to other exotic places. The Cranes obviously had an affinity for the mysterious Levant. The wrought iron had an Arabian quality to it, like Damascus gates from a child's picture-book. The mosaic fountain Iris talked about was tinkling musically in the courtyard. A body moved among the ti leaves. It wasn't a harem girl.

An ancient Japanese gardener with a leathery face peered up at me through wire-rimmed spectacles, his long rubber boots slick with

water from the lily pond he had been sloshing about in, clearing out
dead rushes.

"I'm very sorry, sir. There is a sign out front that says 'No
Solicitors' in case you couldn't read it. The lady of the house is most
insistent on that matter."

"Then she's in luck. I haven't a damn thing to sell today." I looked
at the gardener with a smirk. At least it drew the corners of my mouth
up a little. Indulgent smiles were in short supply that day and I had
given my last one away to the communists at The Willows.

The dark beady eyes behind the lenses suddenly softened and the
old man smiled. His teeth were yellow and chipped.

"Oh! I'm sorry! You must be one of Mrs. Crane's friends from the
Palolo Group."

"No, I'm not. But I'm here to talk to her about them." I pulled the
badge out of my pocket and showed it to him. The beady eyes narrowed
suspiciously and I was back to being the illiterate salesman, though I was
about twenty-four hours past caring about it.

"Relax," I said. I mimicked his squint back at him. "I don't care
about the old lady's politics. I'm a homicide detective."

"Oh," he said. The eyes softened again. "In that case, please wait
here in the garden and I will announce you."

"Thank you. Announce away."

"Your name, Detective?"

"Yoshikawa. Francis Yoshikawa."

"Very good, Detective Yoshikawa." He said my name properly,
like the Mikado's own gatekeeper. The little man disappeared quickly
and quietly, leaving me in the idyllic courtyard. I cast an admiring look
about. Somewhere in Cairo a fat rich man in a fez was wondering
who the hell stole his garden. I pulled a Lucky Strike out of a battered
pack and lit up. My breath pulled on the cigarette like the smoke was
somehow keeping me alive, while the sun began its steady descent into

the sea. I had a picture-perfect view of it from my vantage point in the palace garden. It was a view that could be bought with half a million dollars and signed covenants and restrictions forbidding one to sell it to Orientals, Negroes, or Hawaiians not descended from the Royal Line of Kamehameha. This impudent Oriental threw his cigarette butt into the fountain, to be fished out later by the impudent Oriental in the black rubber boots. I put my hands in my pockets and watched the cigarette butt bob about on the gentle ripples over the brilliantly colored tiles. It started to sink when the little gardener reappeared. His black rubber boots were gone, replaced by a pair of brown leather brogues.

"This way, Detective Yoshikawa."

"Lead on."

We stepped into the shade of an awning and through the front double door, a pair of koa monstrosities that would have held their own against a battering ram. They were thrown open to catch the faint breeze. The dark foyer, surprisingly cool, was done in brilliantly colored hand-painted tiles like the baths of the Topkapi Sarayi. I cast a glance around at all of the Levantine artwork on the walls and on alabaster pedestals. There were gilt-framed Ottoman miniature paintings done after the Tabriz school, illuminated pages in the same style, and glazed dishes from Iznik in a thousand different colors. I hadn't entered someone's home; I had stepped into a museum.

The wrinkled little gardener led me past the exhibit in the long hallway and we emerged in the sunlight once again in a smaller garden. The quaint space, elegant and less ostentatious than the big courtyard I had waited in, had its own tiny fountain tiled in the same fashion as the larger fountain and a heavy glass-topped wrought iron table next to it. A woman sipping a martini sat at the table and stared out at the ocean.

She must have been about sixty but didn't look a day over forty-five. The only hint about her true age was a dramatic silver streak that ran through her chestnut hair, fashionably coiffed over a statuesque neck.

Her form was well maintained and sheathed in a simple but flattering white linen blouse and dark slacks. Her shoes looked like a month's salary. She turned her head and regarded me with pale gray eyes. Her smile took another five years off her age.

"Good afternoon, Detective," she said. Her voice was low and gravelly from a lifetime of cigarettes in the pubs and casbahs of the newsworthy world, though not without a unique charm.

"Good afternoon, Mrs. Crane. I apologize for the sudden unannounced visit, but the urgency of my work makes such calls unavoidable at times."

"No need to apologize, Detective. I quite understand. I detect a note of Eastern Seaboard in your speech. Dartmouth?"

"Columbia."

"That's quite a way from home. I almost went to Barnard but ended up at Radcliffe. But I'm neglecting my responsibility as a hostess. Would you care for a drink?"

"Thank you. Scotch," I said, a little too eagerly. The headache was coming back. Beatrice Walker Crane nodded almost imperceptibly and the little gardener disappeared into the gloom of the enormous house. "Will you have a seat, Detective?" She motioned to the vacant iron chair across the table from her. I nodded and sat.

"You told Makoto that you are a homicide detective."

"That's correct." I drew the badge out and showed it to her.

"He also said you wished to discuss some friends of mine."

"That's also correct."

"Are the two related? That is, you being a homicide detective and wanting to discuss my friends."

"Regrettably."

Beatrice Walker Crane turned pale and shivered. She lifted her glass to her face for another dainty sip of her drink, but it shook in her suddenly unsteady hand and she changed her mind and put it back

down on the table. She cast her eyes down at her drink and her voice
came out small and soft like a trace of a half-remembered dream.

"What happened?"

"Did you know Jiro Machida?"

She nodded soundlessly and clasped her hands together in a
ferocious grip until they were white with strain.

"We found him in a cane field yesterday."

I wasn't prepared for the air raid siren she apparently kept in
her throat, the wail piercing and heart rending. I offered her my hand
across the glass table and she gripped it and nearly tore it off my wrist.
Violent sobs wracked her body. Suddenly, I understood. Beatrice Walker
Crane wasn't just Jiro Machida's benefactor and admirer. She had been
his lover. The kind of caterwauling she was doing wasn't something one
would do over a mere pitchman for a cause she threw some money at.
This, a damn sight more than his young wife did over him.

After a while, the grip on my hand slackened a bit and the sobs
grew quieter. I hadn't even a handkerchief to offer her. I gave it away
to my nieces filled with after-dinner mints. Beatrice Walker Crane
eventually composed herself and managed to look at me.

"I'm sorry, Detective. We were very close."

Apparently. "No, ma'am, *I'm* sorry," I said. "I apologize for
having to inform you of his passing this way. I am investigating the
circumstances surrounding his . . . departure. I understand that you had
seen him before he disappeared."

"Yes," she said. Eyes, red and watery, suddenly made her look
her age. The news sucked all of the remaining enchantment out of her.
She reached in her pocket and pulled a slim gold cigarette box out of it
and drew a slim, expensive looking stick out of it. I held my Zippo out
for her and she drew deeply and exhaled, filling the little garden with a
haze and shrouding her grief-ravaged face. "I wondered why he hadn't
called."

Makoto the gardener returned and not a moment too soon with a generous pour of something amber and elegant in a heavy cut crystal old-fashioned glass and another martini. He set the drinks in front of us and withdrew soundlessly. I sipped the excellent scotch as daintily as a thoroughbred at a trough and let it do its magic. The encroaching headache was beaten down once again and the world was a nicer place.

"Could you tell me about Jiro's relationship with Harry Kurita?" I asked when her sobs had quieted along with the drums in my head. Good scotch was all the medicine I needed on most days.

Beatrice Walker Crane smiled and sniffed the last of her tears away. Her natural allure was coming back. Or maybe it was the scotch. "They had the worst case of sibling rivalry I had ever seen from two people who weren't actually siblings. But, like real brothers, I could sense there was an affection and admiration for each other underneath it all. They were both madly brilliant and passionate men, full of ideas to set the world on fire."

All this was shit I had heard before. The Young Radicals. The Wonder Boys of the Hawaii Communist Party. Tristram and Palomides. It was enough to make me want to vomit all that good scotch over the neat little lawn overlooking the sea. Everyone had a take on how damned clever these characters were. I had a pretty good idea of why one might chop up the other and burn the pieces then hop a boat for Asia, but I needed more. I needed means and opportunity but so far all I was getting was motive. I had motive coming out of my ears. Sibling rivalry. Sheesh. Of the Cain and Abel variety, maybe.

She tapped the ash from her cigarette with the kind of studied grace that comes with being born into money. I squashed my butt in the ashtray somewhat less artfully. Sorry, there weren't a lot of finishing schools in Kakaako. I pulled another Lucky Strike from the battered pack in my pocket and lit up. Beatrice Walker Crane stared out over the sea at nothing in particular.

"I understand you made a donation to the Palolo Group before Jiro disappeared," I said.

"Yes. It wasn't much, but I felt it would help finance some of Jiro's and Harry's innovative plans. Did you know about them? The plans, I mean. An insurance fund of sorts for striking workers. That was Jiro's idea. Harry wanted to send someone to China to study Maoist doctrine and educate the unions here. They were just brilliant."

"Insurance and a junket. Doesn't sound very proletariat."

"That was the beauty of those two men. They were such forward thinkers. Always looking to beat the establishment at its own game."

"You think so? It looked to me like they were trying to beat each other. Over the head. Your two grand touched off a firestorm. It plunged their rivalry into a deeper, darker place."

"Good heavens," she shuddered. "Perhaps I should have given five thousand. That would have been enough to fund both of their dreams."

"I don't think it was really about the money, Mrs. Crane. If you had given them five *million* dollars they still would have found a way to come to blows over it."

Beatrice Walker Crane fell silent and looked at me with eyes widening as my point dawned on her.

"Oh, no," she whispered. "No, no, Detective. Are you telling me that Harry was responsible for Jiro's . . . for Jiro?" The slightly salty breeze of the ocean was charged with her silent horror.

"I'm not saying that he was. The money's gone, though, and so is Harry. They both went missing about the same time Jiro did. What am I supposed to think?"

"No," she said again. "Oh, how terrible!"

"I need your help, Mrs. Crane. Was there any indication from either of them that something like this would happen?"

"No ... the rivalry they had was deep and, yes, could be fierce at times but I didn't think either one of them was capable of something like this." The smoke from our cigarettes dissipated slowly in the slight breeze coming off the water below. It shook the lauhala fronds in the gardens gently like a languid, sensual dream seen through the ripples in a scotch on the rocks.

"Was there any indication that Harry was going to go through with his plans to get to China?"

"Of course. He was very passionate and persistent about the idea."

"I mean in an at-all-costs sort of way."

"I guess you could say that Harry was an at-all-costs sort of man. But so was Jiro. It's what made them both so appealing."

Her glowing adoration for the two sanctimonious blowhards was beginning to sicken me. "Sure," I said, with a nasty edge even the scotch couldn't blunt, "I always have a soft spot for premeditated killers who dismember their victims and burn their parts."

"My God, Detective! I didn't think that's what you meant!"

"Sorry, I thought at-all-costs meant anything and everything. I guess your anything and everything is different from the anything and everything I'm accustomed to seeing. Did Harry ever mention how he planned to get to China? For the kind of money you gave the Group he could really go in style."

She let some smoke slip from her lips and eyed me as if I had wounded her in Harry's stead. "I know that Harry could be ostentatious at times and had a flair for the dramatic, Detective, but what he wasn't was a hypocrite," she said adamantly. "The only thing he ever splurged on was his amorous adventures."

"Are you sure that China wasn't one for him?" I pictured him among the pretty young women in their white blouses and their red kerchiefs in the crowded streets of Shanghai offering free English poetry readings with Chivas Regal. There were millions of them. Enough to satisfy his appetite for two lifetimes.

"Oh, Detective, really! He told me that there were any number of fishing vessels and tramp steamers he could hop to cut corners. The bulk of the money would be used to support courses at Renmin University in Peking for a half-year and meeting with party officials." There it was. The *Iwakuni Maru*.

"Well, it seems I've misjudged our dashing Mr. Kurita. You are right, Mrs. Crane. I had the privilege of meeting some of Jiro and Harry's associates and they are quite an impressive group," I lied. I thought of the insipid bunch at The Willows. I looked down at the table and saw that another scotch had magically replaced my empty tumbler. Makoto had stolen up from behind us and just as quietly disappeared into the shadows of the lanai. I gratefully raised the tumbler to my lips and forced myself to imbibe with more manners than I had inhaled the last one.

Beatrice Walker Crane warmed to me again with my last comment. "Oh, yes," she agreed. "There are a number of great young minds in that Group. Especially the women. There is one in particular who impressed me as exceptionally brilliant."

"Would that be Iris Imada?" I asked. I tried not to chuckle as I let the fine, golden liquid slip down my throat and fill me with peace of mind.

"Oh, you met Iris? I think she is outstanding as well, but I was talking about the other one."

"Sally Leong?"

"I haven't met her. I meant Jiro's former girlfriend, the one he let get away in favor of marrying that shallow, conniving sneak. I meant the reporter who was at the *Record* with him."

"Reporter?"

"Ellen Park."

I gagged on the 21-year old scotch as someone yanked the carpet out from under my world.

15

Ellen Park. My sweetheart. My life's ambition and the only thing I really wanted with any amount of certainty. Jiro Machida's ex-girlfriend. Communist?

I had staggered out of Beatrice Walker Crane's palatial abode apologetically, saying that I had to be going. Thanks for your time and concern, Comrade. Oh, and thanks for the wonderful news about my girlfriend. It's all my shitty life was missing to make it complete.

My head was spinning out of control. I pulled in front of a liquor store on Kapahulu Avenue and bought a fifth of Kentucky rye and filled my hipflask sloppily, spilling it on my suit and leather upholstery. I threw the flask in the glove compartment and took swigs from the bottle. A half dozen times or more I walked to the telephone booth to call Ellen, but changed my mind each time. *It's what people do when they care for each other, Frankie Yoshikawa.* What about lying about their past and CP affiliation by . . . by omission? Is *that* what people do when they care for each other?

At that moment, under the recently flicked-on neon in Kapahulu as the sun started dying, I couldn't care less about Jiro Machida's pompous dismembered corpse turned to charcoal in Kunia or catching the windbag lothario who put it there. I could feel my future slipping away. The pretty, spunky little girl reporter I had given my heart to may well be taking it to a federal prison with her when the HUAC got around to hanging Koji Ariyoshi. I knew those haoles. They wouldn't stop at the Hawaii Seven. They'd burn down all their associates too. I'd be powerless to stop them. First my sister, now my sweetheart. How could they be so smart and yet so goddamned stupid? I took a long sloppy pull from the bottle and eyed the green and pink neon in the liquor store window through the amber prism and laughed loudly and bitterly. No wonder she had a list of the cell leaders. No wonder she knew about Harry and Jiro. No wonder she hated Beverly.

Beverly. I looked at my watch. I had less than an hour before my "date" with her at the Pearl City Tavern. I didn't care. She could go to hell with Jiro, Harry, and the rest of them. The whole damned world could go to hell, too.

But what about giri?

What about *what*?

Giri. Obligation. It was something To-san used to talk to me about when I was a kid, all those afternoons watching the sampans at Kewalo Basin. Every man needed to understand it and heed its call. But he didn't tell me just how damned important it was until he lay hacking his life away in a damp, dirty little canvas pup tent on Sand Island.

"Did I ever tell you the story of the forty-seven ronin, Hide-kun?"

"Lots of times, To-san. Try not to talk."

It was a miserable wet day at the makeshift detention camp the Army had set up at Sand Island for all the "dangerous" Japs like my dad. He was there awaiting a boat that would take him to Jerome for the seditious act of teaching calligraphy to grade school kids at the Moiliili Language School. To-san was a mechanic by trade but an aesthete at heart, seeing the broad strokes of the brush on the rice paper of his mind's eye and bringing the kanji to life with his labor-knotted hands. Sumi and washi. Black and white. Wrong and right. This was my father's lens. It was 1942 and Honolulu was in the grips of martial law. Barbed wire everywhere, even on the coral and wrought iron fences surrounding Iolani Palace. I had just graduated from McKinley High School.

"Never mind," To-san wheezed. He was bundled up in the scratchy olive drab blanket the haole soldiers had thrown on him. Ka-san and Violet were waiting outside the tent with camphor for his chest and a steel lunch pail of okai, sharing a bamboo-handled umbrella. They waited in the wet so I could have my time with him. "This is important so pay attention." His voice was thin and weak and crackled with thick moisture.

"Okay," I said.

"They worked hard and waited patiently, the forty-seven, before the moment came to avenge Asano. They waited months. When the time came, they did what they had to. They took Kira's head and cut themselves open."

"I know," I said. "I told you. I heard this before, To-san. Lots of times."

"Do you know why?"

"Why what?"

"Why they did it."

"Yeah. Revenge."

"No."

"No?"

"You said you heard it lots of times, but you never listened once," he croaked. Then he coughed violently again. I placed my right hand gently on his chest and cradled the back of his head with my left. His skin was clammy and he felt incredibly small and frail, like a bird.

"What? Not revenge? Didn't Kira shame Asano into seppuku and make all their lives miserable? Then why?"

"Because they had to."

"Oh," I said, like I understood, but I didn't.

"They had to. Giri. Not revenge. Not love. Not hate. They *had* to."

"Isn't doing all that for revenge . . . or love or hate or whatever . . . doing it because you have to?"

"No. It's not the same thing."

"No?"

"You do because you *have* to. Wakarimasuka?"

"No."

"You will. One day." He smiled widely enough so that I could see the gaps where his teeth had been. His dentures were soaking in a tin surplus cup on an old lettuce crate next to his cot. I got up and took the umbrella from my sister as she and Ka-san entered the tent to feed him. I stood out in the rain and thought about giri—doing something difficult because you have to, not because of some compelling, overpowering emotion that makes you do it. Black and white. Like his calligraphy. To-san's world wasn't colored with the many hues of the heart. Kuranosuke wasn't Lancelot.

I didn't get it that rainy day in my dad's little sodden tent watching him die of pneumonia. I wouldn't understand it until the day I charged uphill into a storm of German machine gun fire in the Vosges woods to rescue some Texans who bumbled into a bad situation. I didn't charge to save their lives or to throw mine away. I charged because I had to. We all did. Giri. Obligation. It was a damn good thing for those cowpokes that a bunch of Japs had been given the order to pull their fat out of the fire; the haole units would have seen the writing on the wall and called it a day.

I looked at my watch. Forty-five minutes to get out to Pearl City. Beverly Machida and her sultry, hooded eyes were waiting at the Monkey Bar with a truckload of pain-in-the-ass. I didn't want to go. I wanted to make a beeline to Ellen and confront her about not telling me about her involvement with the CP. I wanted her to tell me she was sorry and to make the heartbreak go away. I wanted to forget about the burned bones in the cane field. I wanted to forget about the culprit on a Japanese fishing boat. I wanted to tell Gideon Hanohano I needed a break and he could give this one to some other lucky dick in the Detail.

I didn't want to know any more about Jiro or Harry or Beverly or
Marlon Wilde or Beatrice Walker Crane or her gardener or the whole
damn Hawaii Communist Party.

It didn't matter what I wanted.

I had to go on with the case. I *had* to.

I hit the starter and threw the Eldorado into gear and pulled
away from the curb, bound for Pearl City.

Giri.

Shit.

Sometimes I hated being Japanese.

16

Pearl City Tavern was the kind of place that was supposed to remind you of those quaint little Japanese tea houses with the moonlit gardens and the soft, gentle lantern light radiating from the white-paned shoji doors. Exactly like that if you ignored the drunken G.I.s, the gum-cracking girls in the loud floral print dresses, and the monkeys leaping about in the cage behind the bar, ready to sling their turd at some lucky swabbie's shore-leave whites. It was the monkeys who gave the lounge its name; the rest of Pearl City Tavern was a neighborhood restaurant that served Japanese and "American" fare and stuff in between, like teriyaki sirloin with mashed potatoes and a sprig of parsley.

I had arrived with about five minutes to spare, so I squeezed between a couple of punks in bright aloha shirts and pomaded hair and got myself a Four Roses. I cast my glance about the packed Monkey Bar; it was full of Pearl Harbor sailors and young Japanese and kanaka toughs and girls in tight dresses and painted faces with eyes like the cheap rye they were pouring behind the bar. It was a volatile recipe for a brawl waiting to happen. I didn't see Gid. Maybe he was running late. Maybe he changed his mind about making the drive out just to watch me make a fool of myself.

I took my drink and parked myself in a corner booth with bad lighting away from the marinated yammering and guffaws. It was still about as quiet as a battlefield. Somewhere I heard Dean Martin's canned jukebox voice slurring something in Italian to the plucky notes of a mandolin, buried under the boasts and dirty jokes and failed propositions. A bunch of haole sailors in loud aloha shirts milled about the cigarette machine impatiently while the big delivery guy in his coveralls and faded red cap moved at a snail's pace filling it up with packs out of brand-new cartons. It made me glad I already had my own smokes. I lit up a Lucky Strike and hung a blue haze in the booth with a few puffs when all the heads in the room turned in a single motion toward the door like leaves on a banyan caught in a sudden breeze. They were all looking at the white dress that illuminated the dingy bar. The dress and the girl in it made their way across the room to me, oblivious to the wolf whistles and leers that followed in her wake.

Her hair was piled high in a luxurious coil, black with red-brown accents courtesy of the Waialua sun. Her dark eyes shone beneath lashes impossibly long and thick. Her blood-red lips, pursed shut in a slight pout, hovered like a fiery apparition above the milky pearls adorning her tanned throat. The snow-white dress clung to her alluring form and moved with feline grace through the cigarette fog and cheap liquor fumes and testosterone. She was the wicked cocktail that promised the death's door hangover, the proverbial flame that consumed one unwitting moth after another. She headed straight for me and it was too late to hide.

I got up out of the padded seat of my secluded booth. I nodded, my hands in my pockets and with a loosened tie and a jawbone that hadn't seen a razor since the sun came up. I was first-date-sharp minus the spit shine plus a hundred thousand miles of wear-and-tear. Too much booze and not enough sleep would knock the "charming" out of any prince, and I was no prince.

"Mrs. Machida."

"Beverly."

"Beverly. Good evening."

She brushed past me so I could feel the heat of her bosom and

smell her perfume. She slid into the same padded bench seat I had been
sitting on. I took a step toward the seat across the table when I felt her
slender hot hand grasp mine and pull me toward her.

"Sit next to me."

"Beverly, I don't . . ."

"Please."

"I shouldn't."

"Do I scare you?"

"Immensely."

She laughed a small tinkling laugh that was vague and empty,
and she didn't look at me while she did it. I allowed her to pull me down
onto the padded bench next to her. My head was filled with her scent,
overwhelming and poisonous as cyanide. I felt the slow burn of her
thigh brushing up against mine and thought distractedly of how she
had looked the afternoon before, out of her clothes, laying gloriously on
her sofa in Waialua waiting for a breeze that never came. She pulled a
cigarette from a small lacquered case, a delicate Japanese thing, as if out
of an ukiyo-e print. I snapped my Zippo open and struck the wheel with
my thumb. She seized my hand absently and ignited her smoke with a
single delicate draw. I thought some more about her without her dress
on when the tired-looking cocktail waitress thankfully broke the spell of
Morgan Le Fay by approaching our booth.

"Drinks, lovebirds?"

"Four Roses. Neat," I said, grateful for the interruption.

"The same," said Beverly. She looked at me and gave me one of
her void smiles.

The waitress dragged her worn form back into the haze toward
the bar and the jittery little monkeys behind it. Beverly picked up my
glass and took a sip, then held it to my lips after marking it with her
lipstick. I took a long pull and tasted the sweet wax along with the
bourbon.

"What did you want to talk about?" I asked.

"Did I want to talk about something?"

"You called me at the station earlier today and asked me to meet you. Was it that long ago or did you get a head start on the drinking?"

"I think *you* got a head start on the drinking. I didn't say I wanted to talk to you. I said I needed you. Or was it that long ago?"

My forehead popped a sweat. She wasn't as vacant as she let on. I thought about Ellen and her painful omissions. Was she *ever* going to tell me? Just what the hell was I doing there, sitting in the goddamned Monkey Bar next to Jiro Machida's poisonous widow with her hand on my leg? Did I think, even in the back of my aching head, that this was *good* for me? I drained the rest of the tumbler and loosened my tie another half inch. I hadn't noticed before, but it was positively sweltering in the Monkey Bar.

"You need me," I rasped. "What for?"

"Why do women usually need men?"

"Don't do this. I'm trying to find your husband's killer."

"Right at this moment?"

"Every moment. Until it's done."

"Why?"

"It's my job." Giri. It's why I'm sitting here catching fire, I thought. I had to pull it together and give it my best shot before I lost my nerve or my head. "When was the last time you saw Harry Kurita?" I asked her.

"You have a strange idea of what to say to impress a girl."

"I'm not in top form at the moment. Answer the question, Mrs. Machida."

"Beverly."

"Answer the question. Beverly."

"Only if you relax."

"I am relaxed."

"I don't think so," she cooed, and her hand plunged into my lap, slender bronze fingers grasping. In my mind I squirmed, but I was having trouble getting my body to do what my brain was telling it to do. In fact, I was having trouble moving at all.

A throat cleared gruffly. Thank God.

The waitress stood above us and set down two more tumblers of bourbon. She looked at me with a weary gaze above the mail sacks under her eyes as I fumbled in my coat for my wallet with fingers like lead fishing weights. It seemed like an eternity had gone by when I finally located it and by then I could see the waitress recede into the stale smoke.

"Too late," said Beverly with an absent grin. "I already took care of it."

"Oh," I said. "Thanks."

She lifted her tumbler to eye level and said, "Cheers."

I grasped my drink and brought it up to meet hers. I had a vague impression of the glasses clinking and the burn of bourbon on my tongue. I didn't even feel it go down, but I could feel my heart pounding in my head and my ears getting hotter and hotter with each beat. I felt like my tie and soaking collar were strangling me but couldn't find the strength to bring my hands up to my throat.

"Harry Kurita," I said again. My voice was nothing but a strangled gasp. I coughed to get more air into myself.

"He's a friend," she said, her voice sounding like it was coming from the inside of a storm drain.

"Your friend, but not Jiro's."

"They had conflicting personalities. It happens sometimes."

"When did you see Harry last?"

"A while ago. A couple of months. He was speaking at some kind of symposium at the university. Something having to do with Lord Byron and the changing world."

"Any idea where he might be now?"

"No."

Again, her hand found its way into my lap. Her other hand worked its way up her dress between her legs. I coughed again and the room spun.

"Are you okay? You don't look so well," Beverly's voice was distant and soft but it echoed and clung to my consciousness. I sweat some more.

"Come on. You need some air," she said. I was faintly aware of rising to my feet and floating toward the door of the bar, her soft, small hand grasping mine and leading me out. The white dress glided like a ghost and was the only thing I could see in the dingy, smoky half-light of the bar then the cool black of the night. The muffled sound of a car door being opened tickled my left ear and Beverly's gentle arms eased me into the passenger seat.

"Rest here," she said, her voice getting farther and farther away. I couldn't move or speak. Then suddenly the heat of her face and the floral punch of her perfume loomed enormously and I tasted the sweet wax of her lipstick again, softer than the first taste on the edge of the glass—much softer—and felt the dart of her tongue on my teeth and the whole world was plunged into a thick, velvety blackness and my head felt as heavy as an anvil, falling rapidly into the stygian abyss.

17

I had the strange sensation of floating, of drifting ethereally through thick air. The world drifted in and out of focus. All at once my senses were flooded with Beverly, the hot, perfumed bosom pressed against my face, the weight of her body squirming and writhing in my lap. I was unable to move anything except, I thought, my mouth, which gasped for air between being filled with her perspiration and her probing fingers and tongue. When I managed to gulp a breath, the world became lightless and the sensation of falling came back with a vengeance. I plunged downward into the void at an indeterminate speed.

My head stopped falling, though I couldn't be certain just how long it had been. With a muscular effort, I opened my eyes and the blackness gave way to a very faint blue light. I could make out shapes in the gloom, the white dress that looked pale blue-gray in the thin illumination from the moon through the windshield. Dark shadows on the dress. I saw Beverly's face turned toward me, her eyes closed. I struggled to lift my arms but couldn't. Something seemed wrong with the way my body was situated on the passenger seat; my weight didn't feel as if it rested correctly.

I tried to focus on Beverly and was giving myself a headache in the attempt. Something wasn't right about her dress. I strained my eyes in the poor light and then realized what was wrong. The shadows. Her white dress was *stained* black over her chest by the neckline. And so was her neck. Not shadows. Not black. Not if there had been more light to see by. Red. Blood. She lay perfectly still behind the wheel.

I tried to reach for her again but couldn't lift my arms. My head hurt enormously. I tried to speak but not even a strangled whimper would come out of my dust-dry throat. My eyelids grew unbearably heavy again and the blackness claimed me once more. My head grew heavy and fell down that bottomless pit.

I didn't know how long my head fell or if the rest of my body followed it. A disembodied head, like Jiro's missing skull. Maybe the rest of me was burned to fertilizer in a cane field, too, for all I knew because I couldn't feel a thing. Not until the sting on my cheek came from the slap.

"Sheik. Sheik."

I opened my eyes slowly. Another slap. Another sting.

"Sheik."

Another slap. That one really hurt. I opened my mouth to yell at the slapper to stop, but all that came out was a parched croak. I focused my eyes and peered at the slapper. I saw the cap and the coveralls. I wracked my brain. The cigarette machine at the Monkey Bar. The slow delivery guy.

"Sheik. You okay?"

The delivery guy. Gid. He had been there. Discreet. Like a mouse. I wanted to laugh at the improbability, but my throat felt like it was filled with sand.

"Beverly," I rasped.

"Who?"

"Beverly Machida. Blood. Throat cut."

"Nobody's here, Sheik. You're all alone in a ditch in Waipahu."

"What? Beverly. Where's Beverly, Gid?"

"Not here. I saw her load you into a car then drive away. I followed, but lost her going ewa. I doubled back and saw the tracks going off into the kiawe and found you. The car's gone. She's gone. I didn't see anybody else."

"How long?"

"Huh?"

"How long since we left the bar?"

"Two hours, maybe. It took me a while to find the tracks. I drove up and down this stretch of road for a while after I found out she couldn't have gone into Waipahu town when I talked to the old man at the service station there. He didn't see any cars come past before I got there."

"Beverly. I saw her with blood all over her. Someone cut her throat."

"You've been doped, Sheik. Take it easy."

My head spun. I flopped it to the side and vomited. Gid pulled my chest over a knee and patted my back.

"Good. Get it out," he encouraged. I vomited again. "That's it," he said, "get it out."

I sat back up with difficulty and wiped my mouth with the back of my hand. My head hurt and my mouth was full of cotton. Doped. The lipstick. Doped by Beverly Machida. *Why?* I wiped my mouth again.

"She's dead, Gid. I saw her. She was sitting right next to me with blood all over her."

"You're delirious. She's gone."

"I saw her."

"Okay, Sheik. Just take it easy."

Gid was kneeling, cradling my head. I could feel the grit and dead grass on my coat. Someone had driven the car away after dumping me in the ditch. I was suddenly seized by panic. I felt for my gun. It was still there, ensconced in its holster and painfully digging into my ribcage. I felt for my credentials and badge. Still there. I checked my hands. No blood. I relaxed a little.

"Come on, Sheik. I have to get you up and into my car. Can you stand?"

"I don't know."

"Let's try." I could feel myself rising, levitated by Gid's powerful arms. He threw my right arm over his neck and I stepped dizzily toward his Ford Crestliner, dark and shiny in the distant streetlight. I felt as if I were floating as Gid half dragged and half carried me to his car. After a long time of awkwardly scraping my heels through the roadside dirt, he placed me gently in the passenger seat of his car and shut the door. I slumped over it and lolled my head out of the open window. I was aware of the car dipping under Gid's weight as he got behind the wheel and the muffled sound of the driver's door closing and the scratch and hum of the engine starting. Then the movement of the vehicle came, the slow rumble beneath my body that made me want to lurch and vomit again. The wind caught my hair as my head hung out of the passenger window and made me feel better.

Gid pulled over at a gas station and got out. He left the motor running and the garish fluorescents from over the pumps hurt my eyes. I stared at the pumps sideways from the angle of my limp neck hanging out over the passenger door. They looked like Hollywood robots from some low-budget flick that played too long at the Princess Theatre. I heard the driver's door open and again I felt the dip of the vehicle as Gid settled in. He threw the car into gear and we streaked off into the darkness, away from the harsh white lights of the gas station.

"Beverly's dead," I said.

"Okay, Sheik. We'll talk about it later. Right now, let's worry about you getting some rest."

"But I *saw* her."

"I know. You told me."

I opened my mouth to protest but nothing came out but a strangled cough. I closed my eyes and let the breeze run over my face and through my hair. I could feel myself falling into blackness again but managed to hold on to the edge of consciousness. I tried to sort out the bizarre images in my head and place them in a neat timetable but it only made my temples throb like I was dying. We moved through the night for an eternity. Then the hum and vibration stopped.

I opened my eyes. The familiar yellow glow of the streetlamp near the corner of Waialae and 10th threw its strange, dingy light on the front of my apartment building. Gid opened the passenger door and helped me out of the seat, then practically dragged me up the stairs to my apartment. He helped me locate my keys and I got the door open with his assistance. The place was still trashed. I guess it was too much to hope for that it would have cleaned itself up in my absence.

"I asked a couple of patrolmen from Pearl City to bring your Cadillac back from the Tavern. They used repossession master keys. I didn't think you'd mind and they were happy to do it—there wasn't anything else going on out there. I called them from the service station in Waipahu. They should be here soon."

"Oh," I said. "Thanks."

"Look, Sheik, I want you to get some rest. Take a shower and go to sleep and forget about coming in tomorrow, okay? You've been through a lot today."

"Don't worry. I'll be fine." Even as I said it I realized that I wasn't fooling Gid because I certainly wasn't fooling myself. My head ached like something alive and angry was trying to bust out of my cranium.

"I'd hang around and play nursemaid to you, but Emma's on the Big Island visiting her sister and I can't trust Little Gid to be responsible for all the younger ones. I have to make sure they all have breakfast tomorrow before they go to school."

"Then get going, Lieutenant. I told you—I'll be okay."

Gid turned slowly and shuffled toward the door. He stopped and turned his head with painful effort and looked at me with one squinted eye over his shoulder.

"Don't come in tomorrow. Stay home and rest. I mean it."

"Whatever you say. And thanks for the lift."

Gid waved a big meaty hand and shut the door behind him.

I thrashed about my kitchen looking for a bottle and remembered halfway through my fruitless search that I had sucked the last of my house booze after finding out my place was ransacked. It was less than twenty-four hours before but it seemed like an age had gone by. I felt for and found my hip flask, still half full of the rye I had purchased from the Kapahulu store. I unscrewed the cap successfully after my third try and poured half of what was in there down my throat. My stomach vaulted off a springboard and threatened to fly out of my mouth but settled down in a moment and my headache eased. I thought about Beverly Machida lying still and bloody in the bluish light but only for a moment. I had replayed that scene ad nauseam and still couldn't get any more of a clearer picture of it. What had I done with her? What had she done with *me*? I couldn't be certain.

As always, I drifted back to Ellen. She fed me a list of CP cell leaders. *Her* leaders. And she never told me anything. Not even when I told her we found Jiro in the cane field. The omission stung. What the hell was I to her, anyway? If it had been *my* remains in the red dirt, would she have bawled the way she did for Comrade Machida? Would she have shrugged it off because I wasn't as brilliant or committed as he was?

I thought about Jiro flirting with Ellen in Korean and peppering his conversation with witty references to Lenin and Mao. I thought about him setting her heart on fire with doctrinal bullshit and telling her for the thousandth time how he was going to make the world a sunnier place for all the working people currently under the boot heel of bourgeois oppressor. I thought about her making limpid, watery eyes at him every time he opened his mouth. It made me want to scream and put my head through my plate glass window, except that I didn't have one. Old Chang was too cheap to install anything more expensive than three-cent jalousies.

I picked up the telephone and started dialing, then changed my mind and threw the receiver back toward the cradle, missing wide by about a foot. I got it on the second try, though, and promptly dropped the entire telephone into the burglar-emptied wastebasket in the kitchen. I wanted to talk to her and yet I didn't.

I took another swig. I couldn't even taste the rye anymore. Ellen. Communist Ellen. The joke was on her. She wasn't the first red I had been with. There was Rachel. Rachel Levinsky.

18

January 1947. Morningside Heights. The sun hung somewhere below the buildings looming above the tree line of Central Park and tinted the sky a deep fiery orange with the mantle of twilight looming vast and purple just above. This was all I could see from the narrow window, which probably looked like one of those arrow slits in a castle wall from the outside. It seemed that every Ivy League campus had dormitories that looked like Tudor manors and gymnasiums that looked like gothic cathedrals. The one Ivy campus in New York City was no exception, though its structures were generally on a larger scale.

"What time is it?" I asked.

"Just after five," she said, turning to face me and pulling the covers up under her arms.

"P.M.?"

"Of course, P.M., silly."

"Oh," I said. "Sorry. I still can't get used to it. Back home, the sun pretty much sets at the same time all year round. This business of short days in winter and long days in summer really screws me up."

"I've never been so close to the equator. The farthest south I've gone is Miami. We went with my folks every year and we thought it was heaven on earth. I'll bet it's got nothing on Hawaii, though."

"I'd say you're right. I've never seen Miami, but it's hard to imagine anywhere more beautiful than home."

Rachel Levinsky lay under the covers of her dorm room bed. She slipped on her brassiere, larger than Jane Mansfield's, under the sheets in a pretense of feminine modesty and regarded me with pale blue eyes under a shock of near-black hair. We had just finished rutting like a couple of animals after a brief discussion on some editorial in *The New York Times*. Rachel had bribed her roommate, the prim Miss Dorothy Vandermeer of Scranton, Pennsylvania, with ballet tickets so that she'd make herself scarce that evening. Dorothy was a French major and played the cello so it wasn't likely that she would resist the offer. Rachel seemed to have an endless supply of ballet tickets, so we met and coupled frequently. On occasion, we'd do it in my room, but because my roommate was also my teammate, the place smelled of socks.

I picked up my book which lay on the rug at the foot of her bed and sat next to her as she lit up a cigarette.

"What's that you're reading?" she asked.

"Malory. *Le Morte D'Arthur*. It's the new Oxford printing of the Caxton Edition."

"Can't you give it a rest, Frankie? Ira has you brainwashed. You're like the high priest of his little cult."

"Little is right. There are only a handful of us, but we *are* devoted. Fanatically so."

Ira Levinsky. Professor of Medieval Literature. Rachel's father. Like all progressives, she called her parents by their first names, like they were best friends or shared a telephone in some secretarial pool. If I ever referred to Ka-san as "Haruko," I'd get the beating of my life with a bamboo switch behind the furo house. Professor Levinsky encouraged the practice. In fact, he insisted after a few meetings that I, too, refer to him as "Ira" instead of "Professor Levinsky." It took me a while to do so, but I finally warmed to the practice. Ira Levinsky was the most brilliant mind I had encountered up to that point in my life, and he remains one of a few, sharing that honor only with Gid and Ellen. Though humble and without the hubris that so many academic gods wore like a badge, after a time, it was difficult to think of him as anything but "Ira."

But make no mistake. Levinsky was an academic god of the highest order. Sat at the top of the pantheon. The son of a Petrograd cobbler, a Jewish student of the Christian world among gentiles, he rose to become a Rhodes Scholar at Oxford. He read and spoke seven different living languages and two dead ones, and his understanding of mysticism in early European vernacular writing remained unparalleled. Ira, red to the core, had been born under Romanov rule, not the kindest place for Jews with brains and fire in their guts. Young and active during the revolution, he saw the world change firsthand, which left a lasting impression on him.

Rachel was born in Oxford when Ira was completing his doctorate there. When she was still very young, he accepted a lecturer's post at Columbia and moved his young family to a cramped little apartment in Canarsie next to the subway line. Though born in Russia and steeped in Oxford tradition, Ira developed a love of baseball, an affinity for what he called the "grand symmetry of the game," something that eluded him with cricket. He took little Rachel to every Yankees game he could afford, watching the likes of Babe Ruth, Lou Gehrig, and the rest of Murderers' Row from the cheap, peanut shell-littered seats high above the Bronx. She, too, developed a love of the game, and the two of them never missed a Columbia home contest, particularly against Ivy League opponents.

This is how I came to be involved with Rachel. I was already in Ira's orbit, hanging on his every word in every lecture and joining him on Friday nights in his cramped little office along with the rest of the "Levinskyites" for vodka and conversation on manifestations of the divine in 13th- and 14th-century poetry. Shit like a troubadour's pining for an unattainable woman as allegory for man's yearning for gnosis. I ate it all up and asked for seconds. When Ira learned that I fought against Hitler and played first base, he became a fan of mine of sorts and arranged for an introduction to his daughter.

He and Rachel waited outside the locker room after a narrow one-run victory over Dartmouth in extra innings. I came out with wet hair in a Harris Tweed jacket and saw Ira standing there with a short, curvy girl with thick, dark hair and eyes like winter sky. He introduced us.

"Frankie is from Hawaii," Ira told her.

"Aloha," she said, her full lips framing a dazzling smile.

"Aloha yourself," I told her. It was on.

A breakneck speed courtship resulted in many nights of reckless lovemaking in Rachel's Dorothy-less room. "What's there to know? You play first base like a linebacker and it's wickedly arousing," she told me. Rachel shared her father's politics, which quite frankly bored me, but I put on a look of mock intensity every time one of her diatribes came out. By the same token, Rachel was put off by my passion for all things medieval because she felt that in the end, my feelings were stronger for her father than they were for her and she was jealous of him. Her assessment wasn't far from the truth; Ira Levinsky could expand my consciousness with a lecture the way none of my rolls in the hay with Rachel ever could.

As I sat at the foot of her bed perusing the new Caxton Edition, I couldn't know it would be the last time we'd ever make love or even speak to one another.

Just before ten o'clock, I sneaked out of Rachel's room before curfew checks and Dorothy Vandermeer's return from the ballet. The trudge back to my own dorm through the snow on the ice-slicked walkways was precarious, but I somehow made it in a single piece. When I got to the lobby, Hank Charles, my roommate, was waiting for me on one of the threadbare sofas.

"Where the hell have you been?" he hissed, bolting up as soon as he saw me pass through the doors.

"What do you mean 'where the hell have I been?' I was at
Rachel's, genius, just like I said I'd be." I looked at Hank. It wasn't like
him to give a shit about my comings and goings in the off-season, and
it sure as hell wasn't like him to wait for me in the *lobby*. He looked
worried. "What's wrong, Hank?"

"There's a couple of guys waiting for you upstairs. I thought I'd
give you a heads-up so you don't walk in blind. They've been waiting for
an hour."

"What guys?"

"One says he's with the FBI and the other one is with something
else."

What the hell could *this* be? I thanked Hank and told him
whatever they wanted probably wouldn't take too long. I climbed the
stairs and let myself into our room. Two tall haoles stood in the middle
of our room in dark suits with their hands in their trouser pockets. One
had light, straw-like hair and glasses; the other was balding with a dark
fringe that reminded me of a Franciscan tonsure. Glasses stood fingering
my Ivy League Championship Series consolation medal. Tonsure
extended his hand and spoke.

"Mr. Yoshikawa? I'm Special Agent Fred Hardesty of the FBI." I
shook Hardesty's hand and looked over at Glasses as Hardesty gestured
toward him. "This is Dan Kierkegaard. He's an investigator with the
House Un-American Activities Committee."

Kierkegaard extended his hand. His grip was clammy and weak
like a fish. "Pleasure, Mr. Yoshikawa. What position?" he asked, inclining
his head down toward the medal.

"First base."

"I thought so. You look like you can take a runner at the bag." He
flashed me a yellow, insincere smile. I smiled back, just as insincerely.
Kierkegaard put the medal back on my desk and smiled some more.

"How can I help you gentlemen?" I asked.

"Can we all have a seat?" asked Hardesty. "This shouldn't take too much of your time if you're the American we know you to be."

"Sure," I said. I sat on my bed while Hardesty and Kierkegaard sat on Hank's. Kierkegaard picked up a valise at the foot of Hank's bed and drew a manila folder out of it. Hardesty opened a small notepad and uncapped a pen. I was still wondering what the hell this was all about.

"Francis Hideyuki Yoshikawa—did I say that right?" said Kierkegaard, reading from the contents of his manila folder.

"Close enough," I said.

"Corporal, United States Army, 442nd Regimental Combat Team," Kierkegaard continued. "Saw action in the European theater, Italy, France. Injured at Vosges, France, during the rescue of the 1st Battalion of the 141st Regiment. Purple Heart. Honorable discharge. G.I. Bill to Columbia University. Does that all sound correct to you, Slugger?"

"Sounds like me," I said.

"You did all this despite the fact that your father, the late Yukihiro Yoshikawa, died of pneumonia at a military facility in Honolulu while awaiting transport to Jerome. It couldn't have been easy. I salute you, sir. You are an exemplary citizen and a true patriot."

"Sure. Thanks," I said. I could feel the set up. I just didn't know which direction the boom would be lowered from.

"Slugger," said Kierkegaard, "we need to ask you to serve your country one more time, to go to bat for America and hit one out of the park the way you did in the war."

Here it comes, I thought. The baseball references were there to soften the blow.

"Sure," I said. "Did you want me to re-enlist? Is there a chance I could finish my degree first? I only have a few more credits . . ."

"Oh, no! Nothing like that!" Hardesty laughed. "We wouldn't dream of asking you to place yourself in harm's way again. You put your life on the line for your country, valiantly. Once is enough, wouldn't you say so, Dan?"

"Yeah. You've done plenty," said Kierkegaard. The insincere smile was back. "What we had in mind is a lot less dangerous and doesn't involve going overseas. In fact, you don't even have to leave this room. Best of all, it will only take a couple of minutes of your time."

"I'm sorry. I don't understand."

"Do you have a professor named Ira Levinsky?" asked Kierkegaard.

"Yes," I said. I smiled, thinking that I had just left his daughter.

"Our records indicate that over the last four semesters, you've taken four of his courses," said Hardesty. "I assume you know him pretty well."

"I think so," I said. I started becoming warier. What *was* this about?

"Let me come straight to the point, Slugger," said Kierkegaard. "Professor Levinsky is of interest to an esteemed congressional committee and we are trying to get a better picture of his . . . views. We're here on campus asking his students who know him well to provide some missing pieces to the puzzle, if you will. Students with a strong sense of loyalty to this country. Students like yourself."

Shit. The HUAC. I wasn't thinking when they first introduced themselves. My blood froze in my veins.

"Is Ira . . . uh . . . Professor Levinsky . . . in trouble?" I asked.

"We're trying to help him, Mr. Yoshikawa," said Hardesty. He was now leaning far off the edge of Hank's bed. His face was so close I could smell the chewing gum on his breath. "You can help him, too, by telling us the truth. You see, if he plays ball with us, we can soften the blow. He need not go to prison."

"And neither does his daughter," interjected Kierkegaard, "Rachel, is it? You're acquainted with her, too, I take it?"

"What do you want?"

Kierkegaard pulled a single sheet from his manila folder. He handed it to me. I read it. There wasn't much to it. All it said was that I have heard on numerous occasions Ira Levinsky stated he was a communist and other such nonsense. My name was typed at the bottom under a line.

"Sign it, Slugger. It's all we want. It's that call to arms for your country we talked about. This time you needn't take a bullet for Uncle Sam the way you did in France. Just sign on the line," said Kierkegaard. The smile had taken on new dimensions of insincerity. I tried to return the smarmy grin but my mouth wouldn't move.

"But . . . this part about advocating the violent overthrow of the United States government," I stammered. "Sure, Professor Levinsky made no secret of his politics, but he never said anything like *that*."

"Sign it, son," said Hardesty. "They *all* advocate the violent overthrow of the government just by being communists. Isn't that right, Dan?"

"It sure is. Sign it, Slugger." He held a pen out to me.

"Ira doesn't go to jail if I do this and neither does Rachel?"

"Scout's honor," said Hardesty, grinning huge. "And you're assured of completing your course of study here at this fine institution and securing that Ivy sheepskin. And won't your mother be proud? I'll bet she was when you came marching home with that Purple Heart pinned to your chest. Do it for her. That woman is the last person in the world you'd want to disappoint, isn't she?" That last statement hung frost in the air. This wasn't just about Ira and Rachel's family. It was about mine. And my future. The implied consequences for noncompliance were so strong I felt like my nose was going to bleed from being hit by them.

With more self-loathing than I had ever felt in my life, I took the pen from Kierkegaard's outstretched hand and signed the document. I practically threw it back at him when I was finished.

"Thanks, Slugger," said Kierkegaard with a wink. They both rose from Hank's bed. I didn't move and I didn't look at them. I stared at the floorboards.

"Your country thanks you, too," added Hardesty. "You are a true patriot, sir."

True patriot. Giri. Duty to my country. Duty to my family. Duty to myself. I might as well have consigned Ira and Rachel to the gas chamber. They'd live, but their lives were over. And mine would go on. I sold out a beloved teacher and friend so that nobody in Kakaako would lose face, because I had an obligation to do so. Giri was about sacrifice; I learned this in France. But this was the first time I had seen its poisonous side. It was one thing to sacrifice myself for giri; it was quite another to burn friends at the altar of duty. Would To-san have been proud? I didn't know. All I knew, I hated myself.

They walked out of the room and closed the door behind them. It was a damn good thing neither had extended his hand for a shake; I would have vomited or punched him in the face. I turned out the lights, collapsed on my bed without undressing or removing my shoes, and curled up facing the wall. I was sick to the very depths of my stomach.

The door opened after a few minutes and I heard Hank's brogues shuffle in.

"Frankie?" he half-whispered. "Are you okay, pal? What did those guys want?"

"Don't talk to me, Hank. I'm evil. Evil to the core."

19

Evil to the core. That's what my insides felt like after I drained the rest of my hip flask. My hazy reminiscences of Columbia and my betrayal of the Levinskys had brought me to three o'clock in the morning. The sky outside of Old Chang's penny jalousies was still black and my head hurt less. I dragged myself over to the window and peered down at 10th Avenue below. The Pearl City patrol guys had dropped off the Eldorado as asked, parking it in front of Chang's store front about ten or so yards from Waialae Avenue. I could stand without falling over, so I might as well get back to work. The *Iwakuni Maru* would be tying up at Pier 32 in a couple of hours. I had nothing better to do, so I jumped in the shower, put on a clean shirt and suit, and made myself a couple of cups of coffee. I looked in the mirror and a ghost looked back at me. Army duffels heavily bagged my eyes that even a cold shower and hot coffee couldn't get rid of.

Bushed, I left the apartment anyway. Looking like a cadaver had never stopped me from going out in public before and, if it were possible, I cared even less about it at that moment than I ever had. I drove to Pier 32 and arrived at just before 4:30 a.m. The gate was already open. Pinky's guys made their rounds early. I parked facing the water, but far enough from the cleats so that errant mooring lines wouldn't snap and decapitate me or worse—dent the Eldorado. I got out and leaned against the fender and burned through three Lucky Strikes. The predawn air was cool and moist and carried the saline odor of the harbor on a soft breeze to where I had parked.

At about five, the sky in the east started to lighten a shade, and the chandler's truck came roaring in through the gates, its bed crammed with foodstuffs and other goods under a tarp. Five minutes later, a customs officer, an immigration inspector, and a quarantine inspector pulled up alongside the truck. I ambled over and introduced myself, telling them I was waiting for the *Iwakuni Maru*. I'd wait until they cleared the vessel before I boarded to interview the captain. While we were making small talk, the ship's agent arrived and let us know the pilot vessel had just passed the first buoys at the mouth of the harbor.

At 5:30 a.m., the *Iwakuni Maru* came into view from around the bend of the harbor off Sand Island. She was diesel fueled and made the noises to prove it. Her spiffy white hull turned red-orange with the glow of the rising sun behind it, and she came alongside and tied up at 5:37 a.m. I smoked two more Lucky Strikes while the federal inspectors did their thing. In about a half hour, they came down the gangway, giving me an "all clear" signal on their way back to their car. A yellow quarantine flag was raised and I trudged up the gangway to the galley to meet with the captain.

A grizzled customer in a crew cut and a smart though faded nautical uniform with gold braid on the sleeves sat alone at a small galley table. The tablecloth was snow-white and pressed. The whole place reeked of dried fish and vinegar and shoyu. Crew Cut had a cigarette dangling from his mouth which he promptly killed when I entered the galley. He stood and bowed, gruff and polite simultaneously as only the Japanese can be. I bowed in return, showed my badge and credentials and introduced myself in my halting child's Japanese.

Captain Tokuichiro Yamada of the *Iwakuni Maru* had been her master for seven years. Before that, he held a commander's commission in the Imperial Navy and served as the first mate aboard a supply vessel ported in Formosa during the war. We both sat, and I graciously accepted his offer of coffee and sake. I found the rice wine cloying and harsh, but it helped to bring the world into focus and stave off the inevitable fatigue-induced headache. I asked him my questions and found that Captain Yamada had a near-photographic memory of everything that ever occurred on his vessel.

Yamada recalled the day Harry Kurita came up the gangway on the *Iwakuni Maru*'s last port call in Honolulu; he showed me his logs in Japanese describing the Nikkei in his smart tailored suit with a leather suitcase who showed him a United States passport in the name of Harold Masanobu Kurita, date of birth September 21, 1918; place of birth Kahului, Maui, Territory of Hawaii. Yamada said Harry's Japanese was "flawless," as if to imply mine was anything but. I swallowed the barb with humility, playing the kohai. Harry had offered Yamada five hundred U.S. dollars to take him to Yokohama. He told Yamada that he would find passage in Yokohama to Shanghai, for it was his intent to "study" in China. Yamada told Harry that five hundred U.S. dollars was a lot of money to take him where he was already going, and Harry replied that he was really going to "meet Chairman Mao" so that the money would also buy the silence of Captain Yamada and his crew. After Yamada had an opportunity to think the proposal through and was convinced that he was doing nothing illegal, he accepted Harry's passage and had a mate show him to a bunk in an officers' cabin. Yamada said he explained to Harry that he would be calling Hilo prior to striking out into international waters and Harry told him that he understood—he knew that the Hilo call was a scheduled stop for the *Iwakuni Maru*.

Yamada described Harry as "quiet" and that he stayed out of the crew's way on the leg to Hilo. When they got to Hilo, Yamada informed Harry that they would be in port overnight, that they were expecting a hard-to-find engine part to be delivered by a local chandler in the morning, and that he was granting shore leave to most of his crew that day. Harry asked Yamada if he, too, could go ashore and Yamada told him that he was a passenger, not part of his crew, so he could do as he pleased, so long as he was back on board before they raised the gangway in the morning. Harry thanked him, said he would be back in the evening and left the *Iwakuni Maru* with a small valise at about two p.m. Neither Yamada nor any of his crew saw Harry Kurita again.

Because Harry told him that he did not wish to arouse any attention regarding his passage to Asia, Yamada made no inquiries locally in Hilo as to his whereabouts. Besides, Harry understood he needed to be back by morning, so Yamada kept Harry's five hundred dollars and shoved off. Yamada told me that he still had Harry's suitcase and that I was welcome to take it if I wanted to. I thanked him and told him that I would.

Yamada had one of his mates take me to the hold where Harry's suitcase was stowed. It was a worn leather thing about twenty years old with tarnished brass hardware. I brought it up above on deck and opened it, giving the contents a quick once-over. The old bag was crammed with all the clothes and toiletries that had been missing from Harry's little Kapiolani Boulevard apartment. It didn't appear there was really anything else in there. The passport, any wallet with cash and any additional identification were gone, presumably on his person when he disembarked in Hilo. The contents of the suitcase were wrinkled and haphazardly thrown in, as if he were in a rush when he packed—a big rush.

I shared one more small porcelain cup of sake with Captain Yamada before formally thanking him for his cooperation and descending the gangway with Harry Kurita's suitcase. I stowed it in the trunk of the Eldorado, lit up another Lucky Strike, got behind the wheel and found myself drifting ewa. I was headed out to Waialua. Again. I *had* to know. The sun now up, illuminated the rolling green sea of sugar cane on the drive up to the North Shore. Seven o'clock, and already the heat was unbearable. I drove with the top down—my hat on the passenger seat next to me so it wouldn't blow off my head—and

I caught the sticky-sweet scent of the smokestack of the sugar mill as I drove through Aiea. It was one of those odors that evoked memories of early childhood in the Waipahu Plantation Village, of being eaten alive by mosquitos and sucking on penny candy from Arakawa's store. While it was a difficult time for To-san and Ka-san and my older sisters, it was a golden time for me. No cares, except for the appearance of the bamboo switch when one of my pranks went south or one of my many unsolicited opinions found its way to adult ears. Then my folks moved up in the world and uprooted us all for a new life in town. Kakaako.

Because To-san owned his own shop, working on the various cars and trucks of word-of-mouth referrals, we lived in our own house on our own lot on Kawaiahao Street while just about everyone else lived in a "camp," a collection of ramshackle, tin-roofed firetraps sleeping five or six to a room with the head of the household taking the parlor sofa as his bed and throne. That pretty much made us Kakaako royalty, which made me and my sisters popular with the camp kids. And we weren't rich by any stretch of the imagination. There were many other Japanese families far more prosperous than we were—grocers and fishmongers and a few who bought out general stores and laundries from the pakes— but we were one of the best known due to the "fame" of my sisters, the "Yoshikawa Garden."

The pink house of my post-Waipahu youth was large by Kakaako standards. My folks had their own bedroom, and my sisters slept two to a room—Violet and Daisy, Iris and Pansy—while I had my very own bedroom, the only boy born to Yukihiro and Haruko Yoshikawa, the Little Prince of Kawaiahao Street. My neighborhood friends came over every day when we first moved in, to build a chief's teepee out of sheets and futon on the bed, or to have a knight's tournament with wooden swords and tinfoil hats. It wasn't bad at first, but as soon as my voice started cracking, To-san commandeered me as his source of free hard labor around the shop. I did shit like stack old radiators

and tires and scrub the shop floor with Boraxo. As a mechanic, I had
nothing on my eldest sister Violet, who had a gift for finding her way
around a transmission, so my days were filled with school and toil in
the shop until dinner. What saved me from it all were sports. Baseball
and football. To-san relinquished his hold on me when I made varsity at
McKinley in the 10th grade. Big and tall for a Japanese boy, I was To-
san's pride and joy. Ka-san was harder to convince. She still had chores
lined up for me, not seeing the point in running around on the grass
with a bunch of other boys chasing a hunk of hide.

The smell of the sugar mill disappeared as quickly as it appeared.
I drove along the edge of Pearl Harbor then followed Kamehameha
Highway north to the other side of the island. Tall, waving cane gave
way to stubby pineapple plants dotting the red dirt fields of Wahiawa,
with more sugar in the background on either side of the road. The air
was hot and moist and mirage lines blurred the highway blacktop ahead.
The blue of the North Shore eventually appeared on the horizon and I
veered left away from the sign indicating Haleiwa Town.

When I drove through Waialua, wheels kicking up rusty clouds
of red dirt dust, it was just about ten minutes to 8:00 a.m. The little
plantation village had been bustling long before then. Leathery faces
looked at my red Cadillac with eyes that had been open since before
dawn. I thought about what I might find at the Machida residence, a
little house that may have lost both of its occupants in the space of a
month. If someone had cut Beverly's throat, who was it and why had
they done it? Why had they left *me* alone? It occurred to me, but only
for a nauseating split second, that *I* might have done it, but dismissed
the possibility after recounting all of the facts. I was dumped out of the
vehicle without a trace of blood on me—mine or hers—and my .38 was
still on my person. Shooting her would have been a more convenient
way of giving her the big send-off, if that's what I really wanted to do in
my stupor, and probably the only way I would have thought to do it. If

someone else had killed her and wanted to make it seem as if I did, her body would have been there for Gid—or someone else—to find with me.

I pulled over at a small general store that had some bottles behind the register and purchased a fifth of rye and a pack of Lucky Strikes from the diminutive Japanese lady in a hairnet and white apron. As an afterthought, I had her throw in a wax-paper wrapped roll of makizushi filled with shoyu-sugar tuna—"poor man's unagi"—eggs and kampyo for my breakfast. As I wolfed down one slice at a time, I realized it was the first thing I had eaten since the chop steak at the Kau Kau Korner the previous day at lunch. With Ellen. An emptiness filled me thinking of her and her deception, and I sloshed down some rye to fill the void. The booze leveled out my world, but made her face clearer, looming large like the sun over the turquoise bay. Ellen. Iris. The ghost of Rachel Levinsky, wherever it was she ended up. Reds, all of them. Smart women, and too smart for their own good. Their CP affiliation was not just their problem. It was mine, too. Why the hell couldn't they see it?

I drove toward the shore and the Machida place, toward more ghosts—and more problems.

20

The old plantation house was pretty much the same as I had left it two days prior, but there were no cars in the driveway. The only sounds in the rapidly heating morning were the surf in the distance and the chickens next door. I pulled my very conspicuous red Cadillac into the dirt driveway and got out, taking the three steps up to the screen-encased lanai and knocking on the front door. No answer. The lanai looked pretty much the same as I had left it, with one glaring exception: Jiro's typewriter was now gone. The scarred old table where it once sat was empty.

I made my way off the lanai, and wandered around the perimeter of the small house. It stood raised up on its foundation of timber stilts about two and a half feet off the ground. The space under the house, replete with plumbing lines and electrical wires, was enclosed by thin, flat redwood boards, which had been spaced about three inches apart so that the space under the house could be easily glimpsed. All around the house, ti stalks with red and green leaves had been planted and blue-gray gravel had been spread around at the base in a neat, two-foot-wide band, like a moat. As I circumambulated the structure I made a mental note as to where the parlor and kitchen had been located, where the bedroom situated.

I stopped at the bedroom windows and squeezed between a couple of ti plants, gravel crunching under my wingtips. I looked in and saw a tarnished brass bed covered with a patchwork futon and something bizarre beyond it. It was so strange I had to look away and look again just to make sure I was seeing what I thought I was seeing: it was a coffin. The coffin was on the far side of the room, parallel to the bed and elevated on a gurney of sorts. It was white with gold trim and its lid, open, revealed white satin padded upholstery on its underside. I stood on my toes, but could not see if the coffin had an occupant. I looked about. The next-door house appeared to be unoccupied as well, and vehicular traffic on the street was minimal to nonexistent at that hour of the morning. I fished for and found my Swiss Army knife in my trouser pocket, opened the blade and slid it under the window frame across the sill, undoing the brass hook. After giving the next-door house another glance, I lifted the lower sash and pulled myself up and into the bedroom.

I was immediately hit by the warm, stale air and the scent of Beverly's perfume. I stepped lightly and gingerly around the bed to the coffin and looked in. It was empty. It smelled very strongly of the same perfume. A dainty pillow was dented where a head rested on it. I lowered my face next to the pillow and took a good whiff. Beverly. She slept in a coffin. I shuddered involuntarily and shook my head. I walked about the room and gave it a quick toss, without upsetting anything or looking too deeply. I opened the top dresser drawer and found it crammed with lingerie, mostly brassieres. I handled one and felt the cool silky contour of the cup, then withdrew my hand. Touching it made me feel dirty. Just standing in that room made me feel dirty. I closed the drawer, opened and closed the others finding pretty much the same thing.

I tiptoed over to the closet and opened it to a rack full of dresses, many of them expensive and all cut to fit Beverly Machida's curves. Also, women's shoes of all colors and styles rested on two pine shelves on the closet floor and, on the top shelf, lay five hat boxes stacked on an oyster-colored suitcase.

I closed the closet door and looked at the vanity and mirror situated just inside the bedroom door beyond the macabre coffin next to the bed. It had a silver tray full of perfume and other cosmetics and three boar bristle brushes from Caswell-Massey in New York and combs of shell and ivory. Little netsuke boxes dangled from silk cords from the mirror frame.

There wasn't a thing in the room that indicated if Beverly had slept there last night or not. Then it hit me. In that very house, I had dropped the news on Beverly Machida, less than 48 hours before, that her husband had been found dead. And yet, there was absolutely no trace of Jiro in that bedroom. No men's clothes, no personal items, nothing to indicate that he even slept there. Ever. Had Beverly obliterated the memory of Jiro that quickly?

I stood by the window, listened, heard nothing but the chickens on the other side of the house, and then climbed back out. I pulled the sash back down and walked back to the front of the house. I stood in the front yard for a moment longer, hearing the distant surf and the not-so-distant chickens over the stillness, then got back into the Eldorado and hit the starter. I uncorked the rye and took a long pull then drove away from the strange little bedroom and the sweltering heat of Waialua.

I thought about Beverly as I drove south, back toward town. It seemed likely that she did not return home. Was she dead? Possibly, though I couldn't be sure I saw what I thought I saw. Gid finding me lying in a ditch and Beverly and her car nowhere to be found didn't make any sense. Then there was her strange little house. The coffin was probably just a weird little fetish, but I found that those with weird fetishes are often prone to other weird behavior. And what the hell happened to Jiro's things? Maybe she didn't want any painful reminders, but erasing all traces of a man in less than two days of receiving the news of his death didn't seem right. A lot about Beverly Machida didn't seem right.

Sooner than I knew it, I was back in town. There was no parking for four blocks around the station, so I ended up stowing the Eldorado in front of a Pake herb shop in Chinatown. I filled my flask from the rye I bought in Waialua and took another good long belt from the bottle. My head had a strange, floating feeling to it as if it had been detached from my body and left to drift above it, lighter than helium. It happened often when I functioned without sleep and fueled myself with booze. Again, the liquor helped to steady the world around me, muting the chaotic background noises and forcing me to concentrate on the task at hand, which in this case was putting one foot in front of the other en route to the station.

I decided to walk down River Street until I hit King. The "river" is Nuuanu Stream, a trench of murky, brown-green water a few yards wide. Old Orientals waded in with their trouser legs rolled up, armed with small scoop nets and buckets hoping to snag supper. Others with bamboo poles sat on the railing at street level closer to where the stream met Honolulu Harbor, waiting patiently for brackish fish to nibble on the raw shrimp tails they hung on their hooks. All of them on their own personal grail quests, seeking the magic cup that would save their own mean little Camelots. My own quest for the truth didn't seem half as noble. Or half as important.

I trudged through Chinatown not even seeing the bustle around me. Twice I caught myself nodding off on my feet. When I finally reached the station, I took a quick swig from the flask to give me enough courage to tackle the tiled stairs from the receiving desk to the Homicide Detail office. The stairs went on forever. I thought my knees would give and I'd tumble down to the landing and through the window onto Bethel Street.

Despite the fatigue though, I managed to make it to the Detail office and opened the door. Delilah was sitting at her desk, long red nails hammering away at the typewriter. She stopped when the door opened and looked up at me. She stared at me the way one stares at an automobile accident.

"Sheik! I thought you weren't coming in today!"

"Why not?"

"Gid said you weren't."

"Why would he say that?"

"Because you were drugged and dumped in a ditch in Waipahu last night."

"Oh. Did he say *that*? I guess he feels it's not enough for me to be simply aggravated when I can be aggravated *and* humiliated. He's generous that way. Speaking of aggravation, give me some of that coffee of yours. I might as well have a stomach to match my head."

"Shut up. While you're here, something came in the mail for you this morning. And your girlfriend called." Delilah handed me an envelope and three pink message slips then stood up to fetch me a cup of her vile coffee. Ellen had called three times that morning. I picked up the phone, changed my mind yet again about calling her, and then looked at the envelope. It was the envelope I had addressed to myself and affixed with stamps from Ellen's mother two nights before. I tore it open and found the ribbon from Jiro Machida's typewriter.

"Hey, Delilah. Sweetheart."

"Don't 'sweetheart' me, Sheik. Not after that crack about my coffee."

"Come on. You know I'm kidding," I said, in a voice that said I really wasn't.

"What do you want, Sheik?" she asked, straight-faced. I wasn't fooling her. I wasn't fooling anybody that morning.

"I need a really big favor."

"What?"

I handed her the ribbon. I could think of no better person for the task. "I need you to take this ribbon apart and transcribe what's on it."

"This is going to take a while, Sheik."

"Please, Delilah. I need this as soon as you can do it." I made the saddest eyes I possibly could at her. It wasn't hard, though they probably only looked tired and bloodshot.

"Okay," she said, softening. Sometimes it pays to look as pathetic as you feel.

"Tell nobody about this. Only me and Gid. I'll be checking with you for it."

"Okay, Sheik."

"Speaking of Gid, where is he?"

"In his office," Delilah said. She inclined her head toward his door, which was uncharacteristically closed. "He has an important visitor in there. Some haole. Federal, I think."

"Federal? Is it about some out-of-town victim?"

"How should I know? He doesn't tell me everything, you know."

"Yeah. He doesn't tell you everything. Just everything about *me*."

Gid's door opened a fraction. He stuck his enormous head through the breach and his tired-looking eyes widened a fraction.

"I thought I heard you out there," he said. "I thought I told you to stay home today, Sheik."

"Yeah, well, you know me. I couldn't sleep anyway."

"Then I guess it's lucky you couldn't and came in. There's someone in here who wants to speak with you. I just got through telling him you weren't going to be here today when I heard you talking to Delilah."

Great. All I needed was a Fed asking me questions about one of my closed cases when I really should have been making a beeline for the airport and getting on the first flight to Hilo. Their follow-ups usually took forever. This character was probably going to ask me stuff his partner asked me while the case was open just to see if I could remember any of it. I often wondered how the Feds ever secured any convictions when they kept asking the same things over and over again.

"Okay," I said. I looked at my watch. 8:30 a.m. If I was lucky, this guy would get done with me just before lunch. I stepped into Gid's office. He shut the door behind me. The haole in the three-piece suit and wire-rimmed glasses sitting in one the chairs across Gid's desk got up and smiled an insincere, yellow smile at me.

"Hey, Slugger. Long time no see. Do you remember me?"

21

Dan Kierkegaard. HUAC. Witch hunter extraordinaire. Most of the world had moved on to bigger and better things. Not him. Chasing down shadows of sedition was his dream come true, and now he was doing it at the other end of America. Seeing him in Gid's office was like a bad nightmare except I was awake, or at least I thought I was. Stinging memories of Ira and Rachel Levinsky came flooding back. And just when I thought my morning couldn't possibly get any worse.

"Of course, I remember," I said, returning the insincere grin and shaking his hand. It was still as weak and as clammy as it was in my dorm room. We all sat down. My stomach did backflips and threatened to produce the Waialua makizushi and rye on Gid's blotter.

"Mr. Kierkegaard was just telling me how you aided a federal investigation when you were in college. He told me chance brought him out here and now he can catch up with you. That's really something," said Gid.

"I've got to say I'm impressed," said Kierkegaard. "War hero to Ivy League All-Star to police detective. You're the kind of American every kid here should aspire to be." You mean every *Jap* kid here, I thought.

"Well, you know. I try. What brings you out here to our fair islands? Vacation with the family?"

"Vacation? This is work, Slugger. No rest for the wicked," Kierkegaard guffawed. I guffawed along with him, though the old chill in my veins was back with a vengeance. "And as for family," he continued, "the only one I've got is called the House Un-American Activities Committee."

Great. You've got no life. What the hell do you want with *mine*? I was beginning to feel worse by the second. I involuntarily reached for the flask in my pocket and squeezed it hard enough to dent the pewter. I needed a drink as soon as I could get one.

"How can I help you, Mr. Kierkegaard?"

"Well, Slugger, it so happens I was out here to monitor the big trial and report on its progress back to Washington when news broke about this Jiro Machida. He was a red of the highest order, an associate of the Hawaii Seven, particularly Koji Ariyoshi. He was also Ariyoshi's employee if I'm not mistaken. I've just been talking to your lieutenant here and he tells me that the prime suspect is another communist, one Harry Kurita. This is hot stuff, Slugger. A scandal like this is just what we need to crush the red menace here in these beautiful islands of yours once and for all. And if that didn't beat all, the good Lieutenant here told me who the detective assigned to the case was. Icing on the cake. I never forgot the way you helped us in New York."

I said: "Great. Hot stuff." I thought: Fuck. Please God kill me now.

"I told Mr. Kierkegaard that he has the full cooperation of the Homicide Detail," Gid said. He moved his mouth but not his eyes. "And the Chief has pledged the support of the entire Honolulu Police Department." Double fuck. This was the last thing I needed. Thanks a lot, Lieutenant.

"Well, I'm just tickled," said Kierkegaard, yellow teeth showing in a skull-like grin. "You helped us break an East Coast subversive when you were in college and now you and I are going to be partners. I couldn't have asked for a happier ending."

"Yeah," I said, "me neither." This wasn't happy and it sure as hell wasn't an ending. It was just here, a world of shit and I was up to my ears in it. This man had come all the way across the country and out of my past to extract another pound of flesh. I couldn't help thinking that this one was going to be more painful than the last.

"Let me lay it out for you, Slugger. I'd like to ride shotgun with you on your homicide investigation. I'd be an additional set of eyes and ears, but tuned to a slightly different frequency. You're looking for dirt on the killing and I'm trawling for something big to throw in the face of the CP and bring them to their knees. This sordid communist-on-communist killing just may be the tip of the iceberg. Maybe dissention has shaken the party ranks. Maybe a leadership struggle. Who knows? But the papers will eat this up and paint them all to be the animals we know they are." He looked down his nose through his glasses at me, all the while smiling his plastic smile.

"Sure," I said, nodding. It sounded a bit insipid, but this was probably the proverbial sheep's clothing for what Kierkegaard really had in mind. I felt the same nausea I felt in college just before he and Hardesty lowered the boom and told me they were in my dorm room to make me rat out Ira Levinsky.

"Have you found out who any of the deceased's associates were? I mean, besides the suspect Mr. Kurita." There it was. Kierkegaard wasn't chasing a scandal so much as he was fishing for more victims to nail to the HUAC's cross.

"No," I lied. "My investigation thus far has been limited to gathering physical evidence and determining the whereabouts of Harry Kurita." My mind raced. Ellen. Iris. If Kierkegaard ever learned who the other cell members were, they'd burn on the same pyre as Wilde, Fujioka, and the rest of them. Kierkegaard was just the kind of asshole who lived to take credit for something like turning the Hawaii Seven into the Hawaii Twelve or Thirteen. No life. He wasn't here for the dramatic surf or the dramatic rum drinks. What the hell was I going to do?

"Well," he said, "that's a good start. We should start turning up the heat on getting some names, though, don't you think, Slugger? You know those reds—it's always a conspiracy with them and a conspiracy by definition is more than one person. I doubt if this Kurita acted alone."

Moron. Then again, it's not like he really cared how Jiro Machida died or even why. He was after something else or, more accurately, *someone* else. I opened my mouth and delivered the best curve ball I could.

"You know, you may be right. I should go back and look at my investigative notes and see if any leads are hidden in there somewhere. I've got a couple of days leave to take, though, and I know that the trial is in full swing at the moment. Maybe we can meet and talk about it when I get back? It looks like Harry Kurita blew town for the Orient and Jiro Machida certainly isn't going anywhere." Gid raised his eyebrow when I mentioned "leave," but didn't say anything.

"That sounds like an excellent plan, Slugger." A swing and a miss. He bit on the curve. I was far from striking him out, though. The next pitches would have to be even trickier. "Two days, then. I'm looking forward to working with you." Kierkegaard stood up, shook hands with me and Gid and walked out of the office. I listened for the Detail office door and Kierkegaard's footsteps away and down the tile stairs before looking at Gid.

"A couple of days leave?" he asked.

"I'm tired, Gid. I should've stayed home today like you said." I really meant it, too. Running into the Ghost of Christmas Past in the form of a HUAC investigator was the last thing I needed.

"Yeah," said Gid. "Taking a break for a couple of days might be the most sensible thing you've done all week. The work will still be here when you get back. It always is. I think I told you that before, but I think this is the first time you've shown me you were listening."

"You sound like my dad."

"I *feel* like your dad. Sometimes you're just as stubborn as Little Gid. When he gets it in his head to do something, he doesn't take a break until it's done."

"Sounds like a good kid." I smiled. Gid pulled up a corner of his mouth in his version of a smile.

"Something wrong with the Fed, Sheik?"

"Why would you say that?"

"Na'au." Gid patted his ample midsection. "I know you weren't thrilled to see him." Right. If I couldn't even fool Delilah that morning, what made me think I could pull the wool over the eyes of The Great Hanohano?

"It's a long story. The 'help' I gave him in college wasn't one of my finest moments. I'll tell you all about it some time."

"Sure," he said, letting it go out of mercy. "Get some rest over the next two days. What are you going to do to relax?"

"I was thinking of visiting some relatives I haven't seen in a while."

"Oh yeah? Where?"

"Off island. I have an aunt in Hilo."

PART III

Holy Grail
Hilo

22

48 hours. It's all I had to figure everything out, before Kierkegaard crashed the party and dug up everything. 48 hours to save Ellen and Iris. 48 hours to exorcise the demons of the past—Jiro's and Harry's, Ellen's, *mine*. Breaking the case was my only chance to keep Kierkegaard's mitts off the matter and off Ellen and Iris.

I tore down the tiled stairs and blew past the receiving desk and ran all the way up Bethel to Beretania Street and my Eldorado. I hurdled the driver's door without opening it and settled behind the wheel. I hit the starter and plowed my way to the *Honolulu Record* on Sheridan Street. I pulled up to the curb fronting the little weekly's office and burst in through the front door.

Ellen was chatting with Ida Furuta, the *Record*'s secretary, when she turned and looked at me.

"Well, good morning, *Detective*," she said icily. "I only stayed up all last night waiting for a call that never came and left three messages for you this morning."

"Please, Ellen. Not now. We really need to talk."

"What makes you think I *want* to talk to you, Frankie Yoshikawa? Whatever happened to doing what people do when they care for each other? I am really feeling stupid right now. I thought you were different. Boy, was I wrong."

That tore it. I unleashed. "Different from *whom*, darling? Jiro Machida? Your cellmate and boyfriend? What else haven't you told me?"

"Where did you hear *that*?"

"Beatrice Walker Crane. Yesterday."

Ellen fumed in silence. She paced the small floor of the *Record*'s reception area, high heels clicking on the linoleum in an angry staccato. Ida stared uncomfortably, looking away when either of us looked in her direction. Suddenly, Ellen came to a halt in front of me. Her fists were clenched and she stared at her feet.

"How dare you," she said softly, still looking at her feet. "How dare you bring that up as if it has anything to do with the way you just treated me. All of that was over long before we even met. How can you believe it justifies your lack of respect for me?"

"Were you *ever* going to tell me?"

"Was it *ever* any of your business?"

"It is now."

"And just how is *that*, Frankie Yoshikawa? When did you assume ownership of my person? Why does any of that stuff matter to you when all I am is a good time to you? Did you care about the pasts of any of those girls you romanced during the war? Or in college? It's clear to me I'm just the next chapter. I'll give my past to the one who wants me for keeps, not to someone who pops in and out of my life at his convenience."

I was stunned momentarily. Was this what her strange moods were about? Did she really think I thought so little of her? For a forward-thinking, intellectually superior person, Ellen could behave as impetuously as the vapid teenage girls she scorned. Ida continued to stare. She wasn't even pretending to be disengaged at all anymore.

"That's not what I meant, darling," I said, much more calmly than I had before. "It's my business now that all of this has come out in relation to that turd of a case of mine and complications have arisen. Bad ones. Complications that threaten to ruin your life. And mine."

A tear escaped her eye and ran down her cheek. She finally looked up and made eye contact with me.

"What *are* you talking about?"

"We need to talk about it and I need to know everything. But you need to tell me while I drive back to my apartment to pack, then I'll drop you off here or at home on my way to the airport. I need to know because I have two days to break this case and resolve it. If not, there's a HUAC investigator waiting to commandeer the whole thing from me and all of Jiro Machida's past associates could be arrested on Smith Act charges. *All* of them."

Ellen, stunned: "What's this about the airport? Where are you going?"

"Hilo. I have a lead on Harry Kurita."

Ellen wiped her face with the back of her hand and looked at Ida.

"I'm taking the rest of the day off," she told her.

"Okay," said Ida, barely managing to get the one word out of her slack-jawed face.

We walked out to the curb and got into my car. I hit the starter and headed for King Street and Kaimuki. Neither of us said anything until we were on King. When we crossed over Keeaumoku Street, I spoke first.

"Do you really think that all you are to me is a good time?"

"What else am I supposed to think when you make your own rules about when you call me and when you don't?"

"First off: how can you be just a good time to me when you're so much more, like a bad time, too? Like you're being right now? Secondly: I didn't know there *were* any rules on calling, whether I made them or not."

"Was I talking to myself yesterday? Weren't you there? Didn't we discuss your inconsiderate non-contact when your apartment got broken into? And what about your promise to call me when you were finished with your business? What happened to that?"

"That's an easy one to answer. I wasn't finished with my business, and I'm still not finished with my business. That's why we're talking right now, darling. It's personal, but unfortunately, it's also business. Since I saw you last, I've learned that my sister Iris, your comrade, is a member of the Palolo Group of the Hawaii Communist Party. But you already knew that. You just didn't tell *me*. I learned that Jiro and Harry came to blows over money that was donated by an old lady who lives on the slopes of Diamond Head and I drove to see her. She tells me that my sweetheart, the esteemed Ellen Park of the *Honolulu Record*, was also a member of the Palolo Group and Jiro Machida's ex-girlfriend. All this after I filled in the daruma's eye."

"What? *What's* eye?"

"Never mind. I'll explain the daruma thing later. Suffice to say I was upset because you told me all about Wilde and the Palolo Group and some stuff about Jiro and Harry but you never bothered to tell me about your involvement in the CP—or with Jiro. Hurt wasn't the word to describe how I felt. I drove out to Pearl City to meet with Beverly Machida because she said she wanted to see me. I thought she had information regarding Jiro or Harry or both. Gid came along as back-up in disguise. She didn't tell me anything. All she did was drug me and dump me in a ditch in Waipahu. It took Gid a couple of hours to find where she dumped me, but by the time he did, she and her car were long gone. Oh, I almost forgot. She's probably dead. In my stupor, I saw her behind the wheel with her throat slit."

"You went out to see *her*? After I told you . . . wait. Did you say she's *dead*?"

"Yes. Probably. Unless the whole thing was a hallucination, but why would I imagine something like that?"

"But she's gone."

"Yes."

"Oh."

"Gid dragged me home and told me to stay there and recover. I couldn't. The *Iwakuni Maru* was due in port in just a couple of hours."

"The *what?*"

"*Iwakuni Maru.* Harry Kurita's getaway boat to the Orient. I had a talk with the ship's master and he told me they took Harry as a passenger for five hundred bucks but had to make an overnight call in Hilo before returning to Japan. Harry got off the boat and didn't come back, so the boat left without him. Hence my trip to Hilo."

"Harry's in Hilo?"

"It seems. Or that's where his trail ends for the time being."

"So, you're going to look for him. What's the rush? He's been there for over a month or was last seen there over a month ago."

"I wasn't finished. I drove back out to Waialua to see if Beverly was still alive. Nobody was home. I took a quick poke around the house and found that Beverly has some strange coffin sleeping fetish. And there is conspicuously no trace of Jiro in that house, despite the fact his widow only found out about his demise two days ago. Still, nothing in there told me if she was dead or alive or even set foot in the place after she dumped me in Waipahu, so I drove to the station. The package I mailed myself after dinner at your house the other night finally arrived. It's the ribbon from Jiro's typewriter. Delilah's transcribing it for me."

"And you need to hurry up with this because . . ."

"I was just getting to that. While I was at the station, Gid calls me into his office. There's a Fed in there who wants to talk to me. His name is Kierkegaard and he's a HUAC Investigator. He's here for the Hawaii Seven trial but he got wind of Jiro's remains being found, so he senses an opportunity to latch on to my investigation in the hopes of rooting out all of Jiro's associates and putting them up on Smith Act charges like Koji and company. I managed to stall him, said I was taking a two-day leave of absence, and we could start working together on the case when I got back. That's why I have a deadline. On top of that, I know Kierkegaard. I've dealt with him before, when I was in college."

I pulled up in front of Old Chang's building while Ellen mulled the whole thing over. She spoke as we walked up the steps to my apartment.

"You said you've had dealings with this HUAC man before—in college. What's that all about?"

I opened my apartment and we stepped in. Ellen gasped at the mess. I took her by the elbow and led her around the piles of trash in the foyer.

"Darling, I'm going to tell you something I've never told anybody. I feel it's time and I think that it's necessary right now."

I proceeded to tell her everything about Rachel and Ira Levinsky and how I ratted them to the HUAC presumably to spare them a prison sentence and, more to the point, to preserve my own future. I told her about all of my self-loathing and how I've lived with it for years. Ellen was silent throughout my confession. It was crazy to tell her. She was a progressive who didn't compromise her principles and I had compromised everything when I served Ira up to the HUAC. I'd probably lose her but it had to be done.

"So, there you have it," I told her when I was finished. "If you hate me now, I can't say I blame you. I hate myself. I wanted to never have to tell another living soul but you need to understand why I'm doing what I'm doing and how much is at stake here, right now. If this makes you hate me so much you can't possibly love me anymore, so be it. I just needed you to know that duty or no, I will not do it again. Not to my sister. Not to you. I won't sell you to the HUAC the way I sold the Levinskys. If Kierkegaard wanted to arrest you on Smith Act charges, I'd be powerless to stop him. And if that happened, I couldn't live. I love you, Ellen Park. More than you know."

She still remained speechless. Though I was afraid to, I lifted my head to look at her face. I had to know if I'd see the rejection, the loathing, the disgust. In short, the same things I saw when I looked in the mirror whenever I thought about what I had done.

I saw tears. Ellen's eyes were wet and the tears ran freely down her cheeks. She took her glasses off.

"That's it, Frankie Yoshikawa. *That's* what I wanted to hear. I wanted you to tell me these things, the things that affect you. *That's* what people do when they care for each other. And I love you, too. More than you know."

She threw her arms around my neck and we kissed frantically, wet with each other's tears, until the urgency of the case wormed its way back into my consciousness.

"You don't hate me, then, for betraying my friends?"

"Why should I? It's in the past, and you're different now. I guess I'm lucky that I'm the one who got the new you and not Rachel Levinsky, or maybe she'd be standing here with you in this messy apartment. And speaking of the past, I guess it's time I told you about mine, too. You're right. It is your business, just like yours is mine. We belong to each other, Frankie Yoshikawa, whether you like it or not."

So, she told me. Everything.

23

As we stood near the front door just outside the kitchen, Ellen told me that she became involved with Jiro Machida in 1951 when she had first been hired by Koji Ariyoshi at the *Honolulu Record*.

"I was barely a year out of college. I was riveted by the events of the dockworkers' strike of 1949 as they were reported by the *Record*," Ellen said. "I had a job at the *Honolulu Advertiser* doing menial clerical tasks at the time; even though I had been the editor-in-chief of the University of Hawaii's daily newspaper, I couldn't land a job as a cub reporter because I was female and Oriental. I held on to the vain hope that my clerical position was somehow a foot in the door to better things for a couple of years, dutifully filing away morgue photographs and back editions in the reading room, waiting for my opportunity,"

"What happened?"

"It never came. Young haoles fresh out of mainland colleges kept materializing out of nowhere to take every in-house reporter vacancy I put in for, despite being popular with many of the editors as a 'good girl and good worker' who promised to put a 'good word' in for me. The writing was on the wall, but I refused to give up."

"I know," I said. "Surrender's not in your nature."

"Maybe common sense isn't. My self-esteem was taking a daily beating," Ellen said. "There were reminders everywhere, from the photo morgue to the newsroom that all I'd ever be used for was filing and making a fresh pot of coffee. About three years into the humiliation I saw it: a small ad in the *Record*. It was tiny and unassuming and tucked away between a large ad for a Hilo florist and a downtown funeral home and I almost missed it. The ad called for an unpaid intern to work half days every day and full days on Wednesdays, the day the weekly went to press before hitting the streets on Thursday."

"You took an awful chance," I said. I kicked an empty sardine tin away from the front door; the floor was still strewn with all kinds of detritus. Garbage was mingled with non-garbage. It was kind of like my life. "You could have ended up being the coffee girl, but at a much smaller office."

"I know," said Ellen. "But I somehow felt that Koji and his people were different from the cigar-smoking haoles whose idea of acknowledgement was patting my head or my okole. I called the exchange in the ad, spoke with Koji Ariyoshi himself, and arranged an interview that afternoon. After five minutes of chatting, he asked when I could start. I resigned from the *Advertiser* immediately. When some of the editors there learned I was leaving to accept an unpaid internship at a small pro-labor weekly, they tried to talk me out of it."

"I guess they didn't make you any red-hot offers," I said.

"What do you think? I told them that walking away from a career as a clerk was not the same as throwing my life away and if they were serious about not wanting me to go, they could give me a reporter's job. None of them blocked the doorway as I walked out."

She told me that her first days at the *Record* were filled with wonder and hard work. She did everything from proofreading copy to cold-calling potential ad clients to assisting with pre-press layout. After less than a month after her taking on progressively more complex tasks, Ariyoshi allowed her to pen her first article—coverage of an AJA league game between Kakaako and Moiliili.

"I knew next to nothing about baseball," she said, "but I managed to turn myself into an expert in two and a half hours before the first pitch that evening. I read my brothers' sports magazines and got a crash course from them. You know, I even remember seeing your name on the roster. I committed both line-ups to memory."

"Well, that's funny. I don't ever remember seeing a pretty girl reporter in the bleachers. If I did, I probably would have hung around at the park a lot longer after the last inning. Why didn't you introduce yourself?"

"Why would I? I didn't know if there'd be any difference between Francis Yoshikawa and Franklin Yoshimoto. You all looked alike under those caps."

"Right," I said. "I'm about four inches taller than Yoshimoto and a lot better looking. What did Koji think of your coverage?"

"Koji was impressed. My article went to press and I was offered a ten-dollar-an-article arrangement. I filled in when other reporters could not make their deadlines. Opportunities for writing were sparse at first but when they presented themselves, I took full advantage. I graduated from sports and neighborhood events coverage of AJA games, bon dances, flower shows, and penny carnivals to occasional analysis of Territorial Legislature session voting and courthouse reporting. In less than a year, I was a part-time reporter for the *Honolulu Record*, pulling down a hundred dollars a month while I helped out at my folks' grocery in Kapalama."

I hadn't known any of what she had told me until that moment. I was ashamed that I hadn't asked her. Like many other people I knew well in most other aspects, but not their histories, I idiotically assumed that Ellen had somehow always been that way. The irony is that I knew the life stories inside and out of murder victims and suspects, and these were people I didn't personally know well at all. I silently vowed at that moment to ask Ellen to tell me all about herself and not just the superficial stuff I observed. Well, first things first—I should make it a point to just listen to her.

"Sounds like a real turning point," I said. I forced a smile and tried to make it nonchalant. I didn't want her to catch me thinking too hard.

"It was a wonderful, exciting time. I got to know Koji and the other staff reporters. Koji's political theories and verbal editorializing were thoughtful and inspiring. And I loved Frank Marshall Davis's diatribes on race relations in America and even his anecdotes recounting his lurid sexual escapades. They were more poetic and entertaining than vulgar."

"Lots of fascinating personalities," I said. It was time for the hard part for me. I bit the bullet. "But I guess Jiro Machida was the most fascinating of all."

Ellen pulled a half-smile, a little wistful, a little absent. "Jiro was handsome and charismatic and spoke with authority," she said. "He was almost fifteen years older than me and was what I thought of as someone 'worldly.' He had been all over Asia during the war with the Military Intelligence Service as an interpreter. He had a gift for languages and prior to that, he had studied in Moscow at the Sun Yat Sen University. Jiro's politics had been shaped by growing up on a sugar plantation on the Big Island. He was educated at the camp school at the Olaa Plantation where the teachers learned he had a gift for words, in both English and Japanese. There was a secret core of agitators among the Japanese laborers at Olaa who would later become the organizers and leaders of the Olaa strikes of '46 and '48, and these men had taken up a collection to send young Jiro to Moscow."

I held my face in a polite mask of indifference. I was cringing inside. I guess in that moment I felt more than a tinge of despair that in Ellen's eyes I'd never be any match for a revolutionary with a vision. Jiro Machida, full of fire and ambition. Me? Change the world? I had trouble changing my mind.

Ellen looked up at me from under her lashes. She probably sensed that I was sick with jealousy under the nervous grin, so she continued haltingly. "When he came back from Russia, Jiro enlisted with the Military Intelligence Service. He wanted to help fight fascism."

Great. Again, the noble sacrifice for the greater good. I enlisted so the government wouldn't drag my family to a camp on the mainland in my father's place; he had inconveniently died of pneumonia. My world was limited to the four walls of the house I grew up in, my altruism reserved only for those I knew. How the hell could I compete?

"While in Asia," she continued, "Jiro met and befriended Mao Tse Tung. When he came back, he returned to Olaa and was an active organizer for both strikes. He became Koji Ariyoshi's Big Island correspondent during the strikes and moved to Oahu shortly after the Olaa strike of '48 to help organize the stevedores' strike of '49. At that time, he took up residence in Waialua with the help of a relative who was a long-time plantation worker there, continued to report part time for the *Record* and joined the Palolo Group of the Hawaii CP."

It further occurred to me with painful clarity as Ellen recounted Jiro's personal history that aside from our similar origins, the two of us couldn't have been any more different. Jiro stayed rooted in plantation culture while my family fled it for a more "prosperous" life in Kakaako; Jiro's wartime experience took him to the Orient to meet the future leaders of the East while I was on the frontline in Europe trading shots with the Nazis; Jiro's education was a scraped-together trip to an experimental fledgling communist institution, mine was a government-financed Ivy League opportunity. Most of all, Jiro lived by his principles and I sold my friends out, becoming a bird dog for the very establishment that made life miserable for those who looked like me.

"When I met Jiro in '51," Ellen said, "he was reporting on labor issues and writing a book on the condition of the Oriental laborer in Hawaii. He took me to coffee when he was around at the *Record*'s office on Wednesdays." She stopped for a moment and took a breath. "We had a brief affair which lasted for a couple of months. During the time we

were . . . ah . . . intimate, Jiro shared stories of his past, stories of his time
with the Military Intelligence Service during the war. He talked mostly
about Mao and how he was asked from time to time to execute tasks of
a non-linguistic nature, daring cloak-and-dagger stuff like infiltrating
Shanghai nightclubs and restaurants that had been turned into Japanese
military offices and brothels, planting explosive and incendiary devices
he had built to reduce them to rubble and ashes to disrupt their
operations."

"How dashing and madcap," I said. I let a little too much venom
slip into my voice. "Sorry," I said. "Continue."

"While we were seeing each other, Jiro brought me to a handful
of Palolo Group meetings. I met the whole lot, including Harry Kurita. I
was never a member myself."

"Why not? I thought you were pretty taken with the principles
espoused by all those great minds around you."

"I was, but when I actually attended those meetings, they turned
out to be quite different."

Ellen grabbed my hand and gave it a squeeze, probably to
reassure me it was all in the past. She laughed softly and said, "It was
mostly pompous men yelling at each other. But I found a couple of
the women at the meetings intelligent and interesting and formed
friendships with them—Beatrice Walker Crane and your sister, Iris
Imada. I remain committed to improving life for the Fourth Estate, as
Koji called it, but I felt that joining the cell would not be the best way
to do it. I saw through them. There wasn't any point in being a member.
All I would have done there was feed their egos by taking a side in their
bickering. I didn't want to say this at first, but you were right to mock
them."

Ellen had a way of putting me at ease after taking me to the edge.
It was sometimes nerve-wracking but life with her would always be
interesting.

"What about Harry Kurita? What did you think of him?" I asked.

"Self-important and self-absorbed." She laughed to show he meant nothing to her, that he was silly in his efforts. "And he made passes at me while I was in Jiro's company. Harry enunciated his words slowly and purposefully in an almost pseudo-British accent, and bragged more than once about his mastery of what he called his 'true mother tongue.' He said that all other languages were 'deficient' in their ability to express the many 'hues' of the human condition, or something like that. Jiro once told me that Harry said things like that because he didn't have a command of any other language." Ellen allowed herself a little amused smile; it was a pointed barb, coming from a linguist like Jiro.

"I saw the personality conflict between them the moment I first saw them in the same room together," she said. "The two of them were very aggressive and open with their verbal challenges of each other, the insults were nasty and made in bad temper. Often, when they had these exchanges, the room would fall into an uncomfortable silence until Marlon Wilde, ever the peacemaker, would change the subject or scold them for their childish behavior. Both of them would fall into a brooding silence."

"There isn't a room on this island big enough for both their egos," I said.

Ellen laughed. "No, there isn't. They argued about everything, from doctrine to strike organization to wage demands to the artistic merits of novels or movies. A couple of times, their confrontations degenerated into intense shouting and profanity. But it never turned into actual physical violence, at least not that I had ever seen."

"You said you, uh, dated Jiro for only a couple of months?" I asked.

"Yes. Like I told you, it was very short. He ended it. He said he was very busy 'gearing up for the next big one'—meaning the next strike—and that he felt that carrying on with me would not be fair to me because he felt that in the end he was not made for long-term relationships."

"Oh, that must have hurt."

"Of course, it hurt, but I understood, and we continued to be friendly and still met every now and then for coffee on Wednesdays. Jiro would still mentor my reporting career by proofreading my articles and making suggestions for revisions. It wasn't all bad, though, at least I made a couple of friends in Beatrice and Iris and I kept in touch with them though I stopped going to Palolo Group meetings when Jiro broke it off. And during the short time I was with him, I saw another side to Jiro that few who admire him really experience."

"What was that?"

"There was a selfishness and a pettiness under the gravitas he showed the world. He humiliated me verbally when I made factual errors in conversation with him. He wouldn't do things for others unless there was a real benefit he could realize for himself. It was subtle, and nicer folks like Bea Crane never really picked up on it. But I knew. So, when he ended it between us, it did hurt, but it was also a big relief."

I let out a quiet sigh. It didn't sting as badly as I thought it would. Then Ellen bit her lower lip and bitterness flooded her eyes.

"Then she showed up."

"Who?"

"A few months after Jiro told me he couldn't date me anymore, he showed up at a *Record* party at Lau Yee Chai in Waikiki with a girl—and I mean *girl*—on his arm. Beverly Izawa was only a year out of UH and in and out of a graduate program in English Lit. She turned all of the male heads in the room. Okay, I guess she's what most men would call attractive but she struck me as disturbed. Or slow. Jiro said he met her at the stevedores' union headquarters doing volunteer work like stuffing envelopes and telephoning members who actually had telephones. She didn't look smart enough to do either."

I nodded. It was probably best not to make any comment about Beverly, not when Ellen and I were on the mend.

"A week later, Koji told me that Jiro had married this Beverly," said Ellen. "He had made no mention of any plans to do so at Lau Yee Chai and nobody else would have guessed based on their loose and casual interaction with each other."

"Engraved invitations didn't seem like they would be Jiro's thing," I said.

"I guess not. It was hard for me to swallow, especially after Jiro told me he wasn't made for long-term relationships, but I guess he just wasn't made for a long-term relationship with me. It didn't hurt for long, though. I knew that being with Jiro—who was manipulative, self-important, and hypocritical—would be exhausting emotionally. And I threw myself into reporting work. My contact with Jiro cooled to an exchange of pleasant greetings but his appearances, even on Wednesdays, were becoming scarce."

"Why?"

"I'm not sure. Over the next year or so, I'd only seen him a handful of times. And I saw him in Beverly's company even less so. In fact, I had only seen them together twice since: once, about a month after the Lau Yee Chai party, I ran into Beverly purchasing a dress at The Liberty House while Jiro waited on a padded bench outside the ladies' dressing rooms; and a second time a few days before the last time I would ever see Jiro."

"The Liberty House, huh?" I said. "Expensive taste in clothing for the wife of a proletariat champion." I thought of Beverly's wardrobe out in her Waialua closet.

"No kidding," Ellen said. She didn't attempt to conceal her disgust.

"When was that second time? Was this before the fight Jiro and Harry had at the *Record*?"

"Yes, a few weeks ago, just a couple of days before Harry came to the *Record* to call Jiro out. Jiro and Beverly came out of a downtown office building as I was passing by."

Ellen was done confessing her decidedly brief intimate relationship with Jiro Machida and her peripheral involvement with the Palolo Group of the Hawaii CP, whom she found shallow and ineffectual. I kissed her and held her again and thanked her for her honesty. We kissed some more, relieved of the burdens of our pasts and wanting each other badly. We stopped ourselves short of undressing each other; there was no time for that, she reminded me. She helped me pack an overnight valise and tidied up my apartment a bit while I rummaged in my medicine cabinet for toiletries. Ellen was a compulsive cleaner and it bothered her immensely to see my apartment in its ransacked state.

"What's this on the floor?" Ellen asked.

"What's what?"

"This."

She stooped and picked up from among all the trash a circle of smooth wooden beads strung on a silk cord. The cord's tassels were purple and fell luxuriously beneath the beads.

"Is it yours?" she asked. "It's beautiful. It looks expensive."

"No, it's not mine."

"What is it?"

"Juzu," I said. Something connected in my head, making a loud click. "It's a Buddhist rosary. Prayer beads."

"Did they belong to your father?" asked Ellen. "Another family member?"

"No," I said. "They belong to someone I just met the other day."

Shit. I'd been burglarized by a bonsan. Basho.

24

As soon as I was packed, we made a beeline back to the *Record*. I checked the area for any strange vehicles and found none.

"I need you to go in there and find the lists you showed me at Kau Kau Korner," I said. "I need you to destroy them."

"Won't we get into trouble if we do?" Ellen asked.

"I would, because I know they'd be considered Federal evidence," I said. "But you won't, not at this point, because you haven't heard it from me or anyone else, darling. And right now, I don't know a damn thing about them. You never showed them to me, remember?"

Ellen nodded knowingly. "I'll be right back," she said. "Then you can drive me home."

The minutes dragged to a near standstill while I waited for her in the Eldorado, my eyes sweeping Sheridan Street for any strange people or vehicles. I pulled my hat lower over my eyes and threw on a pair of sunglasses from the glove compartment. So far, so good. No Kierkegaard or any other haole in a bureaucrat's three-piece. No rental Packards. I took a slug out of the rye bottle for my nerves then stowed it back in the glove compartment. Remembering I was with Ellen, I chewed a couple of mints after my drink.

I finally heaved a big sigh when I saw Ellen emerge from the front door of the *Record* bearing a large manila envelope. She, too, had donned a pair of sunglasses in lieu of her usual gigantic spectacles and had draped a silk scarf over her head. I got out of the car and opened the door for her.

"Did you get all of them, Mata Hari?" I asked, taking in her get-up.

"All in here," she said, patting the envelope. She gave my low hat and shades a good once-over and smirked. "You're looking pretty clandestine yourself. Too bad you drive a circus fire truck. Not exactly what I'd call the *ideal unmarked*."

I rolled my eyes behind my dark glasses. "*Touché*," I grumbled.

I pulled away from the curb then headed mauka up Keeaumoku Street and hung a right on Beretania. The whole way to Kalihi, I kept an eye out for a tail, though I had no reason to believe Kierkegaard would have figured anything out at that point. There was nothing obvious in my rearview mirror, so I relaxed a fraction. When we got to the Park Grocery on the Kapalama Canal, we got out and Ellen led me across the street to the dirt banks leading down to the water. She dropped the envelope on the dirt and pulled a cigarette out of her purse, fitting it into an ebony holder.

"Got a light, sailor?"

I pulled out my Zippo. She grabbed it, squatted down and ignited the corners of the envelope. The orange flames leapt skyward, barely visible in the late morning sunlight. Ellen lit up her cigarette on the closest flame. She stood, smoothed out her dress and watched the envelope blacken and curl.

"Watch the blaze, will you? I've got to get something inside for you before you go," she said. I nodded and watched the flames get smaller and eventually disappear in a wisp of smoke as the envelope and its contents were reduced to a sloppy pile of loose, curly black ash. I kicked the remnants of the Hawaii CP roll call into the muddy brown water of the Kapalama Canal, watching the charred bits float for a while on the surface as some eventually sunk and some drifted toward Honolulu Harbor. Then I trudged back up the banks to the street, pulled out my own Lucky Strike and lit up.

When I was halfway done with my smoke, Ellen came back out, head still wrapped in a scarf, shades still covering her eyes. She was lugging a suitcase.

"I thought you said you had something to give me before I left," I said.

"Yeah. Me."

"Ellen, no. I've got a job to do and not much time to do it."

"I know. I'm going to make sure you get it done."

"You can't be serious."

"We belong to each other now, Frankie Yoshikawa. Whether you want to or not. Remember? There is no turning back now. I need to see you see this through. Especially because it's me you're trying to save."

I looked at her through my dark lenses. She wasn't moving. I knew I'd have to throw her over my shoulder kicking and screaming to get her back into the house. I leaned over and grabbed her suitcase. She tugged back adamantly. I won and wrested it from her little gloved hand. She stared at me through her dark glasses. I sighed and put her suitcase in the back seat of the Eldorado. She smiled triumphantly.

"Stay out of my way and don't you make this a habit," I warned.

"Don't *you* screw this up, Detective."

"I won't. Apparently, you won't let me."

"You're learning, Frankie Yoshikawa."

We got back into the Eldorado and drove through Kalihi toward the water and the airport. It was about noon by the time we got there. I parked in the dirt lot near the terminal and put the top up and closed the windows. I looked at the amount of dust built up on the other cars in the lot and despaired. Why the hell couldn't they just pave the damn thing?

I carried my valise and lugged Ellen's gigantic suitcase to the ticket counter for Trans-Pacific Airlines and secured two round trip tickets for Hilo. The flight wasn't for another two hours, so Ellen found a sandwich vendor and snagged us a tuna on white and a couple of colas while I tipped a bent old porter to take her suitcase to the DC-3 sitting on the runway. I cast my glance about the waiting area of the terminal for Kierkegaard or anyone that could be one of his HUAC associates. Nothing. I decided to relax and start acting like I was on vacation. Technically speaking, I was.

I filled Ellen in again on the strange monk I had encountered out in Waialua when I went to break the bad news to Beverly.

"It doesn't surprise me that she got a monk to do her dirty work," she said. Ellen made that face of hers that conveyed utter disdain. She made it every time she mentioned Beverly. "What do you think she wanted from your apartment so badly that she'd send her 'spiritual counselor' to go looking for it?"

"The ribbon," I said, remembering. I shot up out of my seat and ran to the pay telephone across the terminal. "I'll be right back," I shouted over my shoulder. I fumbled in my pockets for a coin and dropped it in the circular impression at the top of the chrome telephone and dialed the station. The operator put me through to the Homicide Detail. Delilah picked up after four rings.

"I hope I wasn't interrupting your manicure," I cracked.

"Shut up, Sheik. I thought you were on leave."

"I am. Have you gotten very far with our special project?"

"Why do you think I was doing my nails? It was done an hour ago. You're lucky, you know. The ribbon was practically brand-new and was being used for the first time. If it had gone back on itself and was used over again, I wouldn't have been able to read anything. Plus, there wasn't much on it."

"You're the best, sweetheart. Are you by yourself?"

"Yeah, everyone's out on the road. Even Gid."

"Then let's have it."

"Let's have what?"

"Read it to me."

"Now? Over the telephone?"

"Yes. I have another hour before I get on my plane to Hilo."

Delilah blew out a sigh. "Okay," she said. "You asked for it." And she read.

The first few minutes of her recitation was a couple of short articles Jiro had written for the *Record*; one was coverage and commentary of the cross examinations of John and Aiko Reinecke in the Hawaii Seven Smith Act trial. The other was a piece about shippers conspiring to fix the price of personal freight moving between the islands. Then Delilah started reading data on Jiro and Beverly Machida: last, first and middle names, dates of birth, places of birth, home addresses, occupations, and the like. Jiro's data set was followed by a lot of "yes's" and "no's" and various mentions of things like "asthma," "not applicable" and "infrequently," and "no other conditions." Then she stopped reading.

"Is that it?" I asked.

"That's it."

"Are you sure? There's nothing else?"

"Why wouldn't I be sure? I typed the damn thing."

"Okay. Thanks, Delilah. Put your transcription with the ribbon in a file on Gid's desk with a memo that it's for his eyes only. Tell him to share it with nobody. Not even the Feds." Especially not the Feds.

"Okay, Sheik. Enjoy your trip."

I hung the receiver up and trotted back across the concrete floor of the terminal to Ellen. She looked up at me from over a *Life* magazine.

"What was that all about?" she asked.

"The monk was probably looking for the ribbon I snagged from Jiro's lanai typewriter in Waialua. Beverly probably discovered it was missing after I left. This morning the typewriter was gone, which means she may have examined it before she somehow disposed of it. I had Delilah transcribe what was on it. I just had her read it to me."

"What was on it?"

"Nothing earth shattering. An article about the Reineckes, another about inter-island shipping, and a bunch of identifying data for Jiro and Beverly."

"Oh," said Ellen. "Maybe she wasn't after the ribbon."

"Maybe not. I can't think of anything else she could have been after, though."

Ellen shrugged and went back to reading her *Life* magazine. I sat down next to her, thoroughly exhausted. Something about what Delilah read me bothered me. I was certain Beverly had been after the ribbon and the articles didn't seem like they were any big secret, particularly if they were meant for publication. Then there were the names, dates, and the rest. They seemed so ordinary and nothing Beverly didn't already know about herself or Jiro. What the hell could be so damn important?

An announcement was made over the cacophonous drone of propellers that our flight to Hilo was boarding. Ellen and I held hands as we stood in line along a velvet cordon. I thought about it some more. I leaned my head down to touch my face against the scarf around Ellen's head and breathed deeply to smell her hair and perfume. I closed my eyes. My sweet Ellen. All that drama over something an old lady told me and all that confession, putting my heart on the line and nearly losing it . . . .

Wait. The old lady. Beatrice Walker Crane. She had said something to me about Jiro's plans for the two grand she gave the Palolo Group. I straightened up with a start.

"What's wrong?" Ellen asked. We took a couple of steps every few seconds as tickets were being taken from the passengers in front of us.

"Darling," I said, playing a hunch, "you told me the last time you saw Jiro and Beverly together was just a few days before he went missing, right?"

"Yes. So?"

"You said they were coming out of a downtown building together. Do you remember which one?"

"I had just come out of The Liberty House and was on my way to the bank. I crossed King Street and they came right out of the building and we nearly literally ran into each other. It was the TI&I Building."

We were next in line. Our tickets were taken by a Hawaiian girl in Hollywood makeup, a faux-military uniform and a fat carnation lei around her neck. We stepped out onto the sun-blasted runway and made our way to the staircase leading up to the fuselage of the silver DC-3. I followed Ellen up the stairs and we were greeted by another smile and carnation lei and welcomed aboard. We took our seats.

"TI&I?" I asked her.

"Yes," she said. "Is it important?"

"Territorial Insurance and Indemnity. Jiro was filling out an application for a life insurance policy on his typewriter."

25

The roar of the propellers of the war-surplus-DC-3-turned-passenger carrier was near deafening. Ellen held my hand throughout the flight. I leaned my head on hers and dozed for a couple of hours, exhausted. I missed the complementary pineapple juice and coffee they were serving. I had disturbing dreams of Jiro Machida's head laughing condescendingly, perched on Beverly's bloody lap, while I was being pecked by big black birds with faces like Ira Levinsky from behind bars, Marlon Wilde, Tetsuo Fujioka, and the other Palolo Cell brains looking as insipid as they had at The Willows, and too many others. My soiled, rusting armor did not protect me; I was Sir Percivale on an utterly doomed quest to find the cup that would save a dying world. Too many questions. Not enough answers. The birds pecked viciously.

When Ellen shook me back to consciousness, we had landed in Hilo.

Hilo. Green and black. Wet. Moisture in the air, in your hair, in your shirt, in your shoes. Everything smelled like rain and basalt and compost. Everything smelled wet. The last time I had been in Hilo, I had just finished my sixth-grade year and we had come by boat. We came to visit my Aunt Sachiko, Ka-san's younger sister. It was just me, Ka-san, Iris, and Pansy. Violet and Daisy had to stay back to help To-san with the shop. Aunty Sachiko followed Ka-san to Hawaii from Japan when she was sixteen, also as a picture bride, married a fisherman named Mitsuru Takasawa, and settled in a house in Shinmachi near the water. Uncle Mits had his own sampan and would take my sisters and me for short cruises out of the bay and back. There was nothing to eat but fresh fish for breakfast, lunch, and dinner. I never had it so good.

Aunty Sachiko and Uncle Mits had four sons. The eldest three—Hiro, Tommy, and Charlie—all ended up at the Hilo Ironworks as journeyman welders. The youngest, Herb, two years my senior and Pansy's age, became a Hawaii County Police Officer. Herb came to visit us in Kakaako far more frequently than we had occasion to visit those on the Big Island. We were as close as a couple of cousins on different islands could be—Herb also loved baseball—and more so, once I became a police officer, too. He married his high school sweetheart, a Chinese-Hawaiian beauty queen from Paauilo named Penelope Akana. They built a house next door to his folks, just like his older brothers had. Herb and Penny had four kids and Herb had moved up to the rank of Lieutenant. Having a county cop as a relative was serendipitous to say the least. I had a built-in starting point in my search for Harry Kurita.

I stumbled down the stairs they wheeled up to the fuselage, Ellen following close behind trying to steady me. I felt as wrinkled as my suit. As we crossed over the asphalt to the terminal, it began to rain. Hilo. Perpetual rain. When we got into the terminal, I told Ellen I needed to make a courtesy call to my Aunty Sachiko to let her know I was in Hilo, then I'd call the hotel, and then see if I could secure a cab. Ellen waited by her suitcase and my valise on an old koa bench and took out her *Life* magazine. I found a telephone and called my aunt.

After I finished talking to her, I returned to Ellen.

"Sorry, change of plans. We're not going to the hotel."

"Why not?" she asked. She put the magazine down on her suitcase and smoothed out the pages. Only Ellen would have bothered trying to improve the appearance of a travel-worn magazine.

"My Aunty Sachiko insisted we stay with them. She got really angry when I told her we were headed for a hotel. My cousin Charlie is on his way to pick us up."

"I hope we're not an imposition."

"Heck no. Aunty Sachiko is thrilled to death I've come to visit . . . and brought a girl."

"Oh. Okay. I just don't want to be a burden," said Ellen, beaming.

I was feeling groggy from my fitful nap on the plane. Sometimes getting a little sleep is worse than having none at all. I felt like one of those dried lizards in the herb shop in Chinatown, though I couldn't imagine that grinding me up into tea and drinking it would do anyone any good—not if it made them feel the way I did. I needed another drink but didn't feel like taking one in front of Ellen so early. That meant I couldn't do anything except stand around and look like I had an itch I couldn't scratch.

A half-hour later, an old Ford truck with a faded red paint job came rattling up in front of the terminal. The radio was blaring Alfred Apaka singing "Beyond the Reef," though the volume was not high enough to drown out the driver's off-key accompaniment. My cousin Charlie, skin tinted mahogany and hands calloused like bark, jumped out of the cab. He was wearing denim overalls and a stained undershirt.

"Frankie!" he roared.

"Charlie. Long time, yeah?"

I offered my hand, but Charlie ignored it and threw his arms around me and squeezed. Most Japanese folks aren't very demonstrative with their affection that way but Big Island living made Aunty Sachiko's brood different. It was nice. I squeezed him back.

"My mom told me you just got in. How come you never told us you were coming? We would've made a big party."

"That's okay. And sorry about the last-minute call to Aunty. I didn't even know I was coming until this morning. This is Ellen Park. Ellen, my cousin Charlie Takasawa."

Charlie gave Ellen a hug and a kiss on the cheek just like a kanaka—such was the way of my Hilo relatives. He also asked her if I was "serious" about her—the lack of inhibition manifested itself in not just hugs and kisses but also in tactless personal inquiries. Ellen merely looked over at me and I just smiled uncomfortably. Charlie dispelled the tension by saying I *had* to be serious about her if I brought her along to expose her to his Hilo relatives. I agreed and we all had a laugh about it.

Charlie put Ellen's suitcase and my valise in the bed of the Ford and helped Ellen up into the passenger seat of the cab. I rode in the bed with the luggage, hanging on to my hat and pulling up my lapels against the Hilo drizzle. The ride wasn't very long. Aunty Sachiko's family lived in the Shinmachi district of Hilo, a fisherman's village of sorts with a Japanesey feel to it. Before the tsunami of 1946, it was a really thriving place alive with families and businesses. After much of Shinmachi was literally washed away, those folks who were most tenacious and lucky that there were still some of their structures intact returned to rebuild, but it never really went back to being that bustling place it was before the tsunami. Within ten minutes, we pulled up to the Takasawa compound, a collection of whitewashed houses with tin roofs. All had chimneys—in Hilo, it got cool enough on occasion to build a fire. There was a free-standing bathhouse with a large furo used by all the houses, save for Herb's, which had its own bathhouse. The houses were all nice and new—the old family house and the two others built by Hiro and Tommy were wrecked in the tsunami. Charlie's and Herb's were the newest; the whitewash hadn't even started to show signs of mildew.

Already, preparations for a feast were underway. Uncle Mits was cutting a large ahi at the steel table Hiro and Tommy had fashioned for him. The table stood under a tin roof with glass floats in nets hanging from the rafters. A large taxidermist-stuffed marlin hung from the wall above the cutting table. Aunty Sachiko squatting in high black rubber boots with a hand sickle was cutting a bunch of green onions from her garden. She bore little resemblance to Ka-san, being about three inches taller and having still mostly black hair. As soon as she saw me climb out of the bed of the truck, she yelled an announcement of our arrival for the entire compound to hear and everyone came swarming out of the houses to greet us, smothering us with hugs, kisses, and backslaps. Hiro's wife Minnie even presented us with a couple of orchid leis she had strung herself.

"Frankie!" a voice louder than all the rest boomed. All heads turned to the black and white prowler that had pulled up on the gravel-covered driveway. A stocky uniformed officer got out and ran over to embrace me.

"You're looking good, Herb," I said. I glanced at his uniform and all the shiny brass.

"You're looking wet," he responded, "and tired. What brings you here all of a sudden? Mommy called me up at work and said you just showed up."

"Work," I said.

"Tell me all about it at dinner. You're staying with me and Penny. You got the boys' room and Ellen has the girls'. All the kids will bunk in the parlor. We'll make a fire for them if it's still raining after dinner."

Great. If I had checked into a hotel as planned, I'd be sharing a bed with Ellen. My provincial Hilo relatives saw fit to separate an unmarried couple. I guess I shouldn't complain—I was saving a pretty penny on lodging and I was probably too tired to do anything with Ellen anyway except literally sleep. Ellen just smiled sweetly at me and shrugged. She had already made friends with Herb's daughters, promising to do their hair just like hers before dinner. Everyone was in awe of the pretty reporter I brought along with me and I couldn't blame them.

Dinner brought a brief respite from the Damocles' Sword of a case that hovered menacingly over my head. For such short notice, Aunty Sachiko and her family managed to throw together a grand feast welcoming us to the Big Island. There was sashimi of all sorts—ahi, aku, ono, and some other stuff I didn't even think you could eat raw. All of it made me think of Chester, Iris's raw fish loving husband, who would have been in heaven *if* they had the "right shoyu." Aunty Sachiko made hand rolled makizushi and chicken hekka and every type of pickle imaginable. Uncle Mits brought out his prized bottle of Johnnie Walker Black Label and there were plenty of brown bottles of Primo on ice in a galvanized steel washtub. The folks from the neighboring compound, the Kauhane family, brought some wild pig and haupia. My cousins and the Kauhane boys brought out their guitars and ukuleles and sang one song after another, "Songs of the Islands," "Hilo No Ka Oi," and other tunes I hadn't heard in a long, long time for Ellen and me while Penny danced the hula.

For a couple of hours, my case was blissfully forgotten until Herb came and sat next to me with Uncle Mits's Black Label and a couple of glasses.

"You said work brought you here," he said. He poured a couple of stiff drinks. "Tell me about it."

"A couple of days ago the burned out remains of a guy named Jiro Machida were found in a cane field in Kunia. He was a big deal in local communist circles. Someone clipped him, hacked him up, burned the pieces, and buried them in a cane field. That someone was probably a rival communist named Harry Kurita. Harry jumped on a Japanese fishing boat called the *Iwakuni Maru* with the intention of going to the Orient, got off here in Hilo during an overnight port call and never got back on."

"I know the boat," said Herb thoughtfully. He clinked glasses with me and took a good long sip. "She called about a month ago. I didn't know anyone got off except the crew, and they all got back on."

"Harry paid the master five hundred bucks to take him to Yokohama and keep his mouth shut about his presence on the boat. It doesn't surprise me that you wouldn't have heard anything about a passenger getting off the fishing vessel."

"What did he look like?"

"This," said Ellen, pulling a photograph out of her purse and handing it to Herb.

"Where'd you get that?" I asked.

"The *Record*'s photo morgue. I brought it along in case you didn't have one."

"You think of everything, darling."

"I know. It's my gift."

"Good thing," said Herb. "Frankie only remembers box scores from Yankees games."

Herb looked long at the photograph and then shook his head slowly. "No," he said, "he doesn't look familiar. Do you mind if I borrow this, Ellen? I'll show it in the squad room tomorrow morning."

"Sure," said Ellen. "It's the least we can do. You're doing us all the favors."

"Yeah. Thanks, Herb," I added. "But enough about my case for now. How about you? Working on anything interesting?"

"No. Kids stealing stuff from the sugar mills at night. One or two drunks in the tank. Nothing like your front-page killings. The most interesting thing we've had recently was a jawbone that washed up at Hakalau. Shark attack, most likely. Our Medical Examiner needed some help, so he sent the thing to Honolulu to your M.E."

"You're in good hands. Just have lots of coffee while you review his report. He writes like how he talks."

"*You* should talk, haole-mouth. You came back from New York sounding like Edward R. Murrow."

"Don't let that fool you," said Ellen. "He makes *plenty* of mistakes."

The two of them laughed so heartily that I joined them, though the laugh was at my expense. When it finally died down, Herb poured a couple more drinks and spoke.

"You might be able to help me while I'm helping you," he said.

"Whatever I can do, just ask."

"A couple of weeks ago, the Hongwanji made a complaint about some priest from Honolulu who was around stirring up trouble at the sugar plantations. He took some donations to build a new temple up near Volcano and then disappeared. The old folks who gave money complained to the Hongwanji, but they told them that the priest wasn't one of theirs."

"How do you know he was from Honolulu?" I asked.

"He had to be," said Herb. "He was too strange-looking. Bald, dark glasses, long beard. He never took the glasses off, even at night. He had a strange name, too. Just one name."

"Basho," I said.

26

Who the hell was the weird bonsan who looked more like a jazz musician than a priest? He'd ransacked my apartment and before that he was on the Big Island bilking obaasans out of their precious savings to build a temple on the slopes of Mauna Kea that never materialized. He was spiritual counselor to the even weirder Beverly Machida, an uninhibited man-eater who slept in a coffin. Herb was stunned when I said his name was Basho and I told him the bizarre story of my case. The weird priest was tied in with Beverly Machida and he likely ransacked my apartment looking for the typewriter ribbon I took from the Machidas' lanai. Herb pondered this over more of Uncle Mits's Johnnie Walker Black Label and called the coincidence "interesting." To Japanese folks, "interesting" was often a euphemism for screwed up.

I needed to ponder this development in the place I did my best thinking: the furo. I already had a bath in the "big" bathhouse attached to Aunty Sachiko's house, but I wanted another and Herb was happy to oblige, building a fire the old-fashioned way and heating the water in his own modest furo. I got into a yukata furnished by Penny and threw a clean towel over my shoulder.

"Having another bath?" Ellen asked. She looked up from the floor of Herb and Penny's parlor, where she sat Indian-style playing cards with the kids on their futons.

"You're observant. Care to join me?"

"I wish. I don't think it would go over well with your Aunty."

"You're right. How about a rain check? You can squeeze into Old Chang's tiny shower with me when we get back to Oahu."

One of Herb's daughters made a face. "Eww," she said. "Do you *really* take a bath with *him*, Aunty Ellen? He seems kind of hairy and scratchy underneath, like my dad."

"Eww," said her sister.

"Now that you put it like that, it does seem unpleasant," said Ellen, eyes to the ceiling in mock thought. She winked at me as the girls gagged. I shook my head while I hid a smile and shuffled off to the little furo in the back of Herb's house.

The furo was a modest pine box, about the size of a Labrador retriever's kennel. It was not as deep as the main compound's furo, but the water stayed hotter for much longer. The little bathhouse with its concrete floor smelled of clean dampness. I doused myself twice with the basin, lathered up while sitting on a little pine stool, then rinsed off and eased into the furo. Outside, the rain had started to come down more heavily and assaulted the tin roof of the bathhouse with a million drops in a cacophonous hiss.

I slipped beneath the hot water's surface and the rattle of the rain dulled then came back when I resurfaced. I closed my eyes, put the wet towel on my face, and let my mind wander.

France. Vosges Mountains. October 1944. Cold. Gray. Damp. Pinned down on a bed of dead pine needles on a mountainside. No furo in sight. I could've used one. I hadn't bathed for days. I had developed that film of grime all over the surface of my body, what medieval pseudo-physicians called cultivation of the "protective layer," a critical practice for good health, along with bloodletting using barber's razors and leeches. The night before, I had been having a discussion of all things medieval with my tent-mate, Art. Arthur Kawamura was a kotonk from Fresno. Art's folks had a small vineyard that produced grapes for raisins; they were lucky enough to temporarily deed it over

to a haole neighbor and friend so they wouldn't lose it before they were
carted off to Tule Lake. Art had a book he kept with him all the time—
King Arthur and the Knights of the Round Table. The book was given to
him by a favorite uncle who had a thing for English language books
of all kinds, because they taught him the nuances of the language. Art
loved the damn thing—the protagonist had the same name he did. He
toted it in his pack and he'd read dog-eared pages like a bible every
night before "Taps" in the barracks. For Art, the book had a life of its
own—some kind of talisman or lucky charm. He lent it to me on a
couple of occasions and I had come to understand why he held the book
so dear in my quick read of the story. He was small and determined, just
like the young Arthur who would one day become the King of England.
Perhaps he thought a similar destiny awaited him, if only he believed it
hard enough.

Art Kawamura was a quiet and studious character, shy to a fault
and afraid of the raucous Hawaii boys. He was scared shitless that we'd
make him the butt of our jokes or beat his ass for his loose change so we
could buy beer in the canteen. I had come to his aid one day when he
was being bullied in the chow hall in basic; he tagged along with Wally
and me from that moment. He had taken to calling me Sir Kay, his way
of acknowledging my big brother-like status in his eyes. I found the
name somewhat flattering as I had taken a liking to the little book.

After Wally had gone stateside thanks to a lost leg in Italy, Art
became my tent-mate. Art and I had stayed up a little later than usual
the evening before, talking about what life would have been like for us
had we been fighting in medieval France instead of the France we were
in. We concluded that not much would be different, though the food
might have been a little worse. We were roused a couple of hours later by
the sergeant while it was still dark and told that we'd be going uphill in
a few minutes to rescue the Lost Battalion, a group of Texans from the
141st who had gotten separated from the rest.

The sarge made it sound like a piece of cake. Forget that the 141st had tried and failed—twice—to get their own guys back—we were made of sterner stuff. We were boys who were crapped on by our country but managed to swallow it and made it halfway around the globe to fight for that country. This would be easy, compared to that.

"Tournament time," I told Art. "Have you got my sword?"

"Right here, Sir Kay," he said. He handed me my rifle and I punched his upper arm gently. I fixed my bayonet to the muzzle. Art pulled on his wire-rimmed glasses and fixed his own bayonet. Then he shouldered his pack and he stood there, just looking at me as I lit up a Lucky Strike.

"What?" I asked. "Want one?"

"No thanks."

"You sure?"

"Yeah." Art shifted his weight uncomfortably then dropped his rifle and unshouldered his pack. He squatted down and opened the pack up.

"What're you doing, Art? We muster in less than five minutes."

He fished out his precious book and held it out to me.

"Sir Kay, I want you to have this. I'm grateful for everything you've done for me. You've been a good friend."

"Hey, come on. It's just a little stroll up the mountain. You'll need your favorite book back on that raisin farm of yours so you can read it to all the little brats you're going to make with some pretty kotonk girl."

"Please. Just take it."

I gave him a sneer, but under it I was crying. Art was afraid and I was even more so than he was and it broke my heart to think he thought it was the end for him. He was pretty grim and resolute, though, so I took the book.

"Thanks," I said. "I'll hold on to it until after our business is done today, then I'll give it back to you."

Art nodded and shouldered his pack again and picked up his rifle, then pushed past me out of the tent.

"Come on, Sir Kay," he said. "It's time to go."

Not even an hour later, we lay there face down in the pine needles, German bullets coming at us from above in a violent hailstorm. Art was lying about a yard away, hand on his helmet, shaking.

"This is crazy," he shouted. "The shooting hasn't let up. They must have an endless supply of bullets."

"We're practically on their home field. Of course, they've got a lot of bullets."

"Well, we can't just wait here until they run out."

"They won't run out."

"Then let's get up there, Sir Kay."

Art stood up, rifle held in advancing position. He took a step.

"Art! Get your ass back down! They're going to kill you!"

"Too late. I'm going up."

He took another step and then he bellowed inarticulately like a madman and took about three more steps before breaking into a run. He got about five yards uphill before I heard a whine and a slap and saw Art's neck burst open, spraying red everywhere. Another whine, another slap, and his back exploded in more warm blood spraying. Art's knees buckled and he fell forward on his face.

Arthur Nobuo Kawamura of Fresno, California, was dead.

Without thinking, I stood up. It was time. Art had known this. It was time. Like Arthur riding out to meet Mordred. Like Kuranosuke gathering all the loyal Asano retainers, the 46 who remained, and telling them that the moment was at hand to storm Kira's manor and take his head. *It was time.*

I lowered the stock of my rifle to my hip and pointed the bayonet uphill. An inhuman yell broke out of the confines of my soul and I charged. I was vaguely aware of others around me who had stood up when I had and were running uphill alongside me. I finally understood To-san's little lecture in that miserable little pup tent on Sand Island. I finally understood what it was he tried to impress on me with his lungs full of fluid. Giri. Doing what needs to be done because you *have* to. Art couldn't lie there a moment longer, cringing under the withering barrage of German lead. He stood up and charged because obligation demanded it. Because he couldn't *not* do it. And the rest of us couldn't *not* do it, either. This is why the haoles failed. For them, self-preservation trumped obligation.

I ran uphill as fast as I could. My lungs and legs were burning up. My eyes stung from the chill and the sulfur in the air. All around me, bodies dropped. They hit the slope with sickening thuds, crumpled by the shots that found them. I heard a vicious buzz and felt the heat on my shoulder. I had been hit. My flesh burned where the bullet had ripped it. At the moment, no pain, just the burn, the fiery, searing burn of a bullet wound.

I gritted my teeth and ran even faster, pumping my sore legs and hurtling ever upward.

Suddenly, the ground had leveled and the trees thinned out. Shadowy figures lurked about, moving like fish in a reef.

I staggered into the clearing and came face-to-face with two lanky G.I.s, faces dirty and scruffy with prickly beards. One of them immediately crouched defensively and held his fists up. They were both unarmed. Others from my company started breaking into the clearing. The wary one squinted in the dim forest light, taking in my features.

"What are they? Did the krauts bring 'em in?"

"No, I don't think so," drawled the other, looking at my insignia. His eyes widened with recognition then elation. "They're ours! He's one of our Japs! We're saved!"

"No shit, Hopalong," I said. "I'm one of *your* Japs, yeah."

They both converged on me, embracing me and slapping my back. I felt the pain in my shoulder come on at that moment, after the adrenaline had ebbed away. The bear hugs and backslaps from the Texans sent mind-searing pain from my shoulder to every other inch of my exhausted frame. I collapsed.

"Oh, shit! Sorry, Pard! You're hit! Medic!"

The next moments were a haze of red pain. Someone poured something on my wound that burned it, and then bound it up. I looked around and saw there were others from my company, far more broken than I was. Then it hit me. There weren't very many, broken or not. Where the hell was everyone else?

Art. I saw him fall a few steps away from where we lay flat on the pine needles. He wasn't the only one; there was a ton of them, I learned later. My company started our uphill charge with almost two hundred men. Only eight made it to the Texans unhurt. The 442nd as a whole was just under three thousand men strong before the bloody operation. We lost almost two hundred, nearly three times the amount the 141st had in total casualties. Over two thousand of us were wounded. I was one of them. I was lucky, though. I'd still be able to swing a bat and throw a runner out at third, though it didn't feel like it at the time. And I didn't care at the time, either.

When I was able to, I pulled the book from my pack and opened it. Art had inscribed something inside the front cover:

Sir Kay,
Never stop being the champion of the defenseless.
It's your calling.
Thanks for being mine.
　　　　　Your Pal,
　　　　　Arthur N. Kawamura

I shut the book and held it to my chest with the arm that wasn't in a sling and closed my eyes. That moment started me down the path to Columbia University and a degree in Medieval and Renaissance Literature and a career with the Honolulu Police Department. I read *King Arthur and the Knights of the Round Table* over and over again, just like Art had. I went nowhere without it. Later, when exploring *Le Morte D'Arthur* in Ira's lectures, I was disappointed to learn how loosely the book had based its tale on Malory's opus. The disappointment was momentary, though. The book was my talisman, my shield. It was a piece of Art Kawamura and a reminder of his admonishment to protect those who could not protect themselves, an admonishment I was to disregard shamefully when I sold Ira and Rachel Levinsky to the HUAC. And the tale it contained would remain for all time imbued with the light magic that kept the specters of war at bay for a scared little boy from Fresno and a scared bigger boy from Kakaako.

I brought the book to Hilo, too. I dragged myself reluctantly out of the furo and toweled myself dry. The same exhaustion I felt after reaching the Texans hit me over the head like a sledgehammer. I floated through the parlor in my clean yukata with the towel over my shoulder. The kids were all asleep.

I sneaked into the girls' room where Ellen was lying in the big bed. I leaned down and kissed her on the forehead. I withdrew from the room as silently as I entered it, went to the boys' room and pulled the book out of my valise. I lay down on the covers with the book on my chest.

It's your calling.

Tomorrow, I thought wearily. Take up your sword and champion the defenseless tomorrow.

The heavy black-velvet mantle of sleep descended on me and wrapped me up in its gigantic wings and I dreamed of knights at tournament in bright armor, trailing colored pennants from the tips of their lances in all the hues of the rainbows over Hilo.

27

The rain on the tin roof woke me up. Throughout the night it had battered the metal so steadily that the din became a dull, fuzzy audial blanket for my weary and throbbing head. I slept a deep, black sleep and came out of it feeling more exhausted than I had been when I entered it. The sharp smell of the wet and the drenched ferns and lava rocks reminded me that I was in Hilo and that I had come for a purpose. With that reminder came a momentary panic to seize every possible second in my pursuit of Harry Kurita.

I fumbled about the boys' bedroom clumsily, nearly destroying a balsa wood model airplane in my groggy state while trying to get my legs into a pair of trousers. Herb told me that Harry's face in the photograph didn't look familiar to him. I recalled when I had talked to the master of the *Iwakuni Maru*, he told me had seen Harry strike out into Hilo Town shortly after they made port. Did he simply vanish? He didn't take his suitcase. He must have fully intended to return to the vessel and make his way to the Orient. What the hell happened to him? Where was I going to start looking for him? At the harbor? *In* the harbor? About a full month had gone by since he was last seen.

Maybe I was better off leaving the manhunt to Herb and helping Herb with his obaasan problem, since I was familiar with the weird bonsan in the dark glasses.

Basho.

In Hilo.

Shit.

I bolted out of the boys' bedroom while still knotting my tie. I made a beeline for the front door. Ellen looked up from her breakfast. She was sitting with Penny at the kitchen table chatting about something over coffee. Herb and the kids had already left for work and school.

"Frankie! Sit down and eat!" Penny called at me.

"What's the hurry, Detective?" Ellen asked. She held her coffee cup in feminine fashion with two hands close to her face, letting the steam create a veil in front of her.

"No thanks, Pen. No time," I said. I scanned the front door area for my shoes and found them neatly perched to the side of the jumbled pile of sneakers and mud-caked rubber boots next to Ellen's heels, like they were a stately royal couple.

"I think I know what happened to Harry," I told Ellen. I jammed my feet into my wingtips and laced them up.

"What? What do you mean?" asked Ellen. She stood up from her seat at the table. Penny stood, too, and threw some banana muffins into a clean kerchief.

"He broke into my apartment."

I thought about the strange bonsan and how he was about the same height as the Harry Kurita who had pontificated at my sister's cocktail party and condemned my boorish habit of watching a ball game on television while more erudite minds sucked British dry gin out of effete little glasses and bemoaned the state of the decaying world. I wondered how I could have missed it the first time. Maybe too much television and baseball *were* bad for the wits. Probably no more so than seducing coeds with the same tired poems, I decided, but he pulled one over me nonetheless. The thought of being outsmarted by the self-absorbed radical poser irritated me into moving faster. I had the screen door open before I was done tying my shoes.

"Harry was the priest? Are you sure?" Ellen asked. She slid into her pumps at the door somewhat more gracefully than I had stuffed my feet into my abused wingtips.

"Yeah, how about that? He had been conveniently finishing up his 'spiritual counseling' of the grieving Widow Machida when I came to call with the bad news," I said. "He gets extra points for playing humility so well. It must have been killing him."

Penny ran up and thrust the kerchief of muffins in my hands and gave a vacuum flask of hot coffee to Ellen.

"Make sure he has his breakfast," she told Ellen.

"I'll try," she replied. "He usually loses his appetite when he thinks he's been outsmarted."

"Really?" asked Penny.

"I know. You'd think he'd weigh fifty pounds." They broke out in a giggling fit. I rolled my eyes. Penny gave me a bamboo-handled umbrella and the keys to Herb's ten-year-old Packard. I leaned back and gave her a kiss on the cheek.

"Thanks, Pen," I said. Ellen and I dashed out to the Packard under the umbrella. I opened the passenger door for her and shut it once she was tucked into her seat then ran around to the driver's side and got in. Despite the use of the umbrella, my trousers were soaked from the cuffs to the knees. The wet came down with wrath and beat the tin roofs and ti leaves of Hilo Town, savagely.

After some coaxing, the old Packard's engine turned and I pulled out of the gravel driveway onto the winding asphalt slick with rain that over the years had been dangerously crumbling into dozens of potholes. I made my way through the rambling main thoroughfare of Shinmachi as fast as I dared in the downpour.

"Where are we going?" Ellen shouted over the battering rain.

"South."

"That doesn't tell me anything. What's south?"

"Herb told me a bunch of old ladies complained that some strange-looking Buddhist priest ripped them off. They lived in the shacks on the sugar plantation."

"Is that where we're going?"

"It's probably the best lead I have here on this island as to Basho's—Harry's—first appearance since absconding."

"Don't you think we should check in with Herb first?"

"Why?"

"Because unless you left something out, you don't even know the names of the complaining old ladies."

"Oh. Well. I guess that's why the telephone was invented."

"You're welcome, Detective."

I pulled over in front of the Hilo Theatre on Kamehameha Avenue and used a pay telephone under the protection of its Arte Moderne marquee. Ellen remained in the passenger seat while I placed a quick call to Herb at the station and obtained the names of two old women at the plantation. I thanked my cousin, promised him that we would meet him at May's Fountain on Kamehameha Avenue not far from the theater for lunch, then got back into the Packard and found Kilauea Avenue without much of a problem, then drove over the 4 ½ Mile Bridge and into Panaewa Forest toward Olaa. The rain continued to beat down unabated.

"Which plantation are we headed to?" Ellen asked.

"Olaa," I said.

"Olaa? That's where Jiro was from."

"Oh," I said, remembering. "That's right. Maybe in a perverse way, Harry felt he was still sticking it to Jiro by bilking his old neighbors. Herb told me that he didn't hang around for very long—maybe about a week or so, just long enough to take the old ladies' money and leave. I know he was back on Oahu as of at least three days ago, and still in the same disguise. I guess he wasn't interested in going to China after all. He just wanted to stick around and be with Beverly."

"It doesn't really sound like Harry," said Ellen. She was staring out of the passenger window through the water-streaked glass at the wild green tangle of trees and ferns.

"No, it doesn't. I have to say I'm disappointed."

"Disappointed?"

"Yes, darling, disappointed. I'm disappointed that a self-proclaimed Champion of the People clipped his archrival not for the opportunity to expand his intellectual horizons but so he could hang around Jiro's creepy little wife in the guise of a Buddhist priest. It kind of makes me feel a little sad and empty knowing that even the self-important have motives that are just as base and low as those of a Hotel Street pimp. It makes me want to shed a tear for the inconsistency of this world."

"Don't you mean the *injustice* of this world?"

"No. The inconsistency. The world has always been an unjust place and it will always be an unjust place. It will *never* be just. What it should be, though, is consistent."

Ellen let out her silvery laugh. "Oh, Frankie. This is one of the things I love about you. You're always just on the verge of poetic, even at your jaded, sarcastic best."

"You should see me when I've had a few drinks at a cocktail party full of Harry Kuritas. Poetic doesn't begin to describe it."

I thought about the first time I had met Harry, the year before at my sister Iris's cocktail party at her Kapahulu house. Most of the guests were high school teachers and old UH or McKinley classmates of hers. Iris had invited me because she had been trying to fix me up with one of her younger colleagues, a mousy chemistry teacher named Muriel Kusaka who was in her first year out of UH. Muriel had the small, shiny eyes and buckteeth of a domestic rodent and stringy hair that wouldn't stay out of her face despite the beautician's best efforts. Worst of all, her chin had apparently gone AWOL. I mistrust chinless people because their smiles look forced and painful. I know it doesn't sound fair or rational, but no chinless person had ever done me a noble deed. And if our stilted, forced conversation was any indication, it didn't seem as if one would do so that night. Tristram and La Beale Isoud we weren't.

I ditched Muriel Kusaka next to the folding card table with the white linen cloth draped over it. Iris put out some trays of makizushi and Ritz Crackers decorated with parsley sprigs and little pieces of ham and sliced cocktail olives on this table and I recommended that Muriel try one of my sister's bland little snacks. While she helped herself to the fare, I slipped away to the impromptu bar that Chester had set up on the lanai and proceeded to drain the fifth of Wild Turkey one tumbler at a time. Playing along with my sisters' matchmaking schemes always gave me a headache and a thirst.

When I was nice and numb, I recalled that the Yankees were on the radio that evening and that my sister had a radio. The game had already been broadcast the day before and I read the box score in the morning paper, but the thought of hearing Mantle at the plate in an exciting play-by-play struck me as a better way to spend the sticky Kapahulu evening than trying to impress No-Chin with war stories she wasn't interested in hearing. I took the fifth of bourbon and my tumbler to the parlor and plopped myself down on the rug in front of the radio, cross-legged, and turned it on.

About ten feet away, Harry Kurita was holding court with a bunch of Kaimuki teachers in party dresses and nylons. He was regaling them with tales of his rejection of common academic interpretations of English romantic poetry or some such shit, telling them how the "Establishment" has warped the world's reading of such "raw" emotion. A couple of the party dresses gasped in exaggerated astonishment and tittered with their hands over their mouths at his displays of verbal bravado. They looked like the types that had seen too many Cary Grant pictures and had their mothers sew them dresses based on photographs out of *Harper's Bazaar*. When the sound of the announcer's voice came up, Harry made some crack about the "bourgeois tool" of professional sports having claimed another "victim" and looked at me with mock pity. He told his newfound admirers that they had only to look at me to see how the proletariat is being poisoned by a steady diet of propaganda.

Harry was bragging about how he had shamed an old haole professor in some lecture by challenging his statements about the "horror" of the Crimean War when Mickey Mantle stepped up to the plate.

"Excuse me," I shouted, "could we have a little quiet please? Mantle is at bat. It's the bottom of the ninth."

The party dresses gasped at me. Harry Kurita sniffed and put on a saintly face. The parlor had momentarily quieted down so I could hear the announcer call a first ball then a strike.

"How sad," Harry said. "This is a classic example of the intellectual decay I was just mentioning."

The umpire signaled another ball. I stood up and towered over Harry. I put my face down close to his so he could smell the 101-proof fumes.

"It's not intellectual decay," I said, faintly aware of my slurring. "It's the first game of a double header in The Bronx. Intellectual decay is using overrated dilettante poetry and dry martinis to get into the cotton panties of a couple of high school English teachers who're too picky to date the radiator mechanic next door."

A half-dozen party dresses gulped the hot air of the parlor in a big, simultaneous suck. Harry backed a step. His eyes were soft and wide with fear. I felt that if I hit him, he'd implode and collapse upon himself into a dry husk to be blown under the koa sofa into obscurity. Despite his bravado, Harry Kurita was soft, sensitive, and scared.

"FRANKIE!" Iris shrieked. She pushed me relentlessly with her little hands to the screen door and out onto the lanai. "Get out of my house and go home! NOW!"

I staggered into my shoes and nearly tripped down the lanai stairs onto the front lawn.

"What's the count?" I shouted from the lawn at my sister. She stood just outside the screen door with her hands on her hips scowling.

"What?"

"What's the count? Mantle had two balls and a strike."

"SHUT UP AND GO HOME!"

Iris picked up a wooden geta clog and threw it at me with all the torque and fury her skinny right arm could muster. It missed my head wide left and struck the fender of her husband's Buick . . . .

The rain continued to fall unabated on the road to Keaau. Ellen laughed as I finished my reminiscence of my one and only prolonged encounter with Harry Kurita.

"It sounds just like him," she said.

"Which part? The pompous seducer of high school teachers or the frail soul?"

"Both," she said, then added, thoughtfully: "Do you really think he's capable of doing those horrible things to Jiro? I mean, he despised him, true, but he somehow doesn't seem, well . . . "

"Man enough? Agreed. But I've seen some very timid people do some very violent things with the right . . . stimulus. Little housewives with cleavers, even. They weren't beat up by their husbands or had their lives threatened. They just stood to make a lot of extra money sooner if their rich husbands expired."

28

Olaa was an ocean of green cane under the white mist of heavy rain. I had been afraid that I'd get Herb's Packard mired in the mud before I reached the housing area. Thankfully, the road into the village had been paved some twenty years before. The smokestack of the mill was barely visible in the downpour. When we reached the village, Ellen gasped at the condition of the houses. All were dilapidated wooden shacks with rusting tin roofs, looking more like places to store tools or animal carcasses than human beings. The occupants had fortunately taken the pains to lay gravel all about their rotting huts so that the mud wouldn't claim our shoes.

Herb had given me the names of two of the complainants, the only ones who came forward to speak to the police. Herb told me that there were many more, with most reluctant to make formal complaints because of embarrassment or simply because they wanted to "forget the whole thing." Such attitudes were typical of Japanese of my parents' generation; I had spent too many evenings in Kakaako parlors trying to coax statements out of reluctant witnesses. Being Japanese myself, I usually drew those interviews, but I told Gid repeatedly that it made little difference in getting them to open up. The shame they felt for being peripherally involved in something scandalous, even if they only saw or heard something, had been the key to how they reacted. It was as if they were tainted somehow by their knowledge of something terrible and that talking about it would somehow stain them visibly, like spatters of blood or shit.

That morning, getting the women to give me anything was a matter of patience and persistence, but I was in short supply of the former and had an overabundance of the latter. I only had a couple of days at most until Kierkegaard came charging in with his lance lowered and I needed enough to tell him that the tournament was over, that he could pack up his armor and hit the road in search of more plentiful red targets, preferably as far away from Hawaii—and Ellen and Iris—as geographically possible. *Maine, I understand, is teeming with communists, Mr. Kierkegaard—won't you ride to their rescue?*

Spending the morning chatting up a couple of obaasans about the shameful experience of being fleeced by an ersatz bonsan and the ticks of the clock that I would lose and never get back made me want to pull my hair out.

Yet there I was, standing on the wet gravel outside a dilapidated plantation cottage in Olaa all the same, because I had no other leads. Ellen and I managed to find Hatsue Fukuda's humble abode by asking an old man who turned out to be a blacksmith, bent from carrying a sack of horseshoes to his shop near the mill. Horseshoes. In the 20th century. That's life on an Olaa plantation for you. It was a stark reminder that though I drove a Cadillac Eldorado, I was not too far removed from the medieval lifestyle I saw all about me in the wet muck of Olaa. Modern serfdom. Peasant labor tied to the land. Wretched souls in permanent debt to their liege lord. My parents were little different from the folks huddled in their shacks. No wonder they got the hell out. It made me think about all those knights riding about the English countryside looking for the cup that Joseph of Arimathea brought all the way from Palestine and how it was supposed to save all the wretches like the ones who lived in the tin-roofed shacks like the one we stood before. The Cup of Christ. The King and The Land. Nobody at Olaa looked like they'd be getting a sip out of the Holy Grail any time soon.

I knocked on the rickety door, a motley collection of planks fastened to the rotting jamb by rusting hinges and held shut by a crude bar fashioned from a rotted stick. Ellen clung to me under the bamboo-handled umbrella, locking her arms around my waist under my coat and shivering slightly. I knocked a second time, harder, thinking that the first set of knocks couldn't be heard over the deafening rattle of the rain on the corrugated tin roof. I thought I was going break the thing clean off its hinges. In a few seconds, I saw the stick-on-nail "knob" turn and the door opened.

Hatsue Fukuda was about four-foot-ten and maybe seventy-five pounds if she had eaten breakfast. Her skin was translucent and her tiny eyes were fixed in a perpetual squint. She was probably a rare beauty during the Roosevelt Administration—the Theodore Roosevelt Administration. I spoke, introducing myself, and showed her my gold Honolulu badge, then introduced Ellen, who stood next to me smiling sweetly and patiently. After her entire frame rose and fell a few times with the breaths she took, she asked us to enter in a warbling, labored voice.

The interior of the little hut belied its exterior decay and filth. The wooden floor was warm and clean, swept and mopped regularly by the gnarled little hands that gestured to us to sit at the kitchen table. The sparse furnishings were well maintained, each humble cabinet of lacquerware and cotton cushion a museum piece. The only reminder of the decrepit outside world was the lingering smell of mildew and wet that wouldn't be vanquished, not even when assaulted with burning altar senko. The brooding incense mingled with the damp to produce a pungent scent of slow, wet death. It made me want to bury my head under a dry feather pillow perfumed with Ellen's hair.

Hatsue Fukuda poured us each a cup of hot black coffee. It killed the horrible wet smell of the room when I held it up to my nose. I breathed the steam deeply. It was fresh ground coffee grown on the

Kona side of the island—better than the *Parisien* roast I had in press-
pots in Bruyères or the tiny cups of hot Italian sludge from copper
columns topped with shiny eagles. The best coffee in the whole damned
world! It made me wonder why Delilah's brew at the station was so
awful when this stuff was produced in our very own Territory.

When she had poured her own cup, Hatsue Fukuda sat down. I
began by apologizing for the intrusion and made an earnest plea for her
assistance as there were matters at stake bigger than the defrauding of
honest, hardworking folks at Olaa. In typical old-world Issei fashion,
she hesitated dramatically then started in halting speech, all the while
staring down at her hands. A haole instructor at recruit school, some
veteran of some big city PD on the mainland taught us that lack of eye
contact was a sure sign of deception. Some shit about eyes being the
"windows of the soul." He didn't know a damned thing about Orientals.
Eye contact was a challenge, and a challenge was, in most settings,
disrespect. I watched her face surreptitiously from a bowed head. Ellen
was free to look more directly, being a bystander to our conversation.
She took her small pad and pencil out of her purse quietly and discreetly
scrawled notes in her lap under the table.

Hatsue's tale began about three or four weeks before our visit,
when she had been hanging laundry out to dry. She lived alone in the
little shack. Her husband had died of heart disease a few years ago and
her children, all daughters, had married and moved to the mainland. She
had no help with the chores any more. Hanging laundry had become
particularly arduous.

"I can do that for you, Obasan," a smooth, calm voice had told
her. It appeared out of nowhere. It belonged to a peculiar-looking
bonsan who had somehow managed to steal up next to her without
being heard. She was startled and yet she calmed down quickly once she
realized he was a priest. Something about his demeanor and presence
made her feel secure.

According to Hatsue, the bonsan was a strange-looking character to say the least. He was a small, sturdy man with a completely bald pate and a long, wispy beard under his chin, like a jade carving of an old Chinese emperor. He wore sunglasses with big round, black lenses and dark, worn robes like the wandering priests in obake stories. Hatsue remarked that the bonsan's glasses were so dark she couldn't see his eyes behind them. He picked up her laundry basket and started hanging the remaining items, mostly sheets, which were large and required a lot of effort.

"He was fast. Five minutes," she told us. She smiled and looked up at us briefly.

She invited the bonsan in for tea. He said his name was Basho.

"Good name," Hatsue Fukuda said she told him. "Lucky name. Like the famous haiku poet."

He smiled and nodded but never removed the dark glasses, not even indoors. He told her he had sensitive eyes and that he might go blind if he did not protect them. She let it go. She trusted him. "He told me his story," she said. It went like this:

I was born in a small farming village near Kumamoto in Kyushu, Japan's large south island. I had a common name when I was born. My family was so poor that they could not afford to keep all of their children. My eldest brother stayed with my parents and my two sisters were adopted by relatives. I was left with a monastery at the age of eight and was given the name of Basho by one of the priests there. My chores were to sweep the stone steps leading up through a bamboo thicket and to wash the floors. I learned to read the sutras and stopped eating animals. When I reached manhood, I embarked on a pilgrimage of sorts, visiting all of the temples of Japan then making my way by boat to Siam and Ceylon, living with the monks there and picking up hidden wisdom in the withering heat and drenching monsoons. On my way back to Japan, I wandered China for a little over a year, where I visited Nanshan Temple at Mount Wutai, the legendary home of Manjusri, the bodhisattva of wisdom. There, I received a "shock" into wisdom, a momentous instant attainment of enlightenment called satori by Zen practitioners. It was at that moment I decided I must seek out a mountain of my own.

I spent the better part of the next decade wandering Japan looking for the mountain of my vision, but never found it. Then, while helping to care for the wretched survivors of the Nagasaki atomic bombing, I was told of a great mountain in the middle of the ocean by a U.S. Army interpreter, a Nisei from Kohala. Mauna Kea, this man told me, is really the highest mountain in the world because its foot is at the floor of the sea. Something stirred in my heart when I was told of this mountain. I knew that this was my Wutai.

Hatsue went on to say that Basho told her that he set sail for Hawaii as soon as he could raise the funds to do so. "He arrived a few weeks before he met me," Hatsue Fukuda said, "while staying at a Hongwanji on Oahu and later with a Japanese family on Maui before landing on the Big Island. He told me he needed okane, money, to build a temple like Nanshan by Mauna Kea. A peaceful place." She continued, "He wanted to share his satori with the world. He wanted to build a place in the middle of the ocean by the tallest mountain in the world."

Basho told Hatsue Fukuda that he was seeking the help of any who were willing to help realize his vision. She gave him fifty dollars and he assured her that she, too, would have her moment of sudden enlightenment on a great mountain as he had.

She never saw or heard from him again. After making inquiries around the Olaa Plantation and in Hilo, she had found that she was not the only Olaa resident to donate to the cause of the Mauna Kea Nanshan and that nobody in Hilo had ever seen anyone resembling this character.

"And you believed him?" I asked.

"Of course. He seemed to know all about the places he's been to and he was serious about building this temple."

"But now you think he was lying."

"I haven't seen him in a long time. I don't know what to think."

"You went to the police, though."

"Yes."

"But not most of the others. There were only two of you who talked to the police. Why?"

"I lost more than anyone. Most gave five or ten dollars. We're not rich folks here."

"Why did you give so much?"

"I guess because it's the first time since my daughters left that somebody helped me with the laundry."

"Expensive help. What about the other lady who made a complaint?"

"Setsuko is a busybody. She gossips and makes trouble. She couldn't wait to go to the police." Hatsue Fukuda said that Basho wasn't at Olaa for more than a couple of days before he disappeared. It made me wonder why Herb even cared about an old lady's cold fifty bucks in a month-old case. Maybe it was because he had no other cases. It was Hilo, after all.

Ellen looked at me and gave me a quick smile as she flashed her eyes down at the notepad on her lap, indicating she had written down all that transpired in our little interview.

After she gave us instructions on how to find Setsuko Yoshioka's "house," we thanked Hatsue Fukuda and stepped out again into the rain.

"Poor woman," said Ellen. We clung to each other under the umbrella as we crossed over to the other side of the village.

"You feel sorry for her?"

"Sure. It sounds like she's had a hard life."

"Life's hard when you're stupid and gullible."

Ellen struck my chest with her open right hand and clicked her tongue.

"That's not nice, Frankie Yoshikawa! What if that was *your* mother who got taken for fifty dollars?"

"Ka-san? Not a chance. It takes more than some pretty fable about how much her cash is needed to make the world a better place for her to part with it. Believe me. I know."

We reached the shack described by Hatsue Fukuda as the one belonging to Setsuko Yoshioka. It looked to be in better repair than the one we had just visited, with an actual front door with a brass knob and a brand-new corrugated tin roof.

A couple of knocks brought a woman to the door. She was in her early sixties but vain enough to dye her hair jet black and make her face up with rouge and lipstick and eyeliner, despite the fact that she wore the drab work clothes of a day laborer. Her hair was tied back and tucked under a red bandana and she had the sparkling, piggy eyes of a woman addicted to other people's business.

"Mrs. Setsuko Yoshioka?" I asked.

"Handsome Boy and Pretty Girl," she giggled.

"Close, but those aren't our real names. I'm Francis Yoshikawa, a Honolulu Police Detective, and this is Miss Ellen Park of the *Honolulu Record*."

"The newspaper?" she asked. Her piggy eyes were aglow with excitement.

"Yes," said Ellen.

"Come in!" Setsuko Yoshioka yelled, apparently delighted to potentially be the next Big Thing sandwiched between ad space for a florist and a mortuary. We removed our shoes and stepped into a gaudily furnished space, complete with a broken grandfather clock and a brace of kokeshi dolls on a tin Coca-Cola tray on a faux-Victorian credenza. We sat down on a mushy sofa in what was both the parlor and dining room of the shack and were brought tea in short order.

"Are you here about the next strike?" she asked. She looked about the room as if checking for hidden eavesdroppers. "I don't have anything to do with it, but I know who does."

"No," I said. It took all my patience not to start yelling. "We want to ask you about a complaint you filed with the Hilo Police against a priest named Basho."

"Oh. *Him*," she said with a knowing grin. Then she launched into an unprompted diatribe about the strange donation-seeking bonsan.

It turned out that she didn't give him any money at all. Her complaint was mostly on behalf of her victimized neighbors. She harassed the police regularly about the status of her complaint, which explained why Herb was eager to conclude this thing. Before she started the first of many anecdotes of how various people were bilked and for how much, I interrupted her.

"Excuse me," I said. "If you didn't give this priest any money, why are you so adamant about making a complaint against him? You can tell me it's out of the goodness of your heart, which I'm not doubting, but even good hearts have a more compelling reason to be so persistent."

"Oh. Well, it's because I know he's a fraud."

Ellen perked up at this pronouncement. She started scrawling again.

"How do you know?" I asked.

She blushed. "Do I have to tell you?"

"We can leave anything . . . embarrassing . . . out of my article," Ellen said.

"Okay," Setsuko said. She didn't even pause long enough to give even a passing impression of shame on her part. "He was staying in an abandoned place near the edge of the village. I didn't trust him, so while he was out talking to some of the folks in the fields, I took a look at his things."

"What did you find?" asked Ellen.

"He had a bill from a Honolulu travel agency for first class passage on a Nippon Yusen Kaisha liner from Honolulu to Yokohama. It was a payment due for two hundred dollars. First Class cabin. Open date."

"Two hundred bucks is steep even for First Class," I told her.

"It was for two people, not one."

"Was there a name on the invoice?"

"No."

I hastily thanked Setsuko Yoshioka and we sped back to Hilo as fast as the Packard could get us there. Harry Kurita, it seems, wasn't satisfied with absconding with the Palolo Group's funds for the Orient. He had to go in style. Hatsue Fukuda's fifty dollars and the other odd contributions probably gave him enough for his First-Class passage to Japan and it would appear that he decided to take the not-so-grieving young widow with him. I thought of how Beverly's bedroom was completely devoid of any trace of Jiro and her strange, calm reaction to the news of his death. Was she in on the plan to do Jiro in? It seemed a lot more likely now. I ran all these thoughts past Ellen on the drive back into Hilo Town. She agreed in grim silence, nodding and frowning.

When we finally pulled up in front of May's Fountain on Kamehameha Avenue, we found Herb waiting for us under the white metal sign with the Coca-Cola logo proclaiming the establishment's name in green letters. He was smoking and staring out at the rain on the bay. I got out of the Packard and ran to the passenger side to open Ellen's door for her, but she had already dashed out to meet Herb on the sidewalk.

"Where have you been?" he asked. "I've got some news you'll want to hear."

"I know who your Buddhist con man is," I said.

"Really? Well, that's great, but let me go first."

"Okay," I said impatiently.

"Your M.E. called back this morning. They've made identification on that jawbone from the Hakalau estuary I told you about last night based on dental records."

"Yeah?"

"It's Harry Kurita. Now, you were saying something about that bonsan?"

29

Square one. A damned familiar place. I chased my tail all the way the hell to Hilo just to find out that Harry ended up feeding the sharks. Maybe this was it. Maybe Harry took Jiro down then flung himself off the red ginger studded cliffs into the ocean in remorse. Maybe he was soft that way, like the Harry at my sister's cocktail party who flinched at my drunken challenge. It was a neat little ending. It would be nice to close the case that way and close the books on a couple of egomaniacs that couldn't live in a world where the other one also lived. In the end they both left it and made it a safer place for humility.

The problem with that ending was that while it might have been happy, it wasn't procedurally clean by a long shot. Harry killing Jiro and taking off to Hilo only to end up dead himself were the facts, but selling it the way I thought it played out to the inquest would take a leap of logic on my part and a leap of faith on the judge's part. Too much was missing. And I could be damned sure that Kierkegaard wouldn't let the matter of Harry and Jiro's associates lie with that kind of an incomplete conclusion. All of the Palolo Cell members would be suspects for questioning. If Harry killed Jiro, then who killed Harry? A shark? Dan Kierkegaard, Commie Hunter, wasn't likely to accept that when he had other anti-American conspirators to root out.

I hardly tasted the hamburger at the little fountain counter or the chocolate malt I shared with Ellen, distracted by thoughts of a burned femur sticking out of a red dirt grave in Kunia and a wet jawbone

washed up onto the pebbles by the brackish water of the Hakalau
estuary.

It wasn't over yet. Basho was the key. The queer little monk was
somehow tied to the whole mess; his presence at the Machida house in
Waialua and on the Big Island after Harry's mysterious disappearance
could not have been coincidence. He had been in my apartment, turning
it upside down for a typewriter ribbon. I had last seen him on Oahu.

I had to go back.

Herb told me that our M.E. told him that he believed Harry
had been dead for about a month. It fit the timetable with his Hilo
disappearance. Did Harry take a plunge into the sea? Was it his idea? If
not, whose? There was probably no shortage of spurned lovers or jealous
husbands left in Harry Kurita's wake, but it seemed like even he hardly
had the time to provoke such strong feelings in Hilo. Herb canvassed
the cabbies and the shop owners and the barkeeps and the old men who
hung around under the banyan trees near the bay. No one saw him.

After lunch, we all headed back to Aunty Sachiko's compound,
and Ellen and I hastily packed our bags. We said our goodbyes to all
who were there, apologizing for the abrupt departure. Herb drove us to
the airfield where I purchased two seats on the next flight to Honolulu.
The rain had relented a little, slackening to a drizzle and creating a vivid
rainbow over the bay. Ellen leaned against me on the wooden bench
in the small waiting area and slipped her hand in mine as we admired
the colors over the water. I was struck by the juxtaposition of where
the case had started for me and where it led me: burned bones in the
hot red earth of Kunia to a water-worn piece of a jaw in the wet of the
windward side of the Big Island. All of the leads and ideas had gone that
way, too—from hot to cold.

Ellen and I didn't talk much on the airplane ride back to Oahu.
We simply held hands and let the drone of the propellers lull us into a
light nap filled more with thoughts than dreams. When we returned to

the dusty parking lot where I had left the Eldorado, we found it caked with a layer of yellow-brown dirt and white coral grit. It wasn't anything I wasn't expecting. There would be time enough to wash it later.

I made a fast detour to the Chun Hoon Market off of Nuuanu Avenue and had Ellen pick what she wanted to prepare for our dinner and a little extra, taking care that she was in her scarf-and-dark-glasses get-up. Then I whisked her back to my apartment in Kaimuki.

"You're all provisioned for the rest of the day," I said. I put the grocery bags down in the kitchen counter. The place was still a mess from Basho's visit.

"What do you mean?" she asked. She had already started tidying up, sweeping up broken plates and glasses from the linoleum with a little broom and dustpan my sister Daisy had once left as a "gift."

"I mean I need you to stay put, right here in this apartment and not go out until I get back tonight. Don't open the door for anybody. I mean it, darling."

"You can't be serious, Frankie Yoshikawa."

"I am. I have to be, with Kierkegaard on the island. I will be back as soon as I can."

"Where are you going?"

"To find the bonsan."

"I'm coming with you."

"No."

"What about all the things we talked about? What about the things people do when they care for each other?"

"That's exactly what this is, darling," I told her. I gave her a quick kiss and snapped the brim of my porkpie hat down. "I need to finish this so I can have you free and clear of any worry that you'll end up in a little jail cell like Koji Ariyoshi and Jack Hall and the rest of them. I can't have you along for the ride this time. If I were thinking, I should have left you in Hilo with Herb and Penny and Aunty Sachiko. It won't be long. It *can't* be long. I promise. So please, darling. Please do what people do when they care for each other and trust me."

Ellen kissed me one more time and said, "Okay."

My telephone rang. I picked up the receiver. It was my sister Iris.

"The HUAC has been asking questions here at Kaimuki High," she said.

"A man named Kierkegaard?"

"Yes—how did you know?"

"Long story. Did he talk to you?"

"No, he's mostly interested in the Social Studies and English Departments. One of the teachers might have been arrested yesterday."

"Is this finally enough to make you lay low?"

"Let's get this over with. Say it."

"I told you so. Now will you please keep your head down?"

"Okay."

"Good. It's especially important that you do it immediately."

Jesus. High school teachers. Kierkegaard really did have nothing better to do. It wasn't just labor organizers any more. Now the HUAC was chasing high school teachers. First John Reinecke at Farrington, now my sister's colleagues at Kaimuki. Hairdressers and shoeshine boys would be next.

"Iris?" asked Ellen.

"Yes. I told her to do the same thing I'm asking you to do right now."

I left Gid's home phone number with Ellen and told her that I would call her if I ran into complications.

"So, you have a plan, Detective?"

"I do."

I didn't. I shut the door behind me with one more warning to her not to open it for anybody and got back into the Eldorado. Dusk and cold nausea descended on my stomach with the knowledge that I only had one more "vacation" day to figure everything out. I pulled out onto Waialae Avenue from 10th and lit up a Lucky Strike. I headed ewa out toward Waialua, the only place I could think of to start my search for Basho. I blew through a couple of red lights on Waialae, painfully aware that the sinking sun meant the passage of precious time. I wouldn't sell the ones I loved to the HUAC again. The last time I did it cost me my soul and I'd been trying to fill the void where it had been with whiskey and denial ever since.

Pier 88 on the Hudson River, January 1948. I stood at the foot of the gangway of an economy liner bound for England with Ira Levinsky and two large men in heavy tweed coats, U.S. Marshals or Deportation Officers or some such employees of the federal government. Ira had been raked over the coals before a "special committee hearing" in Washington a few months earlier and spent the remainder of his days on American soil in a federal prison awaiting his fate. He and his daughter were to be deported, it was finally decided, the two of them never naturalized. Rachel was mercifully allowed to stay in the dorms and finish up her course of study at Barnard. The weeks of leading up to that day were tortuous and awkward, the two of us avoiding eye contact when we saw each other on campus. Breakups are always uncomfortable, but no more so than when betrayal is at the heart of it. I was responsible for ruining her life.

Ira and I stood there looking at each other while the tweed coats stood there looking at both of us. I was the only one of the Levinskyites who showed up to see him off for the last time, although, I had learned, I wasn't the only one to sign the poisonous statement that helped to secure his one-way passage out of the country. Every single one of the others signed. I knew because all of them were still in school.

Rachel was already aboard. I had waited until I saw her ascend the gangway and disappear into the crowd on the deck before I emerged from my hiding place.

Ira smiled warmly when he saw me approach. It made me feel like someone had grabbed a fistful of my entrails from within and gave them a violent twist. I managed a weak grin in response.

"Frankie. Thank you for coming."

"You shouldn't thank me for anything, Ira. I'm responsible for this."

"Nonsense. I saw the statements that you and the others signed. They were all the same, prefabricated form. Yours was one of dozens."

"Still . . . if only I had the guts . . ."

"To what, Frankie? Throw your life away? Knock down everything you built with your supreme sacrifice? Everything you built for yourself, for your family, for all those like you? No, I couldn't ask you to do such a thing. I alone made my choice to follow my conscience in a time and place where doing so meant ruin. It isn't the first time in my life I've done this, and it won't be the last."

"But it's wrong. What's happening to you is unjust. And I became a part of that process. I'm sorry, Ira. I'm so very, very sorry."

"You didn't have a choice. I understand this. As for injustice, the world has always been an unjust place and it will always be an unjust place. It will *never* be just. What it should be, though, is consistent. That's the most we can strive for, Frankie. Consistency. In a way, I suppose you could say that's what's happening to me. Unjust though it may be, it *is* consistent. Small minds will never cease to inflict their ignorance on others. The predictability of it all gives me some small measure of comfort." He smiled and chuckled a little. I was falling to pieces inside.

"I appreciate you trying to make me feel better, but I don't. I never will."

"Never is a long time. It took the best the Round Table had to offer a long time to find the Holy Grail. I have no doubt that you'll find yours before the end of never. Of all the young minds I set on that quest, you are most likely to succeed. You are my Percivale, Frankie. I want you to promise me that when you finally find your grail, you will grasp it and drink deeply all the peace it contains."

"Sure. Thanks. Will you please tell Rachel that I'm sorry? I never got the chance."

"As I told you, you have nothing to apologize for—not to me and not to Rachel. She is upset but she's young. She will understand, someday."

I heard it before.

"You do because you have to. Wakarimasuka?"

"No."

"You will. One day."

The frigid wind picked up and blew right through our coats and scarves and sent the gangway rolling up and down like a violin bow. Some of the loose snow on the cleats flew up and scattered into the river. One of the tweed coats, tired of standing around in the cold, raised his wrist to make a pointed glance at his watch. Ira caught the hint and nodded.

"It's time for me to go."

"I guess so."

Ira threw his arms around me and embraced me tightly. I hugged him back, burying my face in his cashmere scarf.

"Goodbye, Frankie. Keep hitting them out of the park."

"Aloha, Ira."

I never saw Ira or Rachel again. Ira forgave me. It didn't change the way I felt about what I had done. It only made it worse. And I don't know if Rachel ever forgave me. I would probably never know. I tried to atone for ruining their lives by seeking a career in public service, by protecting and serving, by defending those who could not defend themselves as Art Kawamura had implored me to when he turned over his precious book before going down. I failed to defend the Levinskys. I betrayed them. I couldn't go back and do things over, but I could set the record straight for myself. Ira and Rachel were gone. Ellen and Iris were here. The same man was after them. I wouldn't let him unhorse me this time.

30

I made a quick stop in town at a jeweler to put in a rush order for a special package then made three calls from a pay telephone on Nuuanu Avenue. I first called the Territorial Insurance and Indemnity, and was lucky enough to have an underwriter staying late to finish a policy pick up on his end. He helped me out without complaint. I made my second call to the travel agency that Basho had made his arrangements with for the NYK liner; an irate secretary on her way out fed me the information I asked for. I then called Gid Hanohano. I told him that I was back on the island and that I'd be wrapping things up on the Jiro Machida matter and that he would get all of the details in the morning. Gid just grunted softly and told me that my timing was perfect because the inquest had been set for the following afternoon.

Then it was off to Waialua. The sky was a fierce orange, as if the entire ewa side of the island was set ablaze in one big cane fire. As I drove into that fire, it slowly cooled at the edges into a melancholy gray-violet, time and death inevitably touching the day as it did all things. I moved the Eldorado with its top down at a pretty good clip up Kamehameha Highway through the cane and pineapple fields past Wahiawa on my way up to the North Shore, when I saw the headlamps of an approaching vehicle in the oncoming lane. Cars headed into town at that hour scarce, I luckily took an idle glance at it as we passed each other.

It was hard to tell the color in the waning daylight, but it was probably something dull and neutral like gray. It was an older model

Ford and I just caught the bald pate of the driver in the corner of my eye. I slackened the pressure on the gas, then hung a U-turn on the highway and followed. Fortunately, my reaction time after realizing who it was that just passed me had put a little distance and a hill between us, concealing my U-turn in his rearview mirror. Basho was no doubt coming from the Machida house. The sun was completely gone by the time we passed Schofield Barracks and all I was to him was a couple of headlamps in the night. He continued to drive toward the lights of Pearl Harbor in the distance.

I stuck close enough to him so that I never lost the red tail lamps that led me makai. I presumed that he was headed into town, but he continued straight into Waipahu. He drove past the ditch where I had been dumped the other night after being drugged by Beverly Machida and I wondered if the location had been a coincidence. It made me think of Beverly again and wonder what had become of her. The Ford led me straight onto Oahu Sugar property. After meandering about on the roads of the Oahu Sugar Plantation, the Ford came to rest, not surprisingly, in front of the grand new edifice of the Waipahu Hongwanji. I pulled over across the street from the temple grounds about half a block's distance away. I found a little pay telephone outside a nearby sundry and liquor place and used my remaining pocket silver to place a call to my cousin Herb in Hilo. When he had confirmed my already building hunch, I thanked him and told him I would see him again soon and hung up. Then I crossed the street and headed for the Hongwanji.

The Waipahu Hongwanji was a place I was very familiar with. When To-san first came over from Japan, he went to work for Oahu Sugar in the cane fields of the Waipahu Plantation, living in squalor with other young men in the camp. After being in the fields for nearly two years, he sent for a picture bride, a girl from his Hiroshima-ken town, whose mother was an acquaintance of his mother. Ka-san arrived a few months later on a boat with a bunch of other picture brides. My parents were set up in their own "house" by the company—a shack with thin walls and a water pump outside shared with another shack containing another Japanese newlywed couple. Ka-san went to work alongside the other new Japanese brides in the fields, besides doing her housework early in the morning and later at night. To-san worked much longer hours in the fields and then helped out in the plantation mechanic's shop in the evening. How they found the time to produce my sister Violet a year later is beyond me.

All of us were born at Oahu Sugar. Daisy, Iris, Pansy, and I followed Violet, each of us two years apart. We attended funerals for all relations from Hiroshima and hanai uncles and aunties at the old Hongwanji, a wooden firetrap with red dirt dust on the pews. The smell of the senko that permeated the place always made me want to take a shower and change my clothes after every funeral. It was the scent of death.

There I was, standing on the old temple grounds again, but this time I was looking at a different building. The new temple was about a year old. It was an impressive edifice done in concrete and glass block with Doric columns supporting the portico flanked by a tower on either side of the stairs resembling modern pagodas. It was a slick looking building, but I was willing to bet that the inside still reeked of the smell-of-death senko I disliked so intensely. The grand temple was illuminated within, soft light emanating from the windows, like the Buddha himself. I ascended the steps and entered.

An old bonsan was moving flowers in tall brass vases from one side of the altar to the other. He stopped after placing the vase down to rearrange the red torch ginger and bird-of-paradise stems so that they would flare out at the top in a brilliant display. I waited for him to finish with his arrangement before I spoke up, bowing politely. I asked him where I could find Basho, and he smiled kindly and toothlessly, and explained that Basho was visiting from Japan and that he was the only current occupant of the dormitory rooms the Hongwanji kept in an annex for visiting priests. The annex was outside the main temple to the rear. The old bonsan told me that Basho had been staying at the Hongwanji for about three weeks and that he had been very helpful with the upkeep of the temple grounds, especially with the gardening tasks.

I thanked the bonsan, complimented him on his flower arrangement and walked down the aisle and out of the front door. I stood for a moment under the portico and looked at the Ford parked in front of the temple. Just out of curiosity, I descended the stairs to the vehicle and opened the passenger door. It wasn't locked. I checked the registration and found that the vehicle belonged to the Hongwanji. I guess a visiting priest is accorded every courtesy, including a chariot.

I made my way from the front of the temple to the rear and saw the annex the old bonsan had told me about. The building was a long wooden structure, of the same kind the old temple had been. Probably as old. I recalled running up and down the long lanai as a small child after the funeral services concluded and refreshments were served out on the lawn between the two buildings. All of the windows were dark save for one at the very end. I walked across the lawn and stood on tiptoes next to the pikake bushes under the window to see inside.

Basho sat on a small cot with his dark glasses off, head down in a book. The sparse room contained only the cot, a small chest of drawers, a table with a mirror and basin and pitcher, and a pine wardrobe. Nobody else was in the small room.

I moved quietly to the steps leading up to the long lanai and ascended them as quietly as I could. When I stood before the door to the room I took a deep breath, inhaling the scent of the sweet pikake and the metallic tang of the red dirt and the burnt sugar in the Waipahu night air. It took me back to my childhood, to the time before my folks packed us up and moved us out to Kakaako for a better life in the city. I couldn't have been more than four years old when that happened, but I remembered the smell of the place more vividly than I remembered the sights. The smells all very exact, I could identify each one in a mixture of them all. The visual memories of the place, on the other hand, were much vaguer, faded at the edges like old photographs in varying grades of brownish gray and yellow-white. In fact, the only color I could recall at all was the rusty hue of the red dirt that was everywhere. It was in the fields and on the buildings and on your clothes and in the air. There was no getting away from it. Like the truth.

I knocked at the door. Soft footsteps padded up from behind it and the old brass knob turned. The door swung outward slowly and the spot where I stood on the lanai was flooded with a yellow light.

Basho had donned his dark glasses again. He looked up at me and smiled, revealing the sturdy teeth I had seen a few days before, framed by the strange, wispy goatee.

"Yes, can I help you?" he said in slow, deliberate Japanese-accented English.

I said: "Hello, Jiro."

31

The bonsan removed his dark glasses and Jiro Machida, minus his hair and plus a long sparse goatee, smiled at me.

"Detective Sergeant Francis Yoshikawa," he said. "You're a lot smarter than you look."

"And you're almost as smart as you think you are."

"Almost?"

"Almost."

"Why don't you tell me about it? Won't you come in?"

"Don't mind if I do. Forgive me for not removing my shoes, though. I'm in a hurry."

"As you wish."

Jiro Machida swung the door wide open and padded back into the small dormitory room. He took a seat on the cot and looked up at me, still with a smirk on his face, his eyes impudently alight with amusement. It was the look of all men who thought they were intellectually superior to their company, which for Jiro was the entire world.

"So, Detective, what led you to me?"

I pulled out my pack of Lucky Strikes and stuck one in my face.

"Cigarette?" I said.

"Why not?"

I held the pack out to him, and he removed a cigarette and put it in his mouth. I pulled out the Zippo and lit us both up. I looked at the strange picture of a Buddhist priest with a cigarette between his lips. It was as strange as the last few days had been.

"We found the bones out in Kunia. You couldn't know when this would happen, but you probably guessed, and correctly so, that it wouldn't happen before you had enough time to lay out the rest of your deception. You killed Harry Kurita and dismembered his corpse and burned it, then buried it out in the middle of the cane field. You kept his head, though, so there wouldn't be any dental records to identify. And you needed it for later. You dropped your dog tags into the fire so that we'd think it was you—and we did, for a while."

Jiro sat and nodded and smoked, looking thoughtful and a little amused, which annoyed me but I didn't show it. I smiled back.

"Interesting," he said.

"You broke into Harry's apartment and packed a bag rather hastily. I examined that bag when I recovered it from the master of the *Iwakuni Maru*. Harry was a meticulous character and even in a rush, he would not have crammed his prized wardrobe into a suitcase the way it was. Furthermore, you left the critical clue in the trash as to which vessel he supposedly took. It was blatant and somewhat transparent, but I bit at first and didn't have a choice anyway because there weren't any other leads as to his 'escape.' After I searched Harry's apartment, I visited your wife to break the news of your demise to her. I ran into you out there for the first time in your Buddhist get-up. I have to say, she's an interesting lady. She took the bad news with astonishing calm. But the best part of my house call was finding the ribbon in your typewriter, which you ransacked my apartment to recover. I took the precaution of mailing the thing to myself at the station in anticipation."

"Brilliant," said Jiro.

"Thanks, but you still made a hell of a mess of my place. I guess I couldn't have stopped *that*. You did leave a calling card, though, and this one, I imagine, wasn't intentional. A real bonsan wouldn't drop his juzu, not even if he were ransacking someone's apartment."

"I suppose not," Jiro conceded.

"You boarded the *Iwakuni Maru* dressed in Harry's clothes with your hair done like his and you wore his glasses. The two of you are about the same size and I don't imagine the captain of a fishing boat who took cash under the table for your passage cared very much about checking Harry's passport. You fed him some line about going to China to see Mao and you knew that the vessel would be calling on Hilo before heading out to Japan, which is precisely why you chose it. The master, however, told me that Harry's Japanese was flawless, when he was known to be disdainful of—and not very proficient in—all other languages but English. When the *Iwakuni Maru* arrived in Hilo, you disembarked with the remains of Harry's head in a valise. You placed the jawbone at the Hakalau Estuary knowing kids go there regularly to swim and it would be found and probably attributed to a shark attack. The dental records would be matched to Harry Kurita, then a neat little story about Harry killing you and then meeting up with some gruesome fate on the Big Island en route to the Orient would emerge to give you the happy ending you anticipated."

"It sounds like a brilliant plan."

"Indeed."

"Why did I do it?"

"This is my favorite part. It's full of irony and it's what tripped you up. As soon as you were able to place Harry's jaw for discovery, you changed into your bonsan persona. You stuck around to raise money for your real passage out of town, a luxury trip on a Nippon Yusen Kaisha liner to Japan. You went to a place you were familiar with, the plantation village you grew up in and organized strikes for—Olaa. I somehow knew it was too close for coincidence. A cousin of mine in the Hilo Police just confirmed for me that the abandoned residence you stayed in while there was the old Machida place. Old habits die hard, even for a big brain like you. You knew the people of Olaa pretty damned well and knew they'd give a little here and there and you could raise enough to get you to Japan in style. What you didn't really count on was that old Setsuko Yoshioka would do some snooping of her own and stir up some attention over your fundraising efforts."

"That Setsuko," Jiro said. He smiled and shook his head. "Always a busybody. But you still haven't told me why I did all this."

"Sorry, I didn't know you were pressed for time."

"I thought you said you were."

"Yeah. But call this a courtesy before I take you in."

"Sure. Proceed, Detective."

"You and Harry never really got along. Oh, what the hell, you hated each other's guts. The matter of one-upmanship between the two of you was so intense and spectacularly annoying that it probably threatened to undo all of the hard work the Palolo Group of the Hawaii Communist Party had accomplished for all us little folks. You competed for everything, including Beatrice Walker Crane's two grand, which she turned over to The Group. And this is what makes me want to shed a tear for the sorry world we live in, Jiro: you killed Harry and set it up so it looked like he killed you for money. You, the esteemed ideologue of the Hawaii CP and champion of the working stiff, sold out and killed a man over money."

Jiro threw back his head and laughed. "Listen to yourself, Detective! That's absolutely ludicrous! You want me to believe that I killed a pathetic soul like Harry Kurita for two thousand dollars? If I don't believe it, how are you going to get a jury to believe it?"

"It wasn't the two thousand itself. It's what you did with it. After you stole the money from Wilde's place, you went to Territorial Insurance and Indemnity and set up a single premium life insurance policy with Beverly Machida as the beneficiary. The policy was to pay out twenty thousand upon your death, but there was an obscure clause that put the payout at five times that much if you were to meet your end by means of foul play. Two grand parlayed into a hundred grand in one, single neat shot. I thought when I had the ribbon transcribed that I was looking at an application for the policy. I just found out today that it was a claim form you were filling out. And it was in your typewriter before I had broken the news to your 'widow' that you were dead. Harry knew you had taken the money from Wilde and confronted you about it at the *Record*. That's when you set your plan in motion. You got rid of the one person who was on to you and used him to set up your fake death. You didn't kill Harry out of your burning hatred for him or your oh-so-important rivalry. You killed him for a big fat payday."

Jiro wasn't smiling any more. He sat on the edge of the cot looking at his feet. The smoke from our cigarettes curled in the still, warm air of the little dorm room and would have been heard clearly if it could make a sound.

"That's impressive, Detective," he said after a while. "Very impressive. You almost got the whole thing right."

"Almost?"

"Almost."

"What did I miss?"

"I didn't kill Harry."

"No?"

"No. Do we have time for a story?"

"Why not?"

Jiro told me a story.

32

Jiro's story, as he told it in that stifling little temple dorm room in Waipahu, started with the birth of a baby girl twenty-three years earlier in a shack on land belonging to the Haleakala Pineapple Company on Maui.

This is what he told me: "A young fifteen-year-old girl, Yoshiko Izawa, the daughter of a pair of Japanese laborers from Olaa Plantation on the Big Island, gave birth to a baby girl, whereupon she died of complications; the midwife, who usually served the Japanese community at Haleakala Pineapple, had gone to Oahu visit a relative. The young woman who had taken her place had only once assisted with the delivery of a child, and before that, all she had done was boil water and fetch things for the real midwife. The baby survived, but Yoshiko bled to death.

"It was probably for the better. Her parents had concocted the elaborate plan to send Yoshiko to stay with relatives working for Haleakala Pineapple, accompanied by her mother. Yoshiko would stay confined there until she gave birth, and her mother would return to Olaa claiming the baby was her own. Their pretext for disappearing from Olaa was that they were both needed to help care for an ailing relation on another island. Yoshiko's unfortunate death was attributed to an accident, and her mother returned with the baby as her own: a daughter lost, a daughter gained.

"Nobody knew who the baby's father was. Yoshiko Izawa was my secret and one true love. We met each other secretly and nobody knew of our relationship, so clever the concealment of our feelings for each other, for I was revered by the entire village community as a bright, promising, and morally upright young man. I would be the first to go to law school. Nobody had any idea that I was having sex regularly with the then-fourteen-year-old Yoshiko Izawa late at night in the cane fields. I myself was only seventeen.

"I was sent to Russia to study at Sun Yat Sen University by the fledgling labor organizers at Olaa. I departed before Yoshiko learned of the pregnancy. She never told me of it, and never told anyone, not even her parents, that I was the father. She took that secret to the grave. I was confused and concerned when I stopped receiving correspondence from Yoshiko after the first two letters. I stayed in Russia, though, and completed my studies and returned to Olaa three years later. When I learned Yoshiko had died, I was heartbroken and depressed and made discreet inquiries as to the circumstances surrounding her passing. As our relationship was a secret, I could not ask too directly, and found Yoshiko's parents to be unusually tight-lipped about it. They had their hands full raising a young girl, Yoshiko's *little sister* whom she never knew."

Jiro said he knew Yoshiko died on Maui. "I went to Haleakala Pineapple and made more inquiries. I discovered there that Yoshiko died just before her mother 'gave birth' and was able to conclude that it was Yoshiko, in fact, who had given birth to the girl, and not her mother, and that Yoshiko had expired in the process. I concluded that I was the father of that child. I was strangely free of any obligation because there was no one who could tie me to the child, but, of course, I was overcome with guilt."

He told me, teary-eyed, that he loved Yoshiko more deeply than he would ever love anyone else and he blamed himself for her passing. He returned to Olaa. He would turn up at the Izawa's cottage and offer to help out, chopping kiawe logs for firewood or using his own money to buy things for the girl. The Izawas, who had no clue that Jiro was their late daughter's secret lover and the father of their secret grandchild, thought that he was some heaven-sent hero. They welcomed and in fact became dependent upon his presence and the help he provided for the little girl. Jiro said if the Izawas suspected that he was the child's father, they never gave any indication that they did.

According to Jiro, they named the girl Beverly and at a very early age she began to do extraordinary things. She was talking in near complete sentences at around her first birthday. She was reading both Japanese and English by the time she was three years old and, by the time she was five, she could read music and had taught herself to play the piano in the luna's house where her grandmother worked. At the little plantation school, she far exceeded the performance of the other children, outdoing even Jiro, her father, when he was a pupil. Beverly was something of a rare genius and even the plantation lunas and haole managers had taken notice.

As a young child, Beverly was shy and introverted and preferred books to the company of other children. Her odd demeanor sometimes made her the target of bullies and the butt of jokes of other children but she never reacted emotionally to the teasing. She excelled in the classroom but remained undeveloped socially. Attempts by her grandparents to have her interact with other children were largely unsuccessful; Beverly would end up wandering away from company and secluding herself.

"My plan was to build a reputation and some small amount of financial security so that I could take care of Beverly," Jiro said. "However, when I reached the point in my life I was able to do this, I found that I couldn't. If I suddenly came out and told the world that I was Beverly Izawa's father, the scandal would ruin my reputation as an up-and-coming young organizer and veteran. It would, in effect, ironically render my ability to care for her impossible.

"And you should have seen Beverly blossom. She had become beautiful and physically desirable as well as intelligent. She learned to communicate more proficiently with her peers, though she was generally viewed by them as something of an eccentric. Where her interactions became much more active was with boys and she had no lack of willing sex partners. Almost all of the encounters, however, ended up in the physical wounding, albeit minor, of either Beverly or the unwitting boy. Much of Beverly's ability to enjoy sex was coupled with an almost aesthetic need to include the infliction of pain or the suggestion of death intertwined with the act associated with the creation of life. While I learned of this behavior later, when Beverly confessed it all to me in a fit of rebellion, none of this ever came to the attention of anyone, perhaps because the injuries caused were too minor, and perhaps because the boys who participated with her were too embarrassed to tell anyone.

"Only one unusual incident came to the surface but was successfully suppressed by the Izawas: an unfortunate Olaa schoolboy ended up with a broken collarbone when she impulsively insisted they couple "hands free" in a moving vehicle on a dirt road. Though the incident was kept hushed, word got around among boys that Beverly was "strange" and she was to be avoided despite her physical attractiveness. In spite of her unusual sexual games, Beverly was generally well-regarded by her teachers and adults and treated by her peers with indifference."

Jiro said that Beverly eventually matriculated at the University of Hawaii on Oahu. He kept tabs on her as he, too, was on Oahu as a labor organizer and reporter for the *Honolulu Record*. He looked after Beverly as her "Uncle Jiro" and provided some financial support as well as using whatever influence and goodwill he managed to build to help her establish herself.

Then again, the dilemma of how to legally be responsible for Beverly without revealing the true nature of their relationship came up.

Jiro, not to be so easily defeated, thought his quandary through and came up with a solution. There was a way, he said, that he could make himself Beverly's legal guardian without having to reveal to the world that he was her father. Because nobody knew who Beverly's father was but him, he could marry her. The beleaguered Izawas were more than happy to agree to the arrangement. Taking up the cause of the girl by becoming legally responsible for her also had the effect of enhancing his reputation further as a saint among the Olaa workers. Jiro Machida was magnanimous as well as intellectually gifted, and it was easy for all of the laborers to follow him into whatever strike he had planned for the future.

"I then explained my plan to Beverly and confessed that I was actually her father. Beverly, in a detached fashion, agreed to go along with the plan. She had always felt some genuine affection for me and this affection only became stronger when she found out that she was my daughter. I swore her to secrecy and she never broke that trust. I set her up in a house in Waialua, and I continued to live in whatever plantation housing I could find while organizing strikes on the various islands. When I returned to Waialua, I slept on the sofa in the parlor."

Jiro set some ground rules for behavior with Beverly. They were legally husband and wife but in fact they were father and daughter and the marriage was only set up so that he could be legally and financially responsible for her. While they had to put up a public façade of being a married couple, Jiro told her it would probably be natural for her to want male companionship on her own and he would not stop her so long as her liaisons were discreet and did not include anything that would get her into trouble. Eventually, when Jiro felt she could be trusted to control herself, he would divorce her and let her seek her happiness with someone of her choice. Beverly agreed, and for a time, everything worked out.

Then came Harry.

"Beverly and Harry met at a Palolo Group function where Beverly had shown up as my 'wife.' The attraction was intense and immediate. This was all to my chagrin. I not only detested Harry but had known of his sexual appetite. I knew this was a recipe for disaster," Jiro said. "The urgency of trying to keep the two of them apart only resulted in the deepening of my rivalry with Harry and Beverly's growing resentment of me. The more I forbade her to see him, the more defiant she became. She was a classic rebellious child but much more extremely so than most, owing to her intelligence.

"Harry, always in search of the newest thrill, found it with Beverly. The 'games' they played during their encounters excited him so much more than sleeping with the naïve coeds he seduced. Both he and Beverly were of a like mind and personality when it came to heightening their pleasure. They were always pushing the boundaries with their sex. They started out playacting, one of them being a corpse and the other its violator. Then they started giving each other small cuts and burns during the act. I knew because Beverly would tell me what she had been doing, in defiance, whenever I scolded her for seeing Harry.

"I became scared and desperate. Beverly was out of control. It was now to the point where other members of the Palolo Group saw it and started gossiping. I frantically searched for ways I could help her and protect her from herself. All I ever wanted was for Beverly to live in peace, free from the gossip of a small place like Hawaii, and free from the distraction of men like Harry Kurita. Then one day, I found a way. Land was cheap and plentiful in Japan, but getting more expensive as the nation's postwar recovery was accelerating. I found a few acres at the foot of Mount Hiei, near the Enryaku-ji Temple. I felt this was the place for Beverly. I would acquire the land and I would relocate with Beverly there."

The problem with the land was that it was becoming more expensive by the week. This made him commit the theft of the Crane donation from Marion Wilde's place. Two thousand wasn't nearly enough to cover the expenses but it would help. The theft had consequences in the Palolo Group and Harry rightly accused Jiro of taking the money, though he could never know the real reason behind the theft.

Then disaster struck.

Jiro came "home" to Waialua to find Beverly sitting on the lanai drinking scotch straight out of the decanter, giggling and staring vacantly at the sky. Something bad had happened. Jiro ran into the house and searched about. In Beverly's bedroom, he found Harry Kurita stark naked on her bed, staring at the ceiling with a cotton yukata belt around his neck. Dead. Harry and Beverly's latest thrill was asphyxiating each other and this time they went too far. In her drunken state, Beverly babbled about Harry demanding that she pull the belt tighter and tighter. Jiro's legs gave out from under him and he sat on the floor of Beverly's bedroom despairing. Everything he worked for was ruined. There was no way to fix this. He despaired some more.

"Looking at Harry's corpse, naked and grotesque, lying on the bed, I realized in a big way that Harry and I were about the same size," Jiro said. The plan formed with lightning rapidity in his head. There was a way to fix this, and a way to make his designs for Beverly and Japan come to fruition in the bargain. He got up, collected Beverly, sat her down in the parlor and explained everything to her. She nodded slightly, showing that she understood.

"I worked quickly, moving Harry's body into the furo house in the back and dismembering it and washing all of the blood down the drain. I took the parts out to the beach and burned them near the water; any passers-by on the road would think it a bonfire. I packed the burnt parts except for the head in a large rice bag and headed to the cane fields of Kunia in the middle of the night. I arranged the dog tags, which I had burned previously, around the neck bones and buried the mess. I returned to Waialua, broke up Harry's head, and saved the jaw parts with teeth, disposing of the rest of it in a pig pen at an Okinawan-owned farm in Haleiwa, where the hogs took care of it."

From there everything went as I had figured out. Jiro broke into Harry's apartment, arranged his passage on the *Iwakuni Maru*, and took out the single premium life policy at TI&I. He typed up the claim form and told Beverly not to file it until she received official word of his death. Then he got into Harry's clothes and disappeared. Beverly, on his instructions, waited for two days before filing the missing persons report. In the meantime, Jiro was already at Olaa in the guise of Basho raising funds for their one-way trip to Japan.

Jiro looked about twenty years older after finishing his story. His last cigarette was out and he sat hunched at the edge of the cot like an overripe mango about to fall to the ground to commence rotting.

I asked him why he went through all the trouble for an out-of-control girl who was only going to be more of a problem for him when he clearly could have let her fall to ruin and never have been associated with her. Was it just out of guilt? He replied that he considered Yoshiko Izawa to be his one true love; there were others he had dallied with after her—Beatrice Walker Crane and Ellen among them—but none of them would ever be what Yoshiko was to him. Nobody would be. So, if not out of guilt, then he did all he did out of love?

"No," Jiro replied.

"Then why?" I asked.

He said just one word: "Giri."

Perhaps at last I was really beginning to understand and my moment of enlightenment on the matter came from the unlikeliest of all teachers.

"Where's Beverly now?" I asked.

"At home, in Waialua, where I just left her."

"She's alive?"

"Of course," he said, puzzled. Then a look of understanding came across his face and he smiled distantly. "Oh. The night she drove you away from Pearl City Tavern. It was one of her games. She took a liking to you and you were just another playmate. I'm in the habit of keeping an eye on her when I can these days, so that what happened with Harry doesn't happen again with anyone else. I pulled you out of her car when I felt the game had gone far enough and had her go home."

"She wasn't there the next morning."

"No, she wasn't. She was in town, filing her claim form at TI&I."

The timing for this was perfect. She had received news of Jiro's "death" from me the day before.

"Oh," I said. My cigarettes, after several and sharing my pack with Jiro, also ran out and so had our time. "It's time to go, Jiro. The way I see it, you'll have to answer for obstructing justice, insurance fraud, and bilking the good people of Olaa for your voyage expenses, but right now I need to get Beverly and bring her in for what happened to Harry. Who knows? Maybe she'll prevail again and they'll rule his death accidental."

"I understand," he said, resigned. "All this has been my mistake. Will you do me a favor, Detective, and just give me a second to get something for you to give to Beverly? It's a sutra she had grown fond of and I'd like to think I can at least provide her with the small comfort that comes with reading it."

"Sure," I said.

He got up and I turned toward the door to wait for him.

That was *my* mistake.

33

I saw the white silk cord pass over my face in a split second then felt it instantly burn the skin around my throat as it tightened violently. Jiro had unbelted it from around his waist when my back was turned. He was smaller than me but incredibly strong for his size and frame and he pulled with the desperation of a man with nothing to lose.

I took a constricted breath and held it; I didn't know when or if another opportunity to breathe would come again. I grasped at the cord around my neck in a futile effort to work my fingers under and somehow loosen it.

"I'm sorry, Detective," said Jiro. His breath barely betrayed the monstrous physical effort he was putting into strangling me. "I can't let you end this. Not when I'm so close."

I tried to respond with something suitably sarcastic but all that came out was a scratchy gag. I silently berated myself for not being able to resist the impulse to verbally come back—not only had I not been able to do it, I also lost some precious air in the attempt. I took a step back into him and lowered my hips, remembering the judo I learned as a kid at the old dojo in Kakaako. I was preparing to throw him over my shoulder and hopefully get him to loosen his grip on the cord. Unfortunately, Jiro was also versed in the "gentle way" and countered by throwing his body out to the side while maintaining his fierce hold.

Little white stars danced in my peripheral vision and I became lightheaded. In my head I laughed at the irony that my life began on

Oahu Sugar property in Waipahu and could very well end there. I'd be another pile of charred bones in a shallow red dirt grave, waiting for the next harvest fire to sweep over my pathetic remains. Jiro was fighting to deprive me of my life out of his sense of obligation to make things right for Beverly. His giri.

I had mine, too.

If I were to go, life would go on for those I left behind, but probably in a shittier fashion than if I stuck around to try to make things right. Ellen and Iris would eventually end up like Ira and Rachel Levinsky, raked over the coals by an inquisitor like Kierkegaard, and all because I was careless enough to leave unfinished business behind.

I couldn't do that. I had to close the case. But I couldn't do it with a silk cord around my neck, squeezing the life out of me.

Then I stopped thinking and had a moment of clarity. Jiro's hands were occupied but both of mine were free. I couldn't reach him with my hands as I had been trying to do, but I could reach something else.

I plunged my right hand under my left arm and pulled my .38 out of its holster. My strength was fading quickly along with my life, so the effort to raise it to head level was much greater than it normally would have been. Jiro couldn't stop me, though. He either had to let go of the cord or take his chances that I wouldn't be able to do what I wanted to do with the gun because I'd go unconscious or die before I had the chance.

He gambled on the latter, continuing to squeeze. With everything I had left, I thrust the .38 upward in one fierce push. It weighed a ton. I pointed it behind me, used the last of my strength to squeeze the trigger and let a prayer loose from the muzzle.

A world-ending roar tore through the Waipahu night and blackness closed in on me, mottled with strange green spots rimmed in red and yellow, like Christmas tree ornaments bobbing about in a vat of crude oil. Then the spots disappeared and there was only blackness, deep and endless.

Was this death? Where was the barge filled with black-clad women and queens to bear me away to Avalon? Maybe it was a privilege reserved for kings like Arthur. Maybe my barge would be a red Cadillac Eldorado ragtop filled with Ka-san, Ellen, and my four sisters yammering about how I should have been more careful and how I never think or plan ahead or help out around the house when I should.

I became aware of a glow and slowly the glow came into focus. Was it heaven or hell? A quick accounting of my life told me it could be either. The glow was a halo around the head of a benevolent and wise countenance—a face that was the embodiment of enlightenment and inner peace. It was a bodhisattva. I guess the Buddhists were right after all.

The bodhisattva spoke: "What happened here?"

"What?" I asked.

"What happened here?"

I looked again. The countenance of benevolence and wisdom was missing teeth. It was the face of the bonsan in the big, new temple, and his halo was the frosted light fixture on the ceiling of the dormitory room—Jiro's dormitory room. I wasn't dead. I probably wasn't even out for very long.

I raised my head. It pounded like the surf. I sat up with some effort. The bonsan helped me.

"Where is he?" I asked.

"Who?"

"Jiro Mach . . . I mean Basho."

The bonsan's eyes moved to a place to my left. Jiro lay on the floor on his side in a pool of crimson. The blood stained the cot and the wall behind him. The bonsan closed his eyes, placed his hands together in his juzu, and mumbled a soft chant. I leaned slightly and picked up my .38 and put it back into my shoulder holster.

"He's dead," said the bonsan after opening his eyes.

"I know. I made him that way."

"You?"

"I didn't have a choice. He was trying to send me to Nirvana with his belt around my neck. I'm a police detective and this man is—was—not a priest from Japan named Basho. Would you do me a favor and call the police? I'd do it myself but I'm not sure if I can even stand up just yet."

"Yes," said the bonsan. He practically flew out of the room.

I sat on the floor staring at the thing that used to be a man named Jiro Machida. The bullet from my .38 had found its way into his head and out again. The brilliant mind, lauded by Olaa laborers, military intelligence officers, and readers of the *Honolulu Record*, now lay splattered all over a little Hongwanji dorm room in Waipahu.

He must have known that it wouldn't end well. Everyone thought he was dead a few days before and now he really was; for most of the world, nothing had changed. Everything he had achieved in life was for the daughter he could never publicly acknowledge. He paid the ultimate price to buy her peace. I didn't have a problem with that, except that he expected me to kick in the same amount.

After a while, I stood up and trudged with leaden steps out to the long lanai. My head felt like it was a mile wide. I pulled my hip flask out of my pocket and took a long burning pull from it. My head stopped expanding and floated a little, but felt better, so I drained the flask. I lit up a Lucky Strike and puffed, watching the smoke fill the Waipahu night along with the distant wail of sirens.

34

It didn't take long for the cavalry to arrive. In a few minutes, the Hongwanji grounds were swarmed by olive drab uniforms, and the white bursts of flashbulbs cut the darkness like lightning. About an hour after the first prowler arrived, Gid Hanohano came lumbering across the lawn to the dormitory annex.

"I thought you were on vacation," he said, by way of greeting.

"I thought I was, too."

"How was Hilo?"

"Wet."

He pulled a couple of Montecristo torpedoes out of his coat pocket and handed me one. We both lit up and walked into the dorm room, pushing our way through the press of lab coats and patrolmen.

Gid looked down at the corpse.

"Jiro Machida?" he asked, almost indifferently.

"In the flesh," I replied.

Gid raised an eyebrow and shrugged. "Good work, Sheik," he said. "Let's step back out and you can tell me about it."

We walked back out to the lawn between the dorm annex and the temple. As I shuffled slowly to keep Gid's glacial pace, I thought about Beverly Machida and how nothing she ever did was really her idea, including being born. It must have been the worst kind of hell to live in, knowing that you didn't ask for it. Any of it.

We came to a halt next to a row of red torch ginger running along a fence, out of earshot of everyone.

"Give it to me short," said Gid. "I know you'll be telling it longer over and over again, so I'll save you some wear on your tongue."

I gave it to him short, but I gave it to him completely, up until the moment I had arrived at the Hongwanji. He nodded silently and grunted in a few places but otherwise didn't change his expression. Same old Gid.

"So how did he end up on the floor with his head all over the place?"

"I didn't have a choice. He tried to strangle me." I showed Gid the raw skin on my throat above the collar. He grunted and nodded.

"Did he tell you anything?" Gid asked.

"Yeah. He told me he killed Harry because he was carrying on with his wife." It wasn't far from the truth. Harry's dalliance with Beverly was really his undoing. But I knew that as soon as the words were out of my mouth it was useless. I let out a huge screen of cigar smoke to put a veil between us, however thin.

Gid eyed me skeptically. It was his na'au telling him that I was full of shit. There wasn't much you could put over the Great Hanohano. But I had to try. I had to try because in that moment I felt that I had inherited Jiro's obligation. His giri became mine. Gid raised an eyebrow and stared at the glowing end of the cigar he held between his massive thumb and fingers.

"That's what he told you?" he asked. He worked to hide the incredulity in his voice, but he didn't work too hard.

"That's what he told me," I said.

Gid looked up from his cigar and our eyes met. I broke into a smile. I couldn't help it. Gid's face cracked in that strange little half-grin of his and he shook his big head.

"And that's how you're going to tell it at the inquest?"

"That's how I'm going to tell it."

"I guess that's how it's going in your report, too."

"You're a mind reader, Gid."

He shook his head again and shrugged, and then he laid one of his massive hands on my shoulder and patted it.

"Okay, Sheik."

Gid lumbered away, dragging his size thirteen Oxfords across the grass and trailing white cigar smoke. He raised one of his hands in a wave without looking back.

"See you tomorrow," he said.

"See you tomorrow, Lieutenant."

I stuck around for much longer than I wanted to, giving statements and answering questions. By the time I was "free to go," the sky had started to change color to a hazy violet. I got into the Eldorado and drove back into town. I got into the Eldorado and drove back to town. When I got to the jeweler, the sky was a thin, bleached blue and downtown was beginning to rouse with peddlers trying to get a jump on the competition and old folks taking advantage of the few daylight hours they had left on earth. Lucky for me, the jeweler fit into both categories. His shop wasn't open yet, but I could see him cleaning a bracelet behind the counter. I tapped on the glass and begged him at the top of my lungs to open. He relented and gave me my package. I got the hell out of there and sped back to Kaimuki.

When I opened the door, I stepped into an apartment I didn't recognize. The trash on the floor had disappeared and everything looked neater and cleaner than it was even before the break-in. Ellen was seated at the dining table, head down and fast asleep. A half-consumed cup of cold coffee sat just beyond her head next to the telephone, which she had moved next to her. I stepped silently around the table, leaned down and kissed her. Her lips responded sleepily, then her eyes opened and she sat up slowly.

"What time is it?" she asked.

"7:00," I said.

"Frankie Yoshikawa! What's wrong with you?" she shouted. She had shaken off the sleep and become fully alert. "You didn't even call like you said you would! I waited up all night for you!"

"Not *all* night, sleepyhead," I pointed out.

She swatted me on the arm with an open palm.

"You know what I mean," she said, still fuming. "I thought we went over this already. I thought you said you understood. Calling. It's what people do when they care for . . . what happened to your neck?"

"I'll live. And I'm sorry for not calling, darling. It wasn't intentional. When it occurred to me to do it, I was being strangled. And worse than that, when I wasn't being strangled anymore, I was made to tell the story of it over and over again to a bunch of cops who got there after it all happened. I figured it was best to just come back to you as soon as I could after it was all over."

"Oh. Well, what happened?"

"I'll tell you all about it a little later, maybe after we've both had a little more rest. Suffice to say I've taken care of almost everything. There's just the inquest later today to get through and a report to write, but the case is pretty much closed."

"What about the HUAC man you're so concerned about?"

"Closing the case out will take care of most of it. But I would like assurances that he has nothing to come after you for, and I do mean nothing. You can help me out with that, and you can help me out right now."

"How's that?"

"I need you to tell me that you'll quit working for the *Honolulu Record*. At least for the time being. But I need you to resign effective immediately. The whole nation is looking at the Hawaii Seven trial and Kierkegaard was going to use the fact that the main characters in my case were tied to the *Record* and to the CP to flush out more indictments. He won't be able to use the case anymore but I need to try make sure that if he goes after other *Record* employees just for the hell of it—and he may—that you won't be one of them. I can't do anything more for my sister except ask her to lay low and keep her nose clean, but I can ask you to do this. Look, I'm not naïve enough to believe that having you remove yourself from the *Record* will completely shield you from HUAC harassment but it would certainly move you down their priority list. The HUAC won't be forever, so please—for me—do this for now."

"You want me to quit the *Record*? You want me to quit *my job*?" Ellen sputtered, exasperated. "What would I do if I didn't have my job, Frankie Yoshikawa? Am I just supposed to work at my parent's store like some shop-girl? Is that what you're saying? Can you tell me? *What would I do*?"

"How about helping me out?"

"Helping you out, how? Do you mean like a partner?"

"Something like that."

"What do you mean? How would that work?"

I pulled out the little box I picked up from the jeweler that morning and opened it for her.

"By saying you'll marry me. Will you marry me, Ellen Park?"

35

It just kind of fell out of my mouth. If I had thought about it, I would have been nervous. Of course, she said yes. That is, after the initial shock wore off. Ellen Aeran Park agreed to become Ellen Yoshikawa and resigned that morning from the *Honolulu Record*. Ellen told me that when the coast was clear, she'd go back to work for the *Record* and type her articles at our dining table. I told her to knock herself out. I had done as I promised Ira Levinsky and reached out and grasped my Holy Grail and drank as deeply of her as I possibly could.

That afternoon, I reported to testify at the inquest. There were a few newspaper reporters there, though I noted with relief, none were from the *Honolulu Record*. That's because Dan Kierkegaard was in attendance in a ringside seat, ready to soak up the proceedings and write down any and all names that appeared in the testimony.

I gave him nothing. I left out Marlon Wilde and the rest of them and omitted my visit with Beatrice Walker Crane. Their interviews were not germane to the conclusion I reached; the *Iwakuni Maru* and the facts I uncovered in Hilo were sufficient to explain how I arrived at the identity of the victim found in Kunia and finding Jiro was a simple matter of tailing him from his Waialua residence to the Waipahu Hongwanji.

Kierkegaard sat there with the expression of a house poodle begging table scraps. His ears would perk up whenever Jiro's or Harry's names were mentioned, but his face fell when the story turned out to be devoid of any supporting characters. The way I told it, there were none.

Except Beverly.

She was there, looking resplendent in a lavish burgundy dress and heels. Her hair was piled up as it was when she first came to the door in Waialua to invite me in to share some tragic news and a couple of drinks. Her insurance people were probably there, too—the veracity of the claim would hinge on the facts that came out of that afternoon's proceedings. The payday wouldn't be as big as Jiro had hoped for with the foul play clause but it would be big enough. I watched Beverly as I gave my testimony. She looked past me with a vague smile. Throughout my statement, there were some audible gasps and conversational buzz when the astonishing facts were revealed about the swap of identities but Beverly sat through it all with the serenity of the gentle breeze through the sugarcane in the fields of Waialua.

When it was all over, my findings were concurred with. Everything was entered into record. I had never perjured myself before, but the truth in this case would have done more harm than good. Beatrice Walker Crane didn't need her two thousand dollars and the Palolo Group of the Hawaii Communist Party would never make a claim for it. The two most insistent proponents for its use were dead and gone. It was nobody's money. There was no point in bringing it up. And the fact of the matter was that Harry Kurita's death was not murder; he bore at least half the responsibility as a willing participant. From what I could guess of him, Harry was probably the one who urged Beverly to squeeze tighter.

Only those folks in Olaa who had been swindled by Jiro were out anything. I resolved to work with my cousin Herb to find a compensation fund of some kind they could make a claim against, especially Hatsue Fukuda, who had lost fifty dollars.

In the end, I believe my omissions served justice. They saved
Beverly from an unfair consequence of the game she played with Harry.
They saved all the members of the Palolo Cell of the Hawaii CP from
an investigation that would have arisen out of a peripheral, but really
unrelated, accidental death. They fulfilled what I believed to be Jiro's last
wish. Most of all, they saved Ellen and Iris and, by making omissions
to save them, I balanced the books for the lie I signed off on that
condemned Ira and Rachel Levinsky. A lie for a lie. If that's not justice,
I don't know what is. And I am convinced that I fulfilled the oath that
Art Kawamura bound me to: I took up my sword to champion the
defenseless with my testimony.

When the inquest adjourned, Dan Kierkegaard approached me.

"You did a hell of a job, Slugger. I must say, you found your niche.
You really have a nose for crime."

"Thanks."

"Did you ever consider doing this for Uncle Sam? You'd be great
at rooting out reds right here in your own backyard. The Committee
could use a guy like you."

"Thanks again but I've got my hands full just dealing with common
criminals. As you can see, we've got no lack of them here. The whole
sedition thing is a little too much for a first baseman from Kakaako."

"Don't sell yourself short, Slugger. You give me a call if you ever
change your mind."

"Are you going somewhere?"

"Hollywood. I'm on a plane tomorrow morning. The Committee
boys have more than they can handle up there right now, what with
all those directors and screen writers churning out propaganda, not to
mention some very well-known faces on the silver screen."

"You mean the *red* screen," I deadpanned.

Kierkegaard guffawed and stuck out his hand. "So long, Slugger,"
he said.

I reached out and shook his hand.

"Happy hunting, Mr. Kierkegaard."

He walked out of the room, making me feel ten years younger and ten pounds lighter. I had a cigarette with Gid and talked baseball with him and the M.E. and a couple of the patrol sergeants who had been at the inquest to testify. We were discussing the frontrunners for the American League pennant when the burgundy dress came floating out into the hallway.

"I'll see you back at the station," I told Gid.

"Take your time," he said.

Beverly stood next to a water cooler, waiting for me. I waved as I walked up to her. She smiled back.

"I'm sorry about your . . . about Jiro," I told her.

"I already told you," she said, "he's one with the entire fabric of existence. It's all he ever wanted. How can you be sorry about that?"

"I'm sorry about how he got there. It wasn't very pretty."

"A lot of what he endured in this passing existence wasn't very pretty. He's free now. Isn't that something?"

"I guess it is. A lot of what *you've* endured in this 'passing existence' wasn't very pretty either. What will you do now?"

"I'm going to a beautiful place at the foot of Mount Hiei. Jiro arranged it for me, and now that his insurance money will be released, I can leave as soon as next week. It's beautiful land, and I was told it's tranquil and soothing. Like paradise on earth."

"Sounds wonderful. I'd never leave it."

"I won't. It's strange, all this fussing they all did over me. My games were just a way of dealing with people. They never understood that all I ever really wanted was to be left alone."

"You're getting your wish. Not one in a million of us can say that. I'm happy for you."

She stood on her toes and gave me a quick kiss on the cheek.

"Thank you. For everything," she said.

"It's my job."

Giri. And this time it felt good, To-san.

"Goodbye, Detective."

"Goodbye, Beverly."

Her heels echoed in the hallway as they carried her out of this passing existence and toward a better place. She was Guinevere off to the peace of Almesbury nunnery after the heartache of a lifetime of scandal in Camelot.

I got back to my desk at the station and picked up the daruma and filled in his second eye with my pen. I gave him a poke and watched him dip and spring back upright on my blotter. Then I picked the receiver up out of the cradle of my telephone and dialed.

My Holy Grail was ensconced in an apartment just off of Waialae Avenue sitting by the telephone, waiting for me to do what people do when they care for each other.

Acknowledgements

A second novel. It really wouldn't have happened if not for some talented, discerning, hard-working, and supportive people. All I did was write the thing.

My undying gratitude to the following:

> To Jayson Chun, Pat Patterson, and Sarah Mattos, for enduring the *Red Dirt* manuscript in its larval stage, even as the future of *Kona Winds* was uncertain. This would never have seen the light of day if you didn't think it deserved to.

> To Juliet Kono Lee and Jean Yamasaki Toyama, for your advocacy of *Red Dirt* before the gatekeepers of Bamboo Ridge Press. This survived because you used your clout to champion it.

> To Juliet Kono Lee, for taking the helm once again and imbuing this book with your brilliance. Truly, I am the luckiest writer in Hawai'i to have had you twice as an editor.

> To Milton Kimura, for weighing in on short notice in an editorial capacity and serving as my conscience when it came to what was and was not believable. Thanks for keeping me as honest as I can be.

> To Gail N. Harada and Normie Salvador, for their discerning copy edits. It's because of you that I look like I know what I'm doing. Thanks for being my smoke and mirrors.

To Ken Tokuno, for writing the grants that make this book, and all Bamboo Ridge Press publications, possible. It's because of your effort and the grants secured that the Sheik can be the Sheik and not something with a "market."

To Tommy Hite, for another perfect cover. I feel like I have to keep writing just so I can get you to keep painting covers for me.

To Jui-Lien Sanderson, for signing on for another tour as our book designer. The package, as always, is gorgeous.

To Dr. William Puette of the University of Hawai'i West O'ahu, for access to the collection of the Center for Labor Education and Research (CLEAR). Apologies for not bringing white gloves for handling the material! Your generosity has hopefully resulted in something with credibility.

To Eric Chock and Darrell H. Y. Lum, for Bamboo Ridge Press. Who else would print a book featuring a Nisei protagonist in an "ugly Hawai'i" (the words of the agents who rejected me, not mine)?

To Kent Sakoda, Mavis Hara, Micheline Soong, Juliet Kono Lee, Wing Tek Lum, Joy Kobayashi-Cintrón, and Gail N. Harada, for being Bamboo Ridge along with Eric and Darrell and providing a home for my stories and a home for the stories of many, many others.

To Misty Sanico, for helping to get the word out about my book to readers I hope will enjoy my work.

To Naomi Hirahara, for being my patron saint. Because of you, people outside of Hawai'i know who I am. And without Mas Arai, there would be no Sheik.

To my family—Arnie, Caroline, and Cole—for making everything possible.

A product of Hawai'i Kai in East Honolulu, Scott Kikkawa is the author of noir detective stories set in postwar Honolulu featuring Francis "Sheik" Yoshikawa, which have appeared in the pages of *Bamboo Ridge, Journal of Hawai'i Literature and Arts*. *Kona Winds*, his début novel, earned him recognition as a recipient of the Elliot Cades Award for Literature. He also serves as a columnist and an Associate Editor for *The Hawai'i Review of Books*. The New York University alumnus is currently a federal law enforcement officer and lives with his family in Honolulu. *Red Dirt* is his second full-length novel.

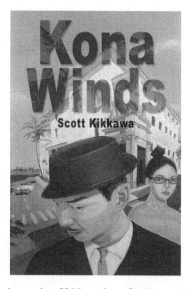

A moody and violent meditation on corruption and class warfare, *Kona Winds* is more than real-life law enforcement officer Scott Kikkawa's noir novel of 1953 Honolulu. Yes, it has a lovely woman's body found floating in the harbor, a diamond bracelet, lowlifes and union toughs, a couple of decadent descendants of a wealthy white plantation family, and a plot that ties old and new political establishments together. But what drives the story and its tarnished knight, detective Francis "Sheik" Yoshikawa, is the private inferno of his trauma fighting in Italy in World War II—and the outrage at a society that has put his and other men's sacrifices aside in pursuit of money, sex, and power. There's nothing like it in local literature—thanks are due publisher Bamboo Ridge Press—and it raises the hope that Kikkawa's unflinching vision opens the door to more stories willing to go down the mean streets of our Island history.

—Don Wallace, senior editor, *HONOLULU Magazine*

Scott Kikkawa's *Kona Winds* is a blast of fresh air that lets Hawai'i's people—both good and bad—speak for themselves in a crime narrative. Homicide detective Frankie Yoshikawa is a revelation. Only he can lead the reader through a harrowing world that is at turns tougher and more multihued than expired SPAM. *Kona Winds* blows past *Hawaii 5-0*—it goes all the way to 11!

—Ed Lin, author of the Robert Chow mystery series and the Taipei Night Market mystery series

Homicide detective Francis "Sheik" Yoshikawa imbibes bourbon every chance he gets, but it's Scott Kikkawa's readers who will be intoxicated by the intricate plot and the whirlwind ride. This noir thriller is notable for its remarkable verisimilitude, its sumptuous reconjuring of Honolulu in the early 1950s.

—Rodney Morales, author of the novels *For A Song* and *When the Shark Bites*

Evocative and riveting, *Kona Winds* grabs the reader from the first page and does not let go until the end. Even then, prepare to be haunted by author Scott Kikkawa's scarred characters, gritty 1950s Honolulu, and layered tale in this elegant noir. I loved it!

—Pamela Rotner Sakamoto, author of *Midnight in Broad Daylight*

Available from BambooRidge.org